THE BEST OF THE WEST 4

INTRODUCTION BY
Ron Hansen

THE
BEST
OF THE
WEST

New
Stories
from the Wide Side of
the Missouri

4

EDITED BY
James Thomas and Denise Thomas

W. W. NORTON & COMPANY · NEW YORK · LONDON

The editors would like to thank Ted Cains for his invaluable assistance in putting together this year's volume, Carol Houck Smith for her unerring direction and outstanding literary acumen, and Nat Sobel for his steady nerves and keen sense of balance.

The Acknowledgments on page 265 are an extension of the copyright page.

Printed in the United States of America.

The text of this book is composed in Goudy Old Style, with the display set in Century Bold Condensed. Composition by and manufacturing by the Haddon Craftsmen, Inc. Book design by Michael Chesworth.

LIBRARY OF CONGRESS CATALOGING-IN-PUBLICATION DATA
The Best of the West 4 : new stories from the wide side of the
  Missouri / edited by James Thomas and Denise Thomas.
    p.   cm.
    1. Western stories. 2. Short stories, American—West (U.S.)
  3. American fiction—20th century. I. Thomas, James
  II. Thomas, Denise   III. Title: Best of the West 4.
  PS648.W4B473 1991
  813'.087408—dc20   91-2352

ISBN 0-393-03018-0
W.W. Norton & Company, Inc., 500 Fifth Avenue, New York, N.Y. 10110
W.W. Norton & Company, Ltd., 10 Coptic Street, London WC1A 1PU

1 2 3 4 5 6 7 8 9 0

Again, and as always, for Jesse and Christopher

CONTENTS

EDITORS' NOTE

The Best of the West series was started in 1987 and attempts each autumn to celebrate between the covers of one book the best "western" stories published the year before (between November 15 and November 15). We also list and honor "other distinguished western stories" we much admired but were unable to include: a list, we are happy to note, that has grown each year.

The criteria for inclusion as "western" is as much subjective as it is technical, with geographical location of the story in the western United States only part of the process of consideration and final selection; what we look for besides literary quality is a sense of the western experience, whether contemporary or historical. The American West, it has often been noted, is as much a state of mind—a *sensibility*, it would seem, borne of both its perpetual newness and its stubborn oldness, both its open hospitality and its ability to be suddenly and brutally hostile, both its beauty and its rawness—as it is a mindful set of states. As the series title is meant to suggest, the stories we're looking for are as much "of" the West as simply "in" the West. Call it a geography of the heart, a geological survey of western literary imagination.

In recent years it has also been often noted that the "western," as a genre of fiction, has taken on new meanings, has "come of age," and has become part of the college of literature as much more than a school of "region." In order to expand further those notes, and to extend the commentary, we are this year initiating "guest" introductions to *The Best of the West*. We are particularly pleased that this year's introductory essay is by Ron Hansen, well known for both his fiction (short and long) and nonfiction inspired and informed by the West.

The process of selecting stories for *The Best of the West* is continuous; we review all magazines that come to us. A list of those publications appears in the back of this volume. We invite editors of other magazines who would like to have their fiction considered for the series to include us on their subscription list. Send to James and Denise Thomas, *The Best of the West*, 4866 Route 68 North, Yellow Springs, Ohio 45387.

INTRODUCTION

Ron Hansen

EVERY NOW AND THEN we grow tired of ourselves and get a hankering to go West. West, to the great lonesome, the badlands, the wide open spaces, to the just plain yonder, the home where the wild oxen roam and the skies are not cloudy all day.

Going there rarely means *going* there. Usually it means a fancy pair of hand-stitched boots that will be a hard penance for our feet until the heels finally go out and we toss them. Or we'll have a sudden, necessary yearning to hunker with a Tequila bottle and hold forth about Gene Autry's soulful way with a song. I have friends who've tried to read Louis L'Amour or affected putting a *peench* of tobacco between their cheek and gum.

And you hear stories about it all getting out of hand: otherwise reasonable people who end up wearing bola ties and turquoise rings, who power Range Rovers down Wall Street, or tenderly recite cowboy poetry with the kind of hammering rhyme and meter that could pound out dents in a car.

Whence comes this fascination? Why does Susan Sontag have over a hundred pairs of cowboy boots? Why is the Sam Shepard who horsed around on a ranch in New Mexico infinitely more interesting than the Sam Shepard who hacks at polo in Virginia? Why has the former Eagle Don Henley, a with-it resident of L.A., lately been singing his hits from a stage set that looks like an old adobe *tortilleria*? Why did an English gentleman like Malcolm Lowry seek his peace in a Mexican *cantina*? Why are Marlboro cigarettes the hottest sellers in Paris? Why did the West German I ran into on a vaporetto to the Lido insist on listing, in halting English, all the American Indian tribes? And why, after all this, did *Dances with Wolves* surprise the movie studios with its grosses at the box office?

We're savvy enough to know that half our notions of the Old

West are purest myth, but that still gives us plenty to think about when city life begins to seem the greatest ill for the greatest number. And it is true, for example, that everything *is* simpler in the West, if only because your radio stops picking up stations just beyond Grand Island, Nebraska, and your night-to-howl options in Idaho may be a hoo-rah in Peg's Bar & Grill or *Robocop* at the picture show. Everything *is* more honest, if only because there are hills you can stand on in Arizona and see a truck heading toward a house forty miles away. And freedom just naturally comes with a territory where no one is crazy, just eccentric, and where all you have for company at high noon are a few discreet hawks and snakes and tarantulas.

Even the titles of the first-rate western stories collected here show that not much has changed in the Great American Desert: "Jackpot," "The Old Hotel," "Back in Aberdeen," "Mud Season," all could be nineteenth-century fictions by Stephen Crane, Willa Cather, Hamlin Garland, Bret Harte. Cowhands now ride horses named Honda, Suzuki, and Yamaha, but they're still tough enough that you can strike a match off the squint in their eyes. Women out there often do have the spunk, independence, and hang-it-all flair of skyrockets on the 3rd of July. Weather is still punishing there, foot doctors and chiropractors far outnumber psychiatrists, guns are enshrined in truck windows, coyotes warily skulk into yards like boys who've stolen their dad's cigarettes, and it's still a long, long walk between towns.

Writing about Montana, Rick Bass says in "Antlers": "Everyone who's up here is here because of the silence. It is eternity up here. Some are on the run, and others are looking for something; some are incapable of living in a city, among people, while others simply love the wildness of new untouched country."

Often in these fascinating pages, though, the West is bleakly pictured as a great vacancy littered here and there with aluminum trailers, plywood tract homes, or, in Larry Levis's "First Water," the "wilderness of the broken" where "rusted cars and trucks would appear in the dawn light, and farm implements beyond repair, and then baby carriages whose black canopies let in too much sky, and mattresses wet and heavy as galleons, and trash of all kinds."

Once upon a time the Old West was thought of as a new Eden, a garden that our forebears would weed and comfortably settle in like a Labor Day picnic spot. We see the persistence of that romance in Thomas Fox Averill's "The Man Who Ran with Deer" when his newly married farmer looks at a house "surrounded by machinery and buildings, everything that contains work and livelihood, everything that makes their life possible" and finally "feels an uncommon joy," or when Gladys Swan's Penny and Jack hold on to their dear old hotel "as though it were their invention out there in the desert."

Working against our forebears' humblest pastoral aspirations was the perplexing anxiety that the American pioneers could be on the brink of creating just another Europe—peaceful, conformist, inhibiting, and dull. Even while they were taming the West, therefore, some people of the nineteenth century were extolling its virtues as a harsh wilderness that tested a person's mettle and strength and self-reliance, making it seem a kind of Marine Corps boot camp based on misrepresentations of Charles Darwin's theory about the survival of the fittest.

And if the fittest demonstrated it with a special aptitude for guns and violence, that was celebrated, too, in dime novels and melodramas about Frank and Jesse James, Wild Bill Hickok, Annie Oakley, The Dalton Gang, Calamity Jane, and Belle Starr, the "Queen of the Outlaws." There have even been theories that revolutions and wars were forestalled while the frontier was still there, because those most angered by injustice and economic oppression put their great hope in the West instead of in protest, and blew off steam by letting out their frustrations in vast open spaces where a stray bit of violence wouldn't hit much more than dirt.

The government of the Old West has seldom been seen in our mythology as being in the hands of sheriffs—*High Noon* and *Gunsmoke* and John Wayne's hocum oaters are the few exceptions—

but in the hands of go-it-alone cowboys whose interior toughness and courage are hidden by their Old World courtliness and a slow and easy grin: *Shane, The Virginian,* Clint Eastwood with his serape and cigarillo, Robert Duvall's Augustus McCrae in *Lonesome Dove,* Ken Smith's anti-hero here in "The Government Man," all as gritty as hard-boiled eggs rolled in sand.

In Dagoberto Gilb's "Ballad," we hear about Cowboy Mike Duran who "got into construction because he thought it was the only work that was still western. He thought it wasn't much different than what cattlemen and trail-drivers, wildcatters and roughnecks did in the earlier days. They were drinking, brawling, whoring, hard-working men whose job tangled them up with the outdoors, men whose clothes were secondary to what was inside them, men whose independence was so dogged they'd do it alone if they had to, without cranes or dozers or backhoes, with two hands if it came down to getting the job done, and who afterwards would drive on without a second thought to the next job."

We still seem to be looking for wranglers like that in our writers, and the job description includes a flair for words and an existentialist interest in the ways our lives are formed. We only want the genuine article, however, not one of them stall-fed tenderfeet who's all hat and no cattle; and so we admire Thomas McGuane not just because of his wonderful novels and screenplays, but also because he's a champion quarterhorse rider who ramrods a ranch in the high country of Montana. We appreciate the fact that Leslie Silko, the critically acclaimed author of *Ceremony,* lives in the rugged foothills above Tucson, Arizona, where she holds a weekly poker game and tries out her extensive pistol collection on a stash of empty bottles from the finest wineries in Bordeaux. We like it that Rick Bass truly lives in Yaak, Montana, a town composed of a general store and a saloon called the Dirty Shame, and that the other fine writers represented here are from places like Albuquerque and Lodi, El Paso and South Dakota, Las Cruces and Salt Lake City. We look at people differently when they've freed themselves from convention and, as Huckleberry Finn would put it, "lighted out for the territories." We imagine them all like Melissa Pritchard's Hallie, "Dumping her past, wind bailing it out the car windows, trashing the roadsides from Cheyenne to here, nothing acknowledged but uncolored calm."

There's a joke about a cowboy telling a foreigner about his outfit: He says he wears the Stetson for shade, the neckerchief to filter the trail dust from his mouth, the chaps to keep the sand burrs off his jeans, and the tennis shoes so "I won't look like some damn trucker."

It's not just the clothes, it's the attitude. Paul Newman and Robert Redford played it, not in *Butch Cassidy and the Sundance Kid*, but in *Cool Hand Luke* and *The Candidate*. And you see it here in the haunted country people in Kent Meyers's "Wind Rower," "the girl who disobeyed" in Joy Harjo's "The Flood," the "I" in Larry Levis's story who confesses the historical truth behind his fictions because "although the altering of facts and the justification of any fabrication because it is 'art' is permitted everywhere now, it is not permitted on the East Side of the San Joaquin Valley, not without the restoration of fact."

Honor, integrity, principles, spirit—we presume it of people who seek out the West. And when we want to get away from it all, it's those half-forgotten, old-fashioned values that we have a hankering for.

WHERE WEST IS

Long before we were born
the people who lived in the world
had their way of finding west
without the use of delicate instruments.

One of them whose duty it was
to find west would begin to walk
in the direction of the setting sun
while chanting the tale of the world
in his head.

When he was finished
he would bend down and
draw a line in the dirt
with his finger.

Beyond this line
everything was west.

—THOM TAMMARO

THE   BEST   OF   THE   WEST   4

Peter LaSalle

A Guide to Some Small Border Airports

"Here we go round the prickly pear."
—T.S. Eliot

1. EAGLE PASS, TEXAS.

Be careful of this one. If there are a half dozen legitimate airports along the border in West Texas, clear out to El Paso, this is the first and the one I learned to trust the least.

When I fly down from Austin I stop there only because at the end of the cracked airstrip one of the stubby red-and-white Phillips pumps serves up automotive gas, "mo-gas." My Cessna 182 is old enough to run well on the stuff. Plus, going west after Eagle Pass everything turns to blond desert, peppered with aqua scrub, restricted military property for thousands and thousands of square acres. It is a stretch where you don't want to run short and have to put down if you are circling for time.

I was there last month and something strange happened.

It is really not much of a setup, just that strip and those pumps, and a decrepit galvanized hangar shed with an office for an enterprise called Bravo Flying Service. I have never been to the town of Eagle Pass, or to the gritty Mexican town across the weeded-over Rio Grande, Piedras Negras. But last month this guy was at the airport again, supposedly waiting to have some work done on his Skywagon. It was one of those single-engine six-seaters that is basically nothing more than a flying bus. I remembered him from my previous trip, and I remembered that then he was also supposedly waiting to have some work done.

He was slim and tall, about my build, in his forties and a bit older than me. He had curly gray hair, a leathery face, squinting too-blue eyes. We were alone there, except for the Mexican guy now up on the aluminum ladder and pumping my mo-gas. There is a camaraderie in these small airports. You talk about the winds and the weather, which was a steely low ceiling that afternoon, a late February blow of blue cold in a place you never think of as being cold. He had his hands jammed in the pockets of a cloth bomber jacket, the wind blew that hair. It wasn't as if he was trying to pump me for information, because he just nodded a lot. When he did talk the words came with some smiling, a cowboy's squint, though this guy wasn't from Texas at all. In fact, though he didn't remember me, or let on that he did, I remembered that he had told me the last time that he was living out there, doing general aviation stuff like flying geologists and rich ranchers, and glad to be away from city life. So many people out there tell you they are glad to have escaped the rush of city life—what else can they say?

"You like that power of the 182," he said.

"Six cylinders is better than four," I said. The Cessna I have is a single-engine overhead wing, built in sixty-seven, and it does pack a load of power. I was looking at his Skywagon, painted a yellow-and-red combo. I was noticing what I had also noticed the last time, how he had removed the fenders to allow for the oversized balloon tires on the landing gear and how the undersides of the wings were crusted with thrown-up cinnamon mud. He had been putting that thing down in some far-out places, places even geologists and rich ranchers didn't go.

"Lets you get right in there for your picture taking," he said.

"Yeah, I guess it does at that," I told him. "Lets me get in and then pull right out for my picture taking."

He nodded. But I hadn't given him my stock line about aerial photography being my trade this time, and that was something that must have come up before. And all the while I had been thinking that he didn't remember me, and now it was obvious to me that he had been playing along, letting me pretend that I didn't remember him. In short, each of us remembered the other, neither admitted it.

In a way, I later thought, we were ghosts, acting out a dream that neither was quite sure of. But I was there and he was there, with his same story about waiting for repairs and with a plane that had obviously been places that a for-hire didn't go.

Like I said, be careful of Eagle Pass.

2. DEL RIO, TEXAS.

This is two hundred miles west of Eagle Pass. Believe me, there is nothing much in between.

It is small, but you can lose yourself in an operation like the one they have. Out in that dust, on the very edge of the town that is principally known for the fact that six-gun-shooting Judge Roy Bean himself is buried there, the little airport is Chamber of Commerce neat. A slate-blue humpbacked hangar with a new lounge wing attached: tinted glass; red wall-to-wall and red Naugahyde sofas and chairs right out of a dentist's waiting room; copies of *Flying* and *USA Today* on glass-topped coffee tables; an alcove with the usual sandwich and chip machines and the more-than-usual Dr. Pepper, rather than Coke, machine, because, after all, you are in West Texas. Nothing really distinguishes it, except for a classic old wall chart of the region, dulled to watercolors, and the bulletin board with maybe an extraordinarily large number of Polaroid shots of planes up for sale. As I said, nobody pays much attention to you, even if you are the only plane stopping to refuel. You get the feeling that those who check in and out are probably Del Rio doctors who took up flying as a hobby, the way local doctors are always taking it up as a hobby.

There was a time. Back in that other world when I myself had actually used the phys ed degree I never thought I would use, and when I had a job teaching gym and coaching track at the junior high serving one of those new Austin subdivisions. I was out of the so-called business then, and though I didn't want to think of the border, think of all that time flying "low and slow" in the swallowing desert without lights, think of putting down sometimes on those rough strips in the mountains that you dropped onto just about elevator-straight, I came out to Del Rio with Lizanne.

She had gotten her sister to take care of her kid, Rosie. Which I thought was a start. The Rosie thing with her had become an obsession by that point, and I was glad that she had at last agreed to leave town with me for a weekend. She was from Corpus, had married while at a j.c. there. Her husband, Billy, owned two galleries in Corpus, and they had met when she found herself at some of the parties of that crowd, seeing she was a beauty and had been modeling clothes since she was in junior high for local department stores, even local TV. But when Rosie was born with the defect of that left leg being slightly shorter than the right, Billy wasn't ready for the responsibility of that. He was gone before long, either Tampa or Jacksonville, Lizanne was never sure which. She eventually moved to Austin where her married sister lived, and by the time I began seeing her, Rosie was ten and had already been through a half-dozen operations to try to get that one leg to match the other. The last had been a substantial bone graft, unsuccessful and in truth only emphasizing that the situation was worse—what had started as a fractional difference at birth was now, sadly, a full two inches. Lizanne had begun taking night courses at the University of Texas for a B.A. and she held down a full-time job typing at the state comptroller's office.

It was true. At that stage I finally thought that the craziness of my life flying in the business was over. I was teaching and the last place I wanted to think about was the Texas border. But Acuna, across from Del Rio, had always been special to me. I liked to rest there a few days. I told Lizanne so much about the spot that we decided to head to it for a weekend, using the little four-cylinder Piper I had borrowed from a pal. (I have always flown, crop-dusting in Pennsylvania as a teenager, later a pilot in the Army.) We set out, stowing ten-speed bicycles in the back. And after touching down at that Del Rio strip, we put what we needed in nylon day-packs and planned to use the bikes for the few miles into town, then across the border. It was this same time of year, true spring. We sped by the squat little bungalows on the dusty cross streets of Del Rio, looped around the central square with its proudly pillared 1930s bank buildings and neat red brick storefronts, all the cascading purple wisteria in full bloom, and continued right down that long final empty stretch of slick asphalt two-lane and the occasional souvenir and money-changing shack, toward Customs and the international bridge. We were well outside Del Rio, a couple of miles from Acuna too. But the day was so warm and so ever-blue. Beyond the arc of the narrow span of the bridge, painted silver, rose the dry yellow hills, the little town with its bone-white cathedral bell tower above the puffs of lime-green trees. Still as slim as she was when she modeled, Lizanne had full lips and dark doe eyes now fringed with incipient lines that made her womanly and maybe more handsome still. She stopped halfway across the bridge. She was wearing white camp shorts and a white T-shirt, and she looked back, straddling her ten-speed while I caught up.

"What?" I asked her.

"Look at it," she said smiling. "I can tell from here it's special. I just wanted to make sure that you knew I knew. Everything you said about it will be true. It will." She smiled some more, and the sun sheened her dark hair blown stringy from riding.

In Acuna we stayed in what was the only real hotel. A place called Mrs. Crosby's, it was on a corner of the main street right after the bridge, a Spanish setup around a central courtyard of gaudy ceramic tiles and well-groomed garden. We must have bought the begging little kids out of their supply of Chiclets when we strolled the streets. We ate at cheap restaurants good enough to make you take an oath you would never even bother with Mexican food outside of Mexico again. In the bruised blue evenings we sat in the park across from the cathedral. The teenage girls in frilled dresses giggled among themselves, and the leathery old men wearing straw cowboy hats played dominoes under the big live oaks that had trunks whitewashed lower down, and the dignified statues of all those blessed heroes of the republic just nonchalantly looked on. At night we drank cool Carta Blanca in the hotel bar with its hypnotizing ceiling fans, the only Americans, and later we made love, moonlight gently washing the floors of that admittedly seedy room, whining mariachi music crackling from the little transistor I had set up on the dresser. Afterward we talked.

On the second night there, the last, we lay silent for a while.

"You're thinking of Rosie, aren't you," I said.

"I was thinking that I hadn't really thought much of her at all," she said. "That scares me."

I kissed her on the forehead.

Rosie suffered brain damage after the next operation. It was the result of an infection, then a fever that the doctors originally claimed they had under control. I had stopped seeing Lizanne before that, but she called to tell me about Rosie. My older brother in Pennsylvania died around the same time. And I was drinking, and I knew I wasn't long for that job at the junior high. I first went back to what I told myself would be just one trip flying in and out of Mexico. Then it was half a dozen. But I promised myself that would be all. Nevertheless, I bought the Cessna, made still more runs, and spent the money fast. And here I am on the border again.

Enough about Del Rio, and Acuna across the long-ago way.

3. LAJITAS, TEXAS.

The story about this trip really starts in Presidio, still further west toward El Paso. But before that is an airport so small that it usually is unmanned, Lajitas.

It is at the far end of Big Bend. That is the national park as large as a couple of small states combined. True badlands of erosion-clawed chocolate mountains, and such heat even in spring that every thermal updraft becomes a jarring speed bump to a small plane like mine. You have to fly with the side windows flapping open against the wings above, just for air. A rich man named Cooke Thompson III came out from Houston not long after the oil embargo, in that time of fast and then faster money in that glass-spired supposed city of the future that was swelling with two thousand newcomers a week by 1980. Cooke Thompson was oil money, Beaumont old, and he saw this patch of land, a literal stone's throw from the Rio Grande, as his chance to develop what Californians had a long time before and what rich Texans finally needed them-selves—another Palm Springs. It is all tucked in by orange mesas, and the sole natural vegetation is the starred yucca and the paddles of prickly pear. Cooke Thompson has built a huge luxury hotel, a rustic takeoff on something in a B-Western, with a gray planked sidewalk out front and inside red silk wallpaper for the lobby and the dozens of rooms upstairs that must go for an easy two-fifty a night. Some sprawling modern houses have gone up on the higher plateaus. There are tennis courts where the play sounds like corn popping in the heat, and an eighteen-hole golf course even more emerald than the composition courts, studded with mop-headed palms. From the air, the ponds and the sandtraps are pieces from a spilled puzzle, tiny carts chug along under candy-striped awning tops.

The strip is isolated, but long enough to handle Learjets. Cooke Thompson's social set from Houston whisks out there for the weekends. They import name singers and famous dance bands to entertain themselves and their blueblood wives in the starry nights, at get-togethers after all the sport and all the booze and all the talk, talk, talk of more real estate and more oil, how they are really going to strike it even bigger than before as soon as OPEC reorganizes and eventual prices make anything seen during the gas-line days seem like only a pittance.

It is a good place to land if you miss the strip in the desert where you were supposed to touch down for your ten-minute drop. Nobody notices you in Lajitas, and they do have fuel pumps, though you have to walk a ways to that new hotel there to find the guy who handles them. In twenty-five years this could all be luxury homes and even freeways, I told myself when I stopped there on this trip. Cooke Thompson surely knows what the rest of us only suspect: money *can* do anything.

4. PRESIDIO, TEXAS.

Yes, this is where the madness of this trip genuinely started, and where I had my suspicions confirmed that I was being watched, ever since the month before and that strange exchange with the pilot of the Skywagon. Be very careful of Eagle Pass.

Presidio is my base of sorts. You can't go much further out on the Texas border, except for El Paso, where the state ends halfway across the bottom of New Mexico. It is as simple as this. Alvarez, a Mexican, supplies and arranges. I simply fly to Chihuahua, a pretty big city in northern Mexico, filing my flight plan with the Mexican authorities. I then fly back to Presidio, filing my estimated time of arrival there with the U.S. Flight Service, who arrange to have a Customs man out at the desolate Presidio airport when I land. All my real work is done in between. I bill myself as an aerial photographer. The plane is overflowing with cameras and lenses, all carefully registered with U.S. Customs right down to the twelve-digit or more serial numbers. I am so up front about everything that openness has become my cover, and who the hell would register a peach basket full of Canons and Nikons to prove he wasn't smuggling them, and then actually be involved in smuggling—dope? It is all marijuana, just ninety-pound bales, and my theory is that because it isn't the big money, the risk is less. I make wages and not much more from Alvarez. His leg men who give me my load on one side and his leg men who pick it up on the other aren't all that hardcore. The surveillance for this kind of operation on both sides has to be lighter, you tell yourself; and so, you tell yourself too, it doesn't seem to be true that if you're bringing something across illegally you might as well make it something with as much value as possible. Once I am in Chihuahua, it is easy to fly out to a desert strip for a pick-up from Alvarez's crew, because nobody makes you file a plan after you are inside the country. And when I announce what time I will be landing in Presidio, I always make it a good six hours ahead of time, which allows me to circle and circle, even put down in a place like Lajitas, if the basic look of the desert strip agreed on for the drop in Texas doesn't seem right.

I worked it smoother than usual this run. I made the delivery, then looped above Presidio a couple of times, taking a roll of full-focus camera shots of the way they have used irrigation to nurture some fragile green agriculture. At least some proof of my pretended trade. I radioed down to Charlie at the little airport operation below, and he said that the Customs man was already there. I slid in easy to the velvety black runway, which is off to one side of the new yellow-enameled metal trailer and the new yellow-enameled metal hangar that Charlie wrangled through some bank refinancing. He has one corner of the hangar set up with a small Astroturf carpet on the fresh concrete, four cheap easy chairs, and a cooler that offers a pool of icy water and only, of course, that cherry-syruped Dr. Pepper. But Presidio is my base. And I had a few Budweisers with Charlie in his dim trailer, while the Customs man wearing his heavy blue uniform stooped into the Cessna with his clipboard and started his thorough inspection. He was new, the way customs men here are always new. Border Patrol men are always older, tougher, headquartered in their pale-green buildings closer to town, beside that lot ringed with chainlink and filled with confiscated "vehicles," bullet holes riddling some of them; it is a detail you don't like to think about.

If I owned a small airport, I think it would be like Charlie's. It is far enough outside of the town that you see only more desert and the low purplish mountains all around you. Charlie is my age, with a gut and sideburns of the ilk that really haven't been spotted much outside of a place like Presidio, Texas, since lying Nixon stalked the oval office. Ruddy-faced from too much beer, he has massive hands and wrists the size of fireplace logs. He smiles a lot too, not so much out of dumbness but maybe out of loneliness, which Charlie seems to savor. He has a Mexican wife who has two kids, with hair as black as crow's feathers, by another marriage. But the trio of them seem to show up only on Sundays. Since that last time I had been there Charlie had gotten a new satellite rig for television reception, and with the doors wide open on that mobile home and the desert sky even more neon blue than when you had last noticed it above the mountains' jagged silhouette, we sat in the front room. The furniture was new, reddish-brown stuff; the carpet was new, reddish-brown stuff. He demonstrated how to use the dial that rotated the dish, and at one point he found what he was sure was a baseball game direct from Boston.

"That's up in your neck of the woods, isn't it?"

"Pennsylvania," I said.

"That's close. Or, I guess it's close if you think about it all from down here. It all seems so far away."

"It all seems so far away," I repeated.

We drank for a while without saying anything, the television off. A couple of hours passed, but I don't think we ever really noticed them. Time that was lost, probably before it was even ours to spend. I borrowed Charlie's pick-up truck, had a meal at the one attempt at a restaurant (really just a barbecue place) in Presidio proper, which can't be more than a thousand in population, and booked into the one motel, new, at the edge of town.

I wasn't tired. I lay on the bed with its yellow nubbed spread. I stared at the thermo-insulated plastic pitcher and the two glasses in clear wrap on the dresser. What was it Charlie had said, it all seems so far away. And it did. Pennsylvania was part of that other world too, and it wasn't a part I could manage to get even a slight grip on, like that whole business with Lizanne and Rosie. In Pennsylvania my father had worked in the coal mines. This was in Wilkes-Barre, up in the northeastern corner of the state. There as a kid in the fifties you actually learned to put your butch-cut head flat on your desk for civil defense drills, and as a teenager in the sixties the Polish and Czech girls you were nervous about and looked at from a distance argued over who among them was really first to own a Beatles' album. But all that aside, football was everything. And my older brother, Al, was about everything in football in our city. It was a place of soot and orange trolleys still sparking their blue, because ordinary buses just couldn't muster the climb into the neighborhoods.

Al was a natural, a running back. Low-browed and heavy in the shoulders. He was maybe a little awkward in some ways, my father's oafishness, but he wasn't bragging. My father surely made up for that, but who could blame him? Here was a son who had not only been wooed by Dartmouth and the University of South Carolina, but, most importantly, Penn State itself. Though the handsome campus where the Nittany Lions played in their massive bowl (showing so much assurance and class that they didn't need anything more than numeral markings on their navy-and-white uniforms) was in a way local, that made it only more impressive. Our heroes went to Penn State, and USC and even Notre Dame were nothing to compare to it, let alone some place totally unheard of like South Carolina. And then *Life* magazine did a piece on Pennsylvania schoolboy football. Ten glossy pages of action photographs and the usual journalese on "tough" kids from "tough" coal and steel backgrounds. My brother's picture wasn't there along with some of the state's true stars, but there was a mention of him and also our high school, where I ran track, somewhat relieved that with a brother as "famous" as mine I felt no need to even try to compete for stardom. One fall afternoon it happened; the school was on its way to the state divisional championship.

Actually, this was the quarter-final in Pittsburgh. The stadium was an old poured-concrete affair, and the day stretched milky,

November dim. Even if the stands were just half full, the crowd seemed enormous, when you remembered this was only a high school game. Our school was indeed one from a supposedly tough coal town, and the opposition's was one from a supposedly tough steel town. Their players were huge, including the backfield. They had on ancient uniforms with black-and-yellow-striped sleeves, bees' markings, and the helmets weren't even plastic, but museum-piece, leather-covered jobs that had been repainted so often that the gloss cracked in spiderwebbing. It was in the fourth quarter, a grinding game of slams and bruises as the score stood stalled at a three-all tie on field goals, and I was right down at the bench with my father. My father, a solid man from those years of mining, shouted himself hoarse, while the band's pep song blaringly re-peated itself over and over, off-key horns and machine-gun drums, and the cheerleaders chanted like lost children in the diluted cold. Al finally took the ball on a quarterback hand-off, and I had seen him zig-zag so often, maybe even in my dreams, that I knew from his acceleration alone that this was going to be it for him. He dodged twin tackles near the line, then jetted loose of the whole crowd, springing into the clear of that frost-lumped field. One of their men was waiting for him, however, the safety, poised and low, and Al really turned it on. . . .

But we would never know if Al could have avoided that last snag. Because just then my father in his bulky Army surplus parka and porkpie hat was already crazed and out on the field tackling that last man himself. The crowd was stunned. The referees called the entire play invalid. Escorted to the sidelines, my father looked dazed, my brother looked dazed.

My brother did break away again. Our team won, but lost in the semi-finals. Al went to Penn State, though never made it much beyond the taxi squad. He went to work in the mines when he dropped out of college, married. For a while in our family the story of my father's mad running onto the field was something we all awkwardly tried to laugh about, but later, after I had left home, my father and brother argued bitterly, about everything. And years later my brother told me, "I think I would have stood a chance at Penn State, if it hadn't been for that. The way the papers reported it and all, and the way it got even worse when it was picked up on TV. But the story of it followed me, and somehow nobody ever remembered that I went on to score again, legitimately winning that game. They just remembered me as a clown, a joke. I truly hate him for doing it."

By the time the knock on the door came there in Presidio, I was half asleep. It was Alvarez's runner, the teenage kid in his hipster's getup. A baggy silver shirt, baggy gray trousers with pleats, fringed loafers. I needed some time to calm down after I heard from him that he didn't have the money, that Alvarez himself was up from Chihuahua and in Ojinaga, across the international bridge. He wanted to see me.

"See me about what?"

"Just see you, man," the kid said.

"Yeah, and I want to see some money. Money for the work I did, paid here, as agreed to."

"You'll get your money, man." Did this kid's acquired English require him to nail "man" on everything? "I'll drive you, man."

"No, I'll drive myself. Where is he, the Estrella?"

"I have a car, a fucking big Monte Carlo." Where was the "man?"

"And I have a pickup, with Texas plates, which makes me feel a lot safer. You know, *man?*"

"I like the Monte Carlo, man. Eet's turbo-charged."

I crossed the new international bridge. The sleepy Mexican guards with their droopy mustaches and fascist-brown uniforms must have recognized Charlie's truck. They waved me through. No problem. Ojinaga certainly isn't an Acuna, where I had spent time so often, and then that weekend with Lizanne. Ojinaga is too far out in the desert, and the old rail line that used to go directly from the town down to Chihuahua has been abandoned, and with it has gone the town's lifeline. Ojinaga is gritty and rough, and in the inky blue of that night I could almost taste its dead-end something in the rotting stink of diesel fumes and bad corn-oil cooking. The junker cars never seem to have mufflers in Ojinaga. The dark men in the usual straw cowboy hats stumble staggeringly out of the bars in Ojinaga. I saw the kid's black Monte Carlo in front of what had formerly been the Estrella. It was now painted glossy orange and glossy yellow on its crumbling stucco outside, and it had been re-named Bikini Bar.

The Bikini Bar still offered a long bar proper, running parallel to the front and stretching maybe a block. The redecorating squad had used more of that glossy orange and yellow inside the dive, which could have been frequented by Pancho Villa when he lived here. Two new posters, framed, on the wall: one of Cheryl Tiegs in a white bikini, maybe a blown-up shot from one of those sports magazine swimsuit issues; the other of the short girl, buxom and spilling long blonde hair, who used to play the wild younger sister on "Dallas" and whose name I probably never knew to begin with, in a black bikini. A couple of old men drank at one end of the bar. At the other end, sitting at a table, were middle-aged Alvarez, and two more teenage lieutenants who certainly had learned everything they knew about haberdashery from overdosing on a lot of MTV along the line—*and* the silver-haired guy I had run into that time a month before in Eagle Pass. That didn't surprise me. I had to admit I knew all along that I would eventually see him. Because on one level, that charade he waltzed through that afternoon in Eagle Pass indeed had the texture of a dream, and as all my life turned less and less tangible lately—marbleized memory as interrupted occasionally by the physical solidity of the booze—it had to get dreamier still.

"Ah, Rafferty," Alvarez said to me. Balding and overweight, he wore a light-blue guayabera and could have been simply another meek Mexican shopkeeper.

I looked around. I didn't want to look yet at the tall guy and his squinting blue eyes.

"What's this Bikini Bar stuff?" I said.

"You like that, man," the kid who had relayed the message

said. "Just looking at those pictures, that leetel broad, and I feel strong, man." He had his fist clenched; he jabbed it upward for a power signal. I nodded, without laughing.

"You like the little one, huh," I said.

"Sit down, sit down, Rafferty," Alvarez said.

"Yeah," I said, and sat.

"You know Mr. McCord?" Alvarez asked.

"I'm not sure that I do."

"And I'm sure that you do," the guy said. "And I'm sure that you know that I'm DEA, a bird-dogger. And I know that you've been spreading that aerial photography bullshit like it was Betty Crock-of-It's cake frosting for too long a time now, pal, and the only thing that it took a while for me to figure out was who you were taxiing for. That gets our life stories out of the way."

It was so direct, such a turnabout, that if I had been dreaming that earlier scene with him, I could in fact have been dreaming this as well. He leaned back. He smiled that sleepy smile, back to the treatment I had gotten in Eagle Pass.

"What is this?" I asked Alvarez.

"Relax, Rafferty. What this is, is business. Hey"—he poked one of the other teenage hipsters, the sallow specimen sitting right next to him—"play some shit."

The waiter brought more Carta Blancas, the jukebox blared some song about a man wanting his heart to fly like a dove to his faraway love, like a paloma. The junk cars and trucks were loud outside, backfiring in rifle shots, and sweat beaded on the brown bottles with their red-and-white labels. The silver-haired guy said no more. Alvarez explained.

It was as simple as this. A particularly troublesome DEA man had gone too far. He had been operating out of Mexico, Chihuahua specifically—Alvarez described it in his decent English—and there had been no reasoning with him. He had been shot by Mexican *federales* sympathetic to the "business," but now the problem was transporting the body back across the border, to the States. The DEA didn't like to let its men just disappear, and they would put pressure on everybody in Chihuahua until they extracted some answers. This could degenerate to an international incident, and with the two DEA men being gunned down in Guadalajara a couple of years before, nobody wanted another international incident, to put the heat on everybody. If found in the States, the body would be evidence of just another sad killing in the line of duty here. Open and easily shut.

"You've got a problem," I told him.

"*Nosotros* got a problem," Alvarez said, using the pronoun to stress his point. The silver-haired guy said nothing. He could have been watching it on television, stupid entertainment.

"*Nosotros* got a problem," the teenager with the Monte Carlo laughed. "That's funny, man."

"Shut up," Alvarez told him. "Rafferty, my friend, let me tell you this again."

This time he tightened his case: this is what McCord needed done, and we should listen to his "wishes"—the word seemed formal, not faring well in translation from the Spanish—seeing that he, McCord, was Alvarez's most important new "associate" in the business—that "associate" seemed formal too. Next, without my saying anything, he anticipated my complaints, that I shouldn't tell him that I was just a taxi for a few marijuana bales, not bigtime shipments, or worse, bodies, and something like this wasn't my problem.

"It's not my problem," I said.

"You know about it now, Rafferty, and it is your problem. Mr. McCord, he knows about you, and he is DEA. He is an American agent, you are an American. Listen, it is as simple as a run with marijuana, but the money is not simple." He named the figure; I didn't hesitate.

"No problem," I told him. I flashed to Lajitas for some reason, how a man not much older than me was turning a desert into a city, and what did I have to show for anything?

"No problem," I said again.

"*Nosotros* got no problem now, man," the kid said, liking that too. His teeth shone like shells.

The sweat was running in genuine rivulets down Alvarez's brownish pate. It was almost as if his fingernail had worn the white enamel off the cheap Carta Blanca table that you find in every one of these cantinas, as if his clawing nervousness had gouged right through to the black underneath, though the nick must have been there for years. Wet soaked under the arms of the light-blue guayabera. I realized now how scared he was himself about this.

"No problem at all," I told him.

The silver-haired McCord, Alvarez's associate, smiled, nodded some more.

5. THE FOREVER COMMONLY CALLED NEW MEXICO.
Let me tell you how beautiful this is.

There is a central valley that runs right up the middle of New Mexico. I am deep in it now, well out of Texas, following the Rio Grande north, truly toward its source. The 182 seems to like the tailwind, and flying like this is easy and special, the needles on the black-faced dials and gauges as steady as stone and nothing much to do except adjust the big elevator wheel now and then for trim. The river below winds silvery; flat orange sands, patterned with huge patches of aqua prickly pear, spread out on either side, for the plain of it. The mountains rise beyond on both sides, hazily blue now that I am this far north, whiter-than-white snow-capped peaks starting to show. The sunlight is a soft presence snagging on the scratches in my Plexiglas windshield, a little warm on my face. I am too far beyond any strip to pick up anything on the radio, which dished out only scratchy static the last time I tried a frequency I got from my sectional chart. I like the hum of the engine, entirely smooth, and the way that olive clouds are starting to pile up, gilded, straight ahead. Beautiful clouds. The corpse is sealed tight in a few layers of black trash bags bound with white nylon line. A lump beside me. But now I have gotten used to having it—no, *him,* here.

I made the pick-up on one of the strips near Chihuahua where I had made my marijuana pick-ups in the past. But I wasn't so stupid as to land again on the strip on the Texas side, as agreed to at the meeting with Alvarez and the DEA man. They just wanted the evidence back in the States, and after that was handled I was obviously expendable. Plus, I was the witness that nobody would want around. If nothing else I knew that I had to avoid any small place, those border airports, where they could close in on me. El Paso was the nearest city of any size, after more desert west of Presidio. (At Presidio Charlie appeared to turn strange around me too when I flew out to begin my errand this morning. Was he working with them? Did he know, and does everybody know what there is to know about everything except for me?) But at El Paso, with its futuristic new international terminal so neat out in that stretch of suburban malls and fast-food places, none of it was quite making sense. I filled both tanks with mo-gas and simply headed up into this big valley, where I am now.

And where I know what I am going to do. Or would that be the thing to do? Because I could still loop and retreat, even though these clouds look like real trouble now. They are closing in from three sides, and there is some chop. And if there is one place you don't want to be in an overhead job like this 182, despite all the power of those six tiger-purring cylinders, it is where one of these mountain storms can swallow you whole.

Money isn't the answer to anything after all. Yet here is what I am wondering. What if you go into a cloud build-up like this, a glare of blowing ice and snow that is already rainbowing a hundred times over up ahead, and what if you and this dead man, all the dead from this world, find that by venturing to that place you have never gone before, all the sadness, all the loneliness, doesn't mean a thing any more. And in that land of quiet and sunny stillness is maybe Lizanne's kid, Rosie, sitting on the edge of a puffy cloud, both her legs fine at last, her mind a cheery whole. And on another cloud you see your brother Al waving, so maybe he wasn't killed in the cave-in in the reopened mine that had supposedly been checked out by company inspectors only two weeks before the crushing collapse, and he calls over to you echoingly that he understood all along that a father once ran onto a football field on a dim day in Pittsburgh because of love and love alone, tells you if you can just find love in your own heart, you—

Damn, is this chop ever bad now. I must have dropped three-hundred feet in the last hit, and the windscreen is icing in layers now. I give it more gargling throttle, straight ahead, too rich at first so I nearly stall out, then I have it right, the semblance of a hum once more. I come out of the next drop better. Then straight in again.

"When I get to Albuquerque," I whisper to him beside me, "nobody will believe we got through this, nobody will believe the wonderful things we have seen." And already I realize that I really do want to make it through this, for once in who knows how long I really do want to live. "This is starting to get interesting," I tell him, my hands tight on the twin grips of the black plastic yoke, bracing myself for that next slam of it all.

The dead and me.

Joy Harjo

The Flood

I t had been years since I'd seen the watermonster, the snake who lived in the bottom of the lake, but that didn't mean he'd disappeared in the age of reason, a mystery that never happened. For in the muggy lake was the girl I could have been at sixteen, wrested from the torment of exaggerated fools, one version anyway, though the story at the surface would say car accident, or drowning while drinking, all of it eventually accidental. But there are no accidents. This story is not an accident, nor is the existence of the watersnake in the memory of the people as they carried the burden of the myth from Alabama to Oklahoma. Each reluctant step pounded memory into the broken heart and no one will ever forget it. When I walk the stairway of water into the abyss, I return as the wife of the watermonster, in a blanket of time decorated with

swatches of cloth and feathers from our favorite clothes. The stories of the battles of the watersnake are forever ongoing, and those
stories soaked into my blood since infancy like deer gravy, so how
could I resist the watersnake, who appeared as the most handsome
man in the tribe, or any band whose visits I'd been witness to since
childhood? This had been going on for centuries: the first time he
appeared I carried my baby sister on my back as I went to get water.
She laughed at a woodpecker flitting like a small sun above us and
before I could deter the symbol we were in it. My body was already
on fire with the explosion of womanhood as if I were flint, hot
stone, and when he stepped out of the water he was the first myth I
had ever seen uncovered. I had surprised him in a human moment.
I looked aside but I could not discount what I had seen. My baby
sister's cry pinched reality, the woodpecker a warning of a disjunc-
ture in the brimming sky, and then a man who was not a man but a
myth. What I had seen there were no words for except in the sacred
language of the most holy recounting, so when I ran back to the
village, drenched in salt, how could I explain the water jar left
empty by the river to my mother who deciphered my burning lips
as shame? My imagination had swallowed me like a mica sky, but I
had seen the watermonster in the fight of lightningstorms, breaking trees, stirring up killing winds, and had lost my favorite brother
to a spear of the sacred flame, so certainly I would know my beloved
if he were hidden in the blushing skin of the suddenly vulnerable. I
was taken with a fever and nothing cured it until I dreamed my
fiery body dipped in the river where it fed into the lake. My father
carried me as if I were newborn, as if he were presenting me once
more to the world, and when he dipped me I was quenched, pronounced healed. My parents immediately made plans to marry me
to an important man who was years older but would provide me
with everything I needed to survive in this world, a world I could
no longer perceive, as I had been blinded with a ring of water when
I was most in need of a drink by a snake who was not a snake, and
how did he know my absolute secrets, those created at the brink of

acquired language? When I disappeared it was in a storm that destroyed the houses of my relatives; my baby sister was found sucking on her hand in the crook of an oak. And though it may have appeared otherwise, I did not go willingly. That night I had seen my face strung on the shell belt of my ancestors, and I was standing next to a man who could not look me in the eye. The oldest woman in the tribe wanted to remember me as a symbol in the story of the girl who disobeyed, who gave in to her desires before marriage and was destroyed by the monster disguised as the seductive warrior. Others saw the car I was driving as it drove into the lake early one morning, the time the carriers of tradition wake up, before the sun or the approach of woodpeckers, and found the emptied six-pack on the sandy shores of the lake. The power of the victim is a power that will always be reckoned with, one way or the other. When the proverbial sixteen-year-old woman walked down to the edge of the lake to call out her ephemeral destiny, within her were all sixteen-year-old women from time immemorial; it wasn't that she decided to marry the watersnake, but there were no words describing the imprint of images larger than the language she'd received from her mother's mouth, her father's admonishments. Her imagination was larger than the small frame house at the north edge of town, with the broken cars surrounding it like a necklace of futility, larger than the town itself leaning into the lake. Nothing could stop it, just as no one could stop the bearing-down thunderheads as they gathered for war overhead in the war of opposites. Years later when she walked out of the lake and headed for town, no one recognized her, or themselves, in the drench of fire and rain. The children were always getting ready for bed, but never asleep, and the watersnake was a story that no one told anymore. She entered a drought that no one recognized as drought, the convenience store a signal of temporary amnesia. I had gone out to get bread, eggs and the newspaper before breakfast and hurried the cashier for my change as the crazy woman walked in, for I could not see myself as I had abandoned her some twenty years ago in a blue windbreaker at the edge of the man-made lake as everyone dove naked and drunk off the sheer cliff, as if we had nothing to live for, not then or ever. It was beginning to rain in Oklahoma, the rain that would flood the world.

Rick Bass

Antlers

Halloween brings us all closer, in the valley. The Halloween party at the saloon is when we all, for the first time since last winter, realize why we are all up here—all three dozen of us—living in this cold, blue valley. Sometimes there are a few tourists through the valley in the high green grasses of summer, and the valley is opened up a little. People slip in and out of it; it's almost a regular place. But in October the snows come, and it closes down. It becomes our valley again, and the tourists and less hardy-of-heart people leave.

Everyone who's up here is here because of the silence. It is eternity up here. Some are on the run, and others are looking for something; some are incapable of living in a city, among people, while others simply love the wildness of new untouched country.

But our lives are all close enough, our feelings, that when winter comes in October there's a feeling like a sigh, a sigh after the great full meal of summer, and at the Halloween party everyone shows up, and we don't bother with costumes because we all know one another so well, if not through direct contact then through word of mouth—what Dick said Becky said about Don, and so forth—knowing more in this manner, sometimes. And instead of costumes, all we do is strap horns on our heads—moose antlers, or deer antlers, or even the high throwback of elk antlers—and we have a big potluck supper and get drunk as hell, even those of us who do not drink, that one night a year, and we dance all night long, putting nickels in the jukebox (Elvis, the Doors, Marty Robbins) and clomping around in the bar as if it were a dance floor, tables and stools set outside in the falling snow to make room, and the men and women bang their antlers against each other in mock battle. Then around two or three in the morning we all drive home, or ski home, or snowshoe home, or ride back on horses—however we got to the party is how we'll return.

It usually snows big on Halloween—a foot, a foot and a half. Sometimes whoever drove down to the saloon will give the skiers a ride home by fastening a long rope to the back bumper, and we skiers will hold on to that rope, still wearing our antlers, too drunk or tired to take them off, and we'll ride home that way, being pulled up the hill by the truck, gliding silently over the road's hard ice across the new snow, our heads tucked against the wind, against the falling snow . . .

Like children being let off at a bus stop, we'll let go of the rope when the truck passes our dark cabins. It would be nice to leave a lantern burning in the window, for coming home, but you don't ever go to sleep or leave with a lantern lit like that—it can burn your cabin down in the night and leave you in the middle of winter with nothing. We come home to dark houses, all of us. The antlers feel natural after having been up there for so long. Sometimes we bump them against the door going in and knock them off. We wear them only once a year: only once a year do we become the hunted.

We believe in this small place, this valley. Many of us have come here from other places and have been running all our lives from other things, and I think that everyone who is up here has decided not to run anymore.

There is a woman up here, Suzie, who has moved through the valley with a regularity, a rhythm, that is all her own and has nothing to do with our—the men's—pleadings or desires. Over the years, Suzie has been with all the men in this valley. All, that is, except Randy. She won't have anything to do with Randy. He still wishes very much for his chance, but because he is a bowhunter—he uses a strong compound bow and wicked, heart-gleaming aluminum arrows with a whole spindle of razor blades at one end for the killing point—she will have nothing to do with him.

Sometimes I wanted to defend Randy, even though I strongly disagreed with bowhunting. Bowhunting, it seemed to me, was wrong—but Randy was just Randy, no better or worse than any of the rest of us who had dated Suzie. Bowhunting was just something he did, something he couldn't help; I didn't see why she had to take it so personally.

Wolves eviscerate their prey; it's a hard life. Dead's dead, isn't it? And isn't pain the same everywhere?

I would say that Suzie's boyfriends lasted, on the average, three months. Nobody ever left her. Even the most sworn bachelors among us enjoyed her company—she worked at the bar every evening—and it was always Suzie who left the men, who left us, though I thought it was odd and wonderful that she never left the valley.

Suzie has sandy-red hair, high cold cheeks, and fury-blue eyes; she is short, no taller than anyone's shoulders. But because most of us had known her for so long—and this is what the other men had told me after she'd left them—it was fun, and even stirring, but it wasn't really that *great*. There wasn't a lot of heat in it for most of them—not the dizzying, lost feeling kind you get sometimes when you meet someone for the first time, or even glimpse them in passing, never to meet. . . . That kind of heat was missing, said most of the men, and it was just comfortable, they said—*comfortable.*

When it was my turn to date Suzie, I'm proud to say that we stayed together for five months—longer than she's ever stayed with anyone—long enough for people to talk, and to kid her about it.

Our dates were simple enough; we'd go for long drives to the tops of snowy mountains and watch the valley. We'd drive into town, too, seventy miles away down a one-lane, rutted, cliff-hanging road, just for dinner and a movie. I could see how there was not heat and wild romance in it for some of the other men, but for me it was warm, and *right,* while it lasted.

When she left, I did not think I would ever eat again, drink again. It felt like my heart had been torn from my chest, like my lungs were on fire; every breath burned. I couldn't understand why she had to leave; I didn't know why she had to do that to me. I'd known it was coming, someday, but still it hurt. But I got over it; I lived. She's lovely. She's a nice girl. For a long time, I wished she would date Randy.

Besides being a bowhunter, Randy was a carpenter. He did odd jobs for people in the valley, usually fixing up old cabins rather than ever building any new ones. He kept his own schedule, and stopped working entirely in the fall so that he could hunt to his heart's content. He would roam the valley for days, exploring all of the wildest places, going all over the valley. He had hunted everywhere, had seen everything in the valley. We all hunted in the fall—grouse, deer, elk, though we left the moose and bear alone because they were rarer and we liked seeing them—but none of us were clever or stealthy enough to bowhunt. You had to get so close to the animal, with a bow.

Suzie didn't like any form of hunting. "That's what cattle are for," she'd say. "Cattle are like city people. Cattle expect, even deserve, what they've got coming. But wild animals are different. Wild animals enjoy life. They live in the woods on purpose. It's cruel to go in after them and kill them. It's cruel."

We'd all hoo-rah her and order more beers, and she wouldn't get angry, then—she'd understand that it was just what everyone did up here, the men and the women alike, that we loved the animals, loved seeing them, but that for one or two months out of the year we loved to hunt them. She couldn't understand it, but she knew that was how it was.

Randy was so good at what he did that we were jealous, and we admired him for it, tipped our hats to his talent. He could crawl right up to within thirty yards of wild animals when they were feeding, or he could sit so still that they would walk right past him. And he was good with his bow—he was deadly. The animal he shot would run a short way with the arrow stuck through it. An arrow wouldn't kill the way a bullet did, and the animal always ran at least a little way before dying—bleeding to death, or dying from trauma—and no one liked for that to happen, but the blood trail was easy to follow, especially in the snow. There was nothing that could be done about it; that was just the way bowhunting was. The men looked at it as being much fairer than hunting with a rifle, because you had to get so close to the animal to get a good shot—thirty-five, forty yards was the farthest away you could be—but Suzie didn't see it that way.

She would serve Randy his drinks and would chat with him, would be polite, but her face was a mask, her smiles were stiff.

What Randy did to try to gain Suzie's favor was to build her things. Davey, the bartender—the man she was dating that summer—didn't really mind. It wasn't as if there were any threat of Randy stealing her away, and besides, he liked the objects Randy built her; and, too, I think it might have seemed to add just the smallest bit of that white heat to Davey and Suzie's relationship—though I can't say that for sure.

Randy built her a porch swing out of bright larch wood and stained it with tung oil. It was as pretty as a new truck; he brought it up to her at the bar one night, having spent a week sanding it and getting it just right. We all gathered around, admiring it, running our hands over its smoothness. Suzie smiled a little—a polite smile, which was, in a way, worse than if she had looked angry—and said nothing, not even "thank you," and she and Davey took it home in the back of Davey's truck. This was in June.

Randy built her other things, too—small things, things she could fit on her dresser: a little mahogany box for her earrings, of which she had several pairs, and a walking stick with a deer's antler for the grip. She said she did not want the walking stick, but would take the earring box.

Some nights I would lie awake in my cabin and think about how Suzie was with Davey, and then I would feel sorry for Davey, because she would be leaving him eventually. I'd lie there on my side and look out my bedroom window at the northern lights flashing above the snowy mountains, and their strange light would be reflected on the river that ran past my cabin, so that the light seemed to be coming from beneath the water as well. On nights like those I'd feel like my heart was never going to heal—in fact, I was certain that it never would. I didn't love Suzie anymore— didn't think I did, anyway—but I wanted to love someone, and to be loved. Life, on those nights, seemed shorter than anything in the world, and so important, so precious, that it terrified me.

Perhaps Suzie was right about the bowhunting, and about all hunters.

In the evenings, back when we'd been together, Suzie and I would sit out on the back porch after she got in from work—still plenty of daylight left, the sun not setting until very late—and we'd watch large herds of deer, their antlers covered with summer velvet, wade out into the cool shadows of the river to bathe, like ladies. The sun would finally set, and those deer bodies would take on the dark shapes of the shadows, still out in the shallows of the rapids, splashing and bathing. Later, well into the night, Suzie and I would sit in the same chair, wrapped up in a single blanket, and nap. Shooting stars would shriek and howl over the mountains as if taunting us.

———

This past July, Randy, who lives along a field up on the side of the mountains at the north end of the valley up against the brief foothills, began practicing: standing out in the field at various marked distances—ten, twenty, thirty, forty yards—and shooting arrow after arrow into the bull's-eye target that was stapled to bales of hay. It was unusual to drive past in July and not see him out there in the field, practicing—even in the middle of the day, shirtless, perspiring, his cheeks flushed. He lived by himself, and there was probably nothing else to do. The bowhunting season began in late August, months before the regular gun season.

Too many people up here, I think, just get comfortable and lazy and lose their real passions—for whatever it is they used to get excited about. I've been up here only a few years, so maybe I have no right to say that, but it's what I feel.

It made Suzie furious to see Randy out practicing like that. She circulated a petition in the valley, requesting that bowhunting be banned.

But we—the other men, the other hunters—would have been doing the same thing, hunting the giant elk with bows for the thrill of it, luring them in with calls and rattles, right in to us, hidden in the bushes, the bulls wanting to fight, squealing madly and rushing in, tearing at trees and brush with their great dark antlers. If we could have gotten them in that close before killing them, we would have, and it would be a thing we would remember longer than any other thing. . . .

We just weren't good enough. We couldn't sign Suzie's petition. Not even Davey could sign it.

"It's wrong," she'd say.

"It's personal choice," Davey would say. "If you use the meat, and apologize to the spirit right before you do it and right after—if you give thanks—it's okay. It's a man's choice, honey," he'd say— and if there was one thing Suzie hated, it was that man-woman stuff.

"He's trying to prove something," she said.

"He's just doing something he cares about, dear," Davey said.

"He's trying to prove his manhood—to me, to all of us," she said. "He's dangerous."

"No," said Davey, "that's not it. He likes it and hates it both. It fascinates him is all."

"It's sick," Suzie said. "He's dangerous."

I could see that Suzie would not be with Davey much longer. She moved from man to man almost with the seasons. There was a wildness, a flightiness, about her—some sort of combination of strength and terror—that made her desirable. To me, anyway, though I can only guess for the others.

I'd been out bowhunting with Randy once to see how it was done. I saw him shoot an elk, a huge bull, and I saw the arrow go in behind the bull's shoulder where the heart and lungs were hidden—and I saw, too, the way the bull looked around in wild-eyed surprise, and then went galloping off through the timber, seemingly uninjured, running hard. For a long time Randy and I sat there, listening to the clack-clack of the aluminum arrow banging against trees as the elk ran away with it.

"We sit and wait," Randy said. "We just wait." He was confident and did not seem at all shaky, though I was. It was a record bull, a beautiful bull. We sat there and waited. I did not believe we would ever see that bull again. I studied Randy's cool face, tiger-striped and frightening with the camouflage painted on it, and he seemed so cold, so icy.

After a couple of hours we got up and began to follow the blood trail. There wasn't much of it at all, at first—just a drop or two, drops in the dry leaves, already turning brown and cracking, drops that I would never have seen—but after about a quarter of a mile, farther down the hill, we began to see more of it, until it looked as if entire buckets of blood had been lost. We found two places where the bull had lain down beneath a tree to die, but had then gotten up and moved on again. We found him by the creek, a half mile away, down in the shadows, but with his huge antlers rising into a patch of sun and gleaming. He looked like a monster from another world; even after his death, he looked noble. The creek made a beautiful trickling sound. It was very quiet. But as we got closer, as large as he was, the bull looked like someone's pet. He looked friendly. The green-and-black arrow sticking out of him looked as if it had hurt his feelings more than anything; it did not look as if such a small arrow could kill such a large and strong animal.

We sat down beside the elk and admired him, studied him. Randy, who because of the scent did not smoke during the hunting season—not until he had his elk—pulled out a pack of cigarettes, shook one out, and lit it.

"I'm not sure why I do it," he admitted, reading my mind. "I feel kind of bad about it each time I see one like this, but I keep doing it." He shrugged. I listened to the sound of the creek. "I know it's cruel, but I can't help it. I have to do it," he said.

"What do you think it must feel like?" Suzie had asked me at the bar. "What do you think it must feel like to run around with an arrow in your heart, knowing you're going to die for it?" She was furious and righteous, red-faced, and I told her I didn't know. I paid for my drink and left, confused because she was right. The animal had to be feeling pain—serious, continuous pain. It was just the way it was.

In July, Suzie left Davey, as I'd predicted. It was gentle and kind— amicable—and we all had a party down at the saloon to celebrate. We roasted a whole deer that Holger Jennings had hit with his truck the night before while coming back from town with supplies, and we stayed out in front of the saloon and ate steaming fresh meat on paper plates with barbecue sauce and crisp apples from Idaho, and watched the lazy little river that followed the road that ran through town. We didn't dance or play loud music or any-thing—it was too mellow. There were children and dogs. This was back when Don Terlinde was still alive, and he played his accordion: a sad, sweet sound. We drank beer and told stories.

All this time, I'd been uncertain about whether it was right or wrong to hunt if you used the meat and said those prayers. And I'm still not entirely convinced, one way or the other. But I do have a better picture of what it's like now to be the elk or deer. And I understand Suzie a little better, too: I no longer think of her as cruel for hurting Randy's proud heart, for singling out, among all the other men in the valley, only Randy to shun, to avoid.

She wasn't cruel. She was just frightened. Fright—sometimes plain fright, even more than terror—is every bit as bad as pain, and maybe worse.

What I am getting at is that Suzie went home with me that night after the party; she had made her rounds through the men of the valley, had sampled them all (except for Randy and a few of the more ancient ones), and now she was choosing to come back to me.

"I've got to go somewhere," she said. "I hate being alone. I can't stand to be alone." She slipped her hand in mine as we were walking home. Randy was still sitting on the picnic table with Davey when we left, eating slices of venison. The sun still hadn't quite set. Ducks flew down the river.

"I guess that's as close to 'I love you' as I'll get," I said.

"I'm serious," she said, twisting my hand. "You don't understand. It's *horrible.* I can't *stand* it. It's not like other people's loneliness. It's worse."

"Why?" I asked.

"No reason," Suzie said. "I'm just scared, is all. Jumpy. Spooky. Some people are that way. I can't help it."

"It's okay," I said.

We walked down the road like that, holding hands, walking slowly in the dusk. It was about three miles down the gravel road to my cabin. Suzie knew the way. We heard owls as we walked along the river and saw lots of deer. Once, for no reason, I turned and looked back, but I saw nothing, saw no one.

If Randy can have such white-hot passion for a thing—bowhunting—he can, I understand full well, have just as much heat in his hate. It spooks me the way he doesn't bring Suzie presents anymore in the old, hopeful way. The flat looks he gives me could mean anything: they rattle me.

It's like I can't *see* him.

Sometimes I'm afraid to go into the woods.

But I do anyway. I go hunting in the fall and cut wood in the fall and winter, fish in the spring, and go for walks in the summer, walks and drives up to the tops of the high snowy mountains—and there are times when I feel someone or something is just behind me, following at a distance, and I'll turn around, frightened and angry both, and I won't see anything, but still, later on into the walk, I'll feel it again.

But I feel other things, too: I feel my happiness with Suzie. I feel the sun on my face and on my shoulders. I like the way we sit on the porch again, the way we used to, with drinks in hand, and watch the end of day, watch the deer come slipping down into the river.

I'm frightened, but it feels delicious.

This year at the Halloween party, it dumped on us; it began snowing the day before and continued on through the night and all through Halloween day and then Halloween night, snowing harder than ever. The roof over the saloon groaned that night under the load of new snow, but we had the party anyway and kept dancing, all of us leaping around and waltzing, drinking, proposing toasts, and arm-wrestling, then leaping up again and dancing some more, with all the antlers from all the animals in the valley strapped to our heads—everyone. It looked pagan. We all whooped and danced. Davey and Suzie danced in each other's arms, swirled and pirouetted; she was so light and so free, and I watched them and grinned. Randy sat on the porch and drank beers and watched, too, and smiled. It was a polite smile.

All of the rest of us drank and stomped around. We shook our heads at each other and pretended we were deer, pretended we were elk.

We ran out of beer around three in the morning, and we all started gathering up our skis, rounding up rides, people with trucks who could take us home. The rumble of trucks being warmed up began, and the beams of headlights crisscrossed the road in all directions, showing us just how hard it really was snowing. The flakes were as large as the biggest goose feathers. Because Randy and I lived up the same road, Davey drove us home, and Suzie took hold of the tow rope and skied with us.

Davey drove slowly because it was hard to see the road in such a storm.

Suzie had had a lot to drink—we all had—and she held on to the rope with both hands, her deer antlers slightly askew, and she began to ask Randy some questions about his hunting—not razzing him, as I thought she would, but simply questioning him—things she'd been wondering for a long time, I supposed, but had been too angry to ask. We watched the brake lights in front of us, watched the snow spiraling into our faces and concentrated on holding on to the rope. As usual, we all seemed to have forgotten the antlers that were on our heads.

"What's it like?" Suzie kept wanting to know. "I mean, what's it *really* like?"

We were sliding through the night, holding on to the rope, being pulled through the night. The snow was striking our faces, caking our eyebrows, and it was so cold that it was hard to speak.

"You're a real asshole, you know?" Suzie said, when Randy wouldn't answer. "You're too cold-blooded for me," she said. "You scare me, mister."

Randy just stared straight ahead, his face hard and flat and blank, and he held on to the rope.

I'd had way too much to drink. We all had. We slid over some rough spots in the road.

"Suzie, honey," I started to say—I have no idea what I was going to say after that—something to defend Randy, I think—but then I stopped, because Randy turned and looked at me, for just a second, with fury, terrible fury, which I could *feel* as well as see, even in my drunkenness. But then the mask, the polite mask, came back down over him, and we continued down the road in silence, the antlers on our heads bobbing and weaving, a fine target for anyone who might not have understood that we weren't wild animals.

Ken Smith

The Government Man

Sometimes in the cooler months the government men spread lye over the carcasses of the cattle they killed. But in summer, when the cattle moved up higher onto the slopes, they usually just shot them and let them lay. Up high the Pinal Mountains are rough and you can't get a truck up there. I guess they didn't want to use mules to pack the lye, which was unnecessary anyway, the days so hot that it didn't take long for a cow to bloat and spoil. The men who shot the cows tried always to do it in an open spot, in high sun, away from any shade.

Everybody knew what was going on and most thought it shameful, a harebrained scheme by Roosevelt and his cronies to raise the price of beef and give the ranchers some profit. Trouble is, the people around here couldn't afford beef even at the lower prices, and me and some of my friends didn't see that it was any-thing but wastefulness. The first time Richard Phillips and I came upon a kill, we stomped around that hillside and cussed. It was an awful thing. Those good Hereford cattle bloated and about to bust and only the coyotes and buzzards getting any good out of them.

I spent most all this past summer in an old cabin on the eastern slope of the Pinals, glassing the road far down into El Capitan Pass, waiting for the green government truck hauling a horse trailer which would pull off and weave its way up to a ranch house. I would watch carefully as the rancher and the government man talked, the rancher sometimes waving his arms and pointing toward the mountains, the government man listening and sometimes stopping to ask a question. When their talking was done, the government man would unload his horse and begin the ride up the mountain. Once I figured the general vicinity he was headed for, I'd climb the little knoll behind the cabin and start my smudge fire. In an hour Richard Phillips and Sandoval would be up on the mountain with me. While I waited I'd watch the government man's progress, try-ing to figure just what trail he would take, what bunch of cattle he was heading for. I know all this country, cowboying as I've done for most all the outfits around.

We did not make much money from our venture. We kept the Phillips family in beef and we helped out Sandoval's big family over in Superior. Of all of us I was the one most in it for money, trying to save enough to get away from the twenty-five acres of bottom-land my dad had left me. He had bought the place when I was twelve, right after Mom took my older sister and caught the train for California. Just on the outskirts of Globe, it's a good enough piece of land if you could count on the creek running all summer. We lived there for six years, and since Dad died I've lived there alone, putting in a few crops and waiting, like my dad did, for some of the state land around to come open, which it never will because the bigger ranchers are keeping tight grips on their leased sections. Dad's dream, and I guess you could say I inherited it, was to some-day have a little cow outfit of our own.

I've had only the one letter from my sis, that in answer to my own letter when Dad died. I guess they're doing fine in California. Sis has married a man with orchards. She didn't say what kind, but I imagine oranges, or grapefruits, or some of those strange fruits they grow on the little hills beside the ocean. She said Mom lived with them and was doing O.K. but that she'd get a flutter in her heart now and then. Sis reminded me of what Dad had always told us, time and again, for as long as I can remember. When things were especially bad, he'd tell us we were better people than our circumstance showed.

I think another reason I got into this business of rustling dead cattle was that it seemed like an adventure, sneaking around and following the government men and butchering out the cattle they thought were just going to lie and rot. At first Sandoval, who we nicknamed Sandy, was nervous about doing it. He's light-skinned for a Mexican, and when he gets scared his face goes almost white. But after we'd done it a few times, he got over his jitters. He even started joking about it, calling us *banditos.*

Richard Phillips I've known as long as I can remember, though I didn't much like him in school. He was moody, sometimes down-right standoffish, and sometimes silly as a clown. From one day to the next you could never figure what his mood would be, or whether you were going to be his friend. Later in high school we got in on a couple of the same shows for schoolboy cowboys, mostly roping, though he did some steer wrestling too, big hunk of a kid that he was. Then after school I took up with Tina, Richard's sister, and for a while I hoped something might come of all that. But she got tired of waiting for me to make something of myself, I guess, and last year she married a soldier from Fort Huachuca. Through all that romance Richard was a good friend to me.

He and his folks live on a little bad-water, bad-graze ranch with Mrs. Phillips's old mother and widowed aunt, the whole bunch of them working to improve the place, and lots of time scraping up just enough to keep themselves and a hundred skinny cows alive. Sandy works for them sometimes, mostly just for his keep.

On this one particular day as I sat watching the government man ride into the Pinals, it seemed like Richard and Sandy took a long time getting up the mountain. I had caught and saddled my horse and tied up the two burros I kept at the cabin. I had checked the pack saddles and thrown them over the corral fence next to where all three animals were tied. It seemed like I watched the government man a long time. He'd go down in a draw and I'd lose sight of him, then pick him up again as he topped the next ridge, heading always west. I had to strain to keep man and horse in my focus as they became specks in the blue distance.

When I finally heard the others ride up behind me, I turned quick and said, "We'll really have to ride. The son of a bitch is heading for Phoenix."

"Keep watching," Richard told me. "Sandy and me'll get your horse and the burros."

They rode off to the corral, each leading a burro they had brought up from the Phillips's place. I went back to my binoculars. At first I couldn't see the government man, then he came out on a high, open ridge and turned south, heading farther up the mountain. He was highlighted there against ragged white clouds far off to the west, and then I saw the cattle he was heading for. O.K., I said to myself, he's going up around that bunch and push them down onto Weber Mesa.

From the cabin we had to climb hard for a quarter of a mile. Then we turned and headed west, crossing the rocky draws near their heads where there wasn't so much up-and-down riding to do. Still we did not make good time. I led two burros and Richard, right behind me, helped to push them by lashing out at their rumps with his catch-rope. We traveled fast, and though we didn't talk, our animals made plenty of noise. But we were high up into the tree line and I figured that even if the government man did hear us, he'd probably think we were a herd of javelina or deer. No way in the world could he have seen us.

When we came to a spot which I judged to be just above Weber

Mesa, Sandy and I left Richard with the horses and started down-hill on foot. Sandy carried my old pump .22 rifle and I had the binoculars. We went a good ways down, then finally broke out, as I knew we would, atop a little bluff overlooking the flat. At first I thought I'd made a mistake, because we couldn't see anything of the government man nor any of the cows.

Sandy's face was scrunched up with a question, and he was getting ready to whisper something to me when we heard a cow bawl. Then the government man came out into plain sight, riding away from the bluff we were on, his back to us, and his rifle across his lap.

We eased back the least little bit and watched. The government man continued out onto the flat a few yards, then turned his horse. His face was red and we could see how fat he was and how the heat was working on both him and the horse. His shirt was soaked, and as he got down the horse shifted a little against all that weight going to one side.

Once on the ground, the man stood still for a minute, looking back at the base of the bluff where he'd pushed the cows he was going to shoot. He breathed deep and then chambered a shell. I figured the cows were right up against the face of the bluff, not thirty feet below us.

Holding the horse's reins in his left hand, he brought his rifle up. He fired four times, his horse jerking its head with each shot, and the 30.06 sounded like a cannon as the shock waves hit against the rocks of the bluff. He paused, then fired again. After he threw the last spent shell from his rifle, he spat on the ground, climbed back on the horse and turned off toward the edge of the mesa, riding slow and heavy in his saddle.

As soon as he went out of sight, Sandy eased down the side of the bluff to follow him and I climbed up into the trees to get Richard and the animals.

Our plan seemed foolproof. Sandy would follow the government man until he was sure the man would not double back. If he did turn back, Sandy would either run ahead to warn us, or he'd fire a shot from the .22 and we'd quick gather up our gear and the horses and burros and get out of there. On that particular day it did not seem we had anything to worry about. The government man was hot and tired and I figured he'd head straight back for the ranch where maybe he could get a cold glass of tea before he loaded his horse and drove off.

So Richard and I set straight to work. We tussled the two best-looking cows around so that their heads were uphill, then each started in gutting one. We worked fast and it was hot, the sun shining off the white dirt of the flat and reflecting off the face of the bluff climbing above us. Strong heat rose into our faces from the cattle, too, once we got them opened up.

We boiled in our own sweat, straightening up now and then to stretch the kinks out of our backs, and we talked some and cussed the heat and the blowflies. We just were not careful.

When the government man came around the bluff leading his horse neither of us heard him. We didn't have any idea he was there until he spoke. I think what he said first was "Damn."

Then Richard and I were both standing, cow blood up to our elbows, trying to wipe the sweat out of our eyes with our upper arms. For a long time nobody said anything. We all just looked at each other.

There wasn't even the hint of a breeze, and sweat ran down the government man's fat cheeks. He squinted his eyes at us and finally said, "I had suspicions about this. I had 'em especially strong today."

He was carrying the rifle in both hands, low across his body. He was not pointing it at us, but I had seen him thumb the safety off.

"What are you going to do?" Richard asked him.

The man tilted his head and looked at us, then at the gutted cows.

"You could just ride on," Richard told him. "Save everybody a lot of trouble."

The man nodded, looking straight into Richard's face. Then he sighed and pulled himself up out of the slouch he had been in.

"You fellas are too old for this," he said. "This ain't no schoolboy prank." He moved the rifle so that he was cradling it in one arm, then he pulled out a bandanna and wiped his face. "What you're doing—however you want to cut it—is against the law. What you're doing is stealing government property."

"It's not exactly stealing," I said. "These cattle are pretty much worth less like they are."

He looked at me hard and I wished I had stayed quiet. "What I want you to do is to get some of that blood washed off. You've got water on those burros, don't you?" He looked over at our horses and burros, and I was surprised that it didn't seem to concern him that we had three saddle horses. He was nervous himself, I guess, and didn't notice.

He raised his rifle in both hands again, the first time he'd made a move that seemed menacing. "Then I'm taking you down to the Tidwell place and what we'll do, I suppose, is send for the sheriff."

Richard started for one of the burros that was packing water in a big canvas bag.

"Don't come back with nothing but a canteen," the government man told him.

Richard turned to look at him. His eyes were dark and he chewed on his bottom lip for a second. "Mister," he said, "we ain't got any guns."

The government man smiled, then, and seemed to relax, his big belly pooching out and his shoulders sagging. I was trying to think of something to say that would make him let us go, some good argument that what we were doing was better than just letting the beef go to waste. I was thinking hard when he asked me, "What do you get out of this, anyway?"

"Damn little," I told him.

Richard came over and started pouring water over my hands and arms.

The government man smiled again, but it was cut short with the sharp, whiny snap of Sandy's .22. I remember thinking that his warning shot was coming a little late, and for a minute I felt like laughing at the whole bunch of us. Then another shot came, kicking up dust between where the government man was standing and the dead cows.

He whirled fast, looking off to his left. He saw Sandy out toward the edge of the mesa. We all saw him running, crouched low, and then he disappeared behind some rocks.

"What's that damn fool shooting for," the government man said, but not like a question. Then another bullet hit close to his feet and he jumped a little. "Well, damn," he said, and he raised his rifle and shot two times into the rocks Sandy had jumped behind, the rolling boom of the 30.06 sounding awful loud after the short low snap of Sandy's .22.

He tilted his head to eye us, still keeping the rifle up to his shoulder. "If that fella's a friend of yours, you better tell him to come on in and give himself up."

Then Sandy was running again, out near the edge of the flat, where the brush grew thick, scrub oak and manzanita and deer brush. The government man shot at him again, though it didn't seem he took aim.

When Sandy disappeared into the brush, the man turned back to me and Richard. "Get into your saddles, now. Let's hurry it."

From the brush we heard Sandy yelling. He was cussing in Spanish, taunting, like he thought he could get the man to chase him. In English he shouted, "Ride on, fat man. This is not your business."

The government man took a step toward Sandy's voice. When Sandy yelled again, he fired three shots into the brush. I stood there and shook, sure we'd find Sandy tangled in the manzanita with a big hole in him, and I started shouting for him to give it up, to run away down the mountain.

"You run," Sandy shouted back. "I'll keep this *pendejo* off you."

I thought about that for a minute, but with the man and his ought-six not twenty feet away and hearing the sound of that thing going off, I wasn't about to move. When I glanced at Richard he didn't seem to have any such ideas either. He just stood there looking out toward the edge of the mesa.

The government man was down on one knee now, shoving more shells into his clip. He said to us, "Why don't one of you fellas go out there and get your friend? Otherwise, I'm afraid I'm going to have to kill him."

He stood up and looked at us both. I was thinking maybe I should go, but somehow I believed that if everyone just stayed still, this whole thing might work out. A good idea would come to somebody.

The man looked off toward the brush. "Goddamn you, throw down and come on out," he yelled. His face was red and the veins in his neck bulged. Every inch of him was wet. "Goddamn you, Mex, can you hear me?"

It was quiet for a minute, then Sandy laughed.

The government man brought his rifle up. It looked like he was having trouble with his sights. "Throw that popper out now and stand up," he said, "before somebody gets hurt."

He stood still for a bit. Then he began to shoot as fast as he could work his bolt. Five, six times, I don't know how many bullets he fired, and all I could hear was that ought-six going off and its echo booming against the rock walls of the bluff.

Suddenly he lowered his rifle and turned to look at Richard and me. His mouth formed the shape of a huge O, and his eyes were red and watery. "I'll be a son of a bitch," he said. Then he turned and started towards his horse, which in all the shooting had spooked off toward the other horses and burros. He just turned his back to us and walked away, but after a few steps he stumbled and had to use his rifle like a cane. We hadn't been able to hear Sandy shooting over the loud roar of the ought-six, but I knew now that he had been.

The government man stumbled again. Before he got to his horse he came to a stunted oak growing right up against the face of the bluff. He paused there a moment, then worked the few steps up to the tree and sat down, leaning there, breathing fast, his rifle across his lap.

He closed his eyes and breathed in deep a couple of times. Richard and I started to go to him, but he moved his legs around and fiddled with his rifle and eyed us in a way I didn't like, so I stopped and held my arm out behind to tell Richard to do the same. I was wanting real bad to do two things at once. One was to turn and run like hell, the other was to go see if I couldn't do something for him.

He edged around to one side, still leaning his shoulders against the trunk of the oak, and looked right at us. "I wish I had the gumption to shoot you," he said. He closed his eyes again and the rifle slipped out of his hands. His eyes opened slowly, and I could tell he was still seeing us, but I thought for sure he was dying.

I started to go toward him, but what I was seeing suddenly went black around the edges and I was afraid I'd fall. I felt my legs shaking. Richard's hand came to my shoulder. He said something but I couldn't hear. It was like nothing inside me was working and all I could see was the government man slumped against that tree with his eyes shut tight and his teeth clenched and sweat running down out of his hair.

In a minute Richard walked out onto the flat, his back to me and his hands cupped so his voice would carry. "Sandy, come on in. Dammit, get in here. This guy is—no shit—hurt bad."

A few seconds later, I was over under the tree, looking at the government man. Sandy was coming in, he and Richard walking across the flat toward me, and Sandy shaking his head and saying, "I hit him?"

The three of us stood there staring. I glanced off to the west where big, puffy clouds were building over that end of the mountain range.

Sandy looked at me, his eyes big and scared like he was wondering whether I would turn against him. "I only meant to scare him," he said. "Honest to God, I thought after a while he would go away."

"Shit," Richard said. "You can't scare a man carrying an ought-six with a twenty-two."

The government man had quit sweating by now. His face wasn't red anymore. It sagged and it was gray.

"I don't see a mark on him," I said.

I hadn't hardly got the words out when the man sat upright and opened his eyes. He reached a hand toward Sandy, who stepped back quick. "You," the man said. "You done this. And I used to work the mines with your daddy." Then he slumped hard against the tree. He stared at Sandy, like his eyes were stuck open, and then I saw the very beginning of a glassiness start to come, and I knew he was dead.

Sandy said, "I never saw this man before. My dad never worked in a mine."

Richard reached over easy with his boot and pushed it against the fat man's leg. He looked down for a minute, then said, "Well, he's for sure dead, anyhow."

"I still can't see a mark on the man," I said.

"Maybe his heart just gave out," Sandy said.

"We got to see," I told him.

Richard grabbed my arm. "Let me get my gloves," he said.

As he walked toward the horses, Sandy shook his head and touched my arm. He looked like he was about to cry. "How in the hell can you kill a man that big with a twenty-two?" he asked. "Especially when you aren't even aiming?"

All I could do was shrug.

His gloves on, Richard bent down and looked the man over close. He unbuttoned the man's shirt and pulled out the tails. There, just an inch to the left and a bit lower than his belly button was a small purple hole. It wasn't half as big around as your little finger and there was not one drop of blood that I could see.

Richard raised up and looked at Sandy. "There," he said. "That's where you hit him."

It didn't seem to me like a .22 bullet could have got through all that fat, but I didn't say anything.

In a minute Richard reached down and eased the man over. "I don't see where the bullet came out," he said. "He sure died quick. I always thought something gut-shot lived a long time."

I straightened and started to back away. Richard said, "Come over here, both of you. Help me look. I'll move him around and we'll see if Sandy didn't hit him twice or something."

"What difference does it make?" I said. "The man's dead. He's dead and we killed him and we better figure out what in the hell we're going to do."

For a moment it was quiet, then Sandy said, "I think we just don't touch him anymore." He spread his arms wide like he was giving up on some idea he had started to have. "I say we just leave him lay and we ride."

"They'll find him," Richard said.

"So?"

"They're going to find those gutted cows and put two and two together."

"They still can't prove it was us."

"There's quite a few folks around that know what we do," I told them.

"That's nothing to say somebody else couldn't have done it this time. God, I'm just as sorry as hell. You believe me? You know I was only trying to scare him?"

I looked down at the man, lying now on his side next to the tree, his shirttails stirring just a bit in the wind. "I'm with Sandy," I said. "We just leave, don't any of us ever touch him again."

After a while we walked away from the government man, over toward the eastern face of the bluff where our horses and burros were tied. We talked for a while. Richard had the idea we should load him on his horse, then ride to an old mine shaft on the mountain's eastern slope. There we could shoot the horse and then throw everything—man, horse, rifle—into the shaft.

"Look," I said, "I got this feeling that the more we try to cover all this up, the worse it's going to be. The harder the law has to look for him, the more they got to piece things together, the more likely it is they're going to find something to tie us in. I think we should just ride, like Sandy says, and pretty quick, too, because some Tidwell cowboy could have been up this way and heard all that shooting."

Sandy nodded.

Richard stared at me. I had a tight, bad-tasting throat, and I could feel my heart beating twice its normal pace.

"Could they track us, you think?" Richard asked.

"Not if we're careful," I told him. "And not if that rainstorm blows up this afternoon."

All three of us looked to the west. The clouds that way were darker and more promising.

"The one thing we have to think about is getting rid of that twenty-two," Richard said.

Sandy looked down at the little rifle in his hands. He seemed surprised to find that he still had it. For a minute I thought he was going to hand it to me. Then he said, "I'm going to Superior to see my family. I'll take the burros and spread them out all to hell. I know the place for this gun. A shaft about halfway there. An old one. Hasn't anybody worked it in years."

I told Sandy I'd come along part way and help with the burros.

Richard decided to go on back to his place, then in the morning he'd get his dad to take him to town and he'd catch the train for New Mexico, where he knew some people he could stay with. "Guess we won't see each other for a while," he said, after we'd got onto our horses. A heavier wind rose up from the west. I was thinking we'd for sure have a storm by nightfall.

"Wouldn't be a good idea," I said.

Sandy cleared his throat, then put his hand up to his forehead. "I'm just as sorry as hell," he said. "I got scared, thinking he was shooting at you. Or that he was going to shoot you. I don't know how I missed him doubling back like that. I guess I wasn't listening so good." Sandy's eyes started going watery again as he talked, and his mouth moved slow like he was having a toothache.

"It's O.K.," Richard said. "We're all in this together. The one thing we got to keep remembering is that."

We made a vow then, a promise to deny everything, even if we weren't believed. "If we just hold to it," I said. I stared for a long time at the others. "Nobody admits to a damn thing."

"Well, I will," Richard said. "I'll hold to it right up until they hang me." He smiled kind of lopsided and shook hands with Sandy and me. Then he headed east alone, going back nearly the way we had come, to finally drop down into El Capitan Pass and on across the river to home.

Sandy and I pushed the burros up higher on the mountain until we nearly crested, then we rode the westerly-heading ridges, cutting out a burro every so often and pushing him down into the draw.

We rode across a lot of slick, rocky places, turning uphill and then down, and we'd have been hell to track. We crossed a creek with shallow stagnant water and stayed in it awhile. By the time we were ready to split up, the first raindrops came spitting out of the sky. They were big and far apart, like they were the leading edge of what was to be a real storm. Before I left Sandy to turn north toward my little place on the outskirts of town, I told him to remember about getting rid of the .22.

"Don't worry," he said, "nobody's ever going to find this gun."

"Well, I'll be seeing you then. It wasn't any more your fault than mine or Richard's."

I turned and rode off, but I hadn't gone far when he called to me. I reined around and looked at him. Raindrops battered my straw hat. It only then occurred to me that I'd left my slicker and some blankets and some other things I might need in the old cabin on the eastern slope.

"You could call it an accident," Sandy said. He had to shout because we were a ways apart and the rain was starting to come on good.

I eased my horse up the ridge to Sandy. "Sure," I told him. "It's what it was." I realized then that Sandy didn't have a slicker either and I wished I had mine to loan him.

He nodded. "They'll know it was us," he said. "Soon as they find him, they'll know."

"Knowing's one thing," I told him. "Proving's another."

He sat there and stared at me, his eyes dark under the brim of his hat. Then he shook his head slow and smiled, and sunlight coming between the clouds lit up his face for just a moment.

"Stop and think, Sandy. Once that gun's down a shaft, there isn't one damn thing that can tie us in." I folded my hands and put them on the saddle horn. Cow blood had dried and caked under my fingernails, and I held my hands out to the rain. Then I said, "They're going to come around with some questions. You can count on that, I think. Just don't get scared and they can't trick you. Don't say nothing about me or Richard or cows. Play it dumb and it won't matter what they think they know."

Sandy smiling surprised me. He was not a man to smile so much. He was not one of your happy-go-lucky Mexicans. He looked off toward the mountains, his lips drawn up hard, like he'd set the smile there and planned to keep it. The rain eased a little, and he looked up into it. Then I heard him laugh, and I knew he was not right. He pushed his hat down so hard it nearly touched his ears.

"It's going to be O.K., Sandy. Nothing at all is ever going to come of this."

"Sure," he said. And the way he looked at me I knew he'd been up on the mountain with the cows and dead man for the last few minutes, and that now he was back. He started to turn his horse down the trail, then stopped. He looked at me for a long time, shaking his head slow. "When they come to ask us about this, they're going to think they're talking to dangerous men," he said.

"If you want, you could bunk at my place tonight. Start out again in the morning when this storm's over."

He shook his head. "No," he said. "It's better for the tracks to just keep riding in this rain."

I watched him kick his horse on down the trail toward Superior. He still had a long way to go. In an hour I'd be home and dry. I'd probably be drinking a little whiskey mixed with water, the way my dad always drank his, though I am not a man taken much to drink. I'd probably check the box under my bed and count the money there. I was thinking I'd better use some of that money to get myself another gun, because a .22 comes in handy around a little place like I've got.

When I reached the shelf above the creek that would take me home, I pulled in under a cottonwood and sat there for a minute, giving myself and my horse a little rest from the drumming rain. I thought about my mom and my sis. I hoped they were all right, that my sis's orchards were bearing good fruit, and that they could sell whatever it was they did grow. But in these bad times there sure are no guarantees. Times when men will jump out of buildings or kill cattle and leave them to the buzzards. Times when men start killing other men. I wondered what my mom and sis would think if they knew I had become a bandito, a for-sure outlaw who had helped to kill a man, a government man. I wondered how my life was going to be now that, like Sandy had said, I was dangerous. I thought about that, but I did not feel dangerous, only scared, and it came to me that scared was what he was when he shot the government man, and I got to thinking that maybe scared and dangerous were the same thing.

After a while, lightning flashed too close and I knew that under that cottonwood was not the place to be. As I rode on, the rain beating down so hard it stung, I thought more about buying a gun, and it came to me that with the way all this could turn, I might better be thinking about one of a bigger caliber.

Larry Levis

First Water

1. WATERS.

In childhood I drank a water so cold it seemed to have been born before anything. Or seemed not to have been born at all, but only there, there in the first place.

No one knew it was there until 1940, when my father and a man named Angel Dominguez, having already decided to build a swimming pool for my mother, decided to drill a new well for it beneath the bleak hundred-year-old stillness of a row of walnut trees, and to then pump the water with an engine and drive shaft that had once driven a ferris wheel, and which they had bought at the public auction of a bankrupt, passing carnival.

Anyone might suppose that the noise from such an engine would obliterate the untouchable, shaded stillness of those trees. Actually, the engine's unvarying hum became only another part of that stillness, a further perfection of it, a sound that was a stillness in itself.

They excavated the pool by harnessing two mules to a dredger, and later on, when the cement and concrete finally dried, they filled the pool with the first water from that well.

A few days after, when they let the water drain out into a surrounding orchard for irrigation, there were over a hundred cracks in the walls and floor of the new pool. By now, of course, the pool has been painted over a hundred times in various shades of blue, pink, green, gold, and the perennial favorite, a bright aluminum. The coat upon coat of paint fills the cracks left by the singlemindedly chilling water at the same time it retards the slowly spreading but disappointingly, chronically perceptible brown growth of algae at the bottom, algae that are now forty-seven years old, in good health, and, in their own remarkably uninteresting way, alive.

When the first water from that well rushed into the pool (water that is still called, each year, first-day water), it was so cold it felt anciently cold, aloofly cold.

Unbridled, wild, it nipped and bit the skin.

It is the kind of water one would find on the page one page before the Bible begins.

2. A SCREECHING.

The ferris wheel itself, which no one had bought or even bid on, stood silently in paint-chipped gray and maroon in an unleased field behind the Roma Winery. Sometimes if the wind was strong enough, it would begin to turn slowly, as if it had suddenly remembered to turn, and the long ungreased steel would rend the air with one unending shriek like the scrape of freight cars in a railyard, and the workers at Roma would have to stuff handkerchiefs or balls of cotton into their ears until it stopped.

It was as if something from childhood had now come back, and sat at the edge of a broad field, and sang in the dead falsetto of its metal.

But no one knew why it had come back, and no one could remember the tune.

And anyway its singing ended forever when they chained the Sedan of Death to one of its gondolas. The Sedan of Death was just a DeSoto, but its owner had knotted himself with his necktie to its steering column before plunging the car into fifty feet of water above the dam at Piedra, and no one found the car for weeks. When they hauled it out, the smell of the decomposing body was so strong no one would buy the car, not even after its unsuccessful fumigation, not even for one dollar, finally—though its body and paint were nearly perfect.

It had brought the car dealer nothing but bad luck: crowds strolled past it on summer evenings, but they did not see a dark green DeSoto; they saw the Sedan of Death, and, in the wary style of their compliments they would say: "It *is* a nice car to look at, though."

Superstition owned the car, and was not selling it.

So there was nothing to do but light the pink slip on fire and drive the DeSoto out in the dead of night and chain and padlock it to the ferris wheel. Gradually, over the years, other rusted cars and trucks would appear in the dawn light, and farm implements beyond repair, and then baby carriages whose black canopies let in too much sky, and mattresses wet and heavy as galleons, and trash of all kinds. The whole wilderness of the broken collected there beneath the wheel and the DeSoto like offerings, and its onslaught grew and spread until eventually the entire three-acre field was only a long dream of rust, of gray mice, of lizards so motionless you could not know they were there.

And although in high school Ronny Collins offered twenty dollars to anyone who could prove he had laid a girl in the Sedan of Death, either no one tried or no one could prove it. For proof required witnesses, and everyone was in high school then; everyone was too old, or too modest, or reticent. But when those who lived in Hell's Hole or La Colonia heard of the offer, those who would never suffer the indignity of having to prove anything to

Ronny Collins, they casually surrounded him one afternoon in their chinos with split cuffs and with their long, flashy watch chains spilling from one of the belt loops nearest the buckle, and waited wordlessly until Ronny Collins handed over the money anyway, and for nothing.

In Hell's Hole and La Colonia they lived with their families in long chicken sheds empty by then of chickens. This is true. And it made them wild.

3. A CLINK OF ICE.

The palms are still, unmoving. Ice clinks in glasses by the pool.

No, not yet. My mother is just now emerging from the house, carrying a tray with two glasses of iced tea out to the pool; one for her, one for the young priest who's come to visit and swim.

By noon, it is 99 degrees.

There, now you can hear the ice clink. My mother puts the tray down and looks around for him a moment, then at the pool, and then a little further into the water where the priest is floating, face down. At first he looks as if he's snorkeling there. His whole body is waving idly, and, in some small way, even suggestively. It waves the way limp weeds wave, and in his new, candy-cane-striped swimming trunks, he looks, for a priest, preposterously casual. And though I would always imagine him afterward in black vestments, steeping in water as if conferring upon it some sacrament, it was not so.

His body rocks a little as if he had suddenly remembered a confession and blurted out laughing at it, only to inhale the water immediately after.

But, in fact, he died of a weak heart and of first-day water, not of drowning.

How strong my mother must have been to haul him out alone! For, once a body is dead, it sags, slides, slouches, falls away as if it's in love with gravity—although, even in those first few seconds, eternity itself must be entering it as a crew of wreckers crowd into a cold house with crowbars and sledges and go to work at once, wasting no time.

But of course eternity has no need of tools, nor of Time, for eternity is just what's there, abruptly, once Time ceases in something.

Eternity like a cold apple in the hand of an emperor, the apple green against the burnished dusk of the throne, and the emperor thinking that the apple is temporary, perishable.

And the apple? No, it is just an apple.

That is, it is still an apple.

The only explanation of eternity is in its refusal to explain.

4. RED ANTS.

But if you are made to wait beside a corpse long enough, you step into another world.

Or else you spend all your time trying not to step into another world.

These are likely, however, only if the death has happened suddenly and accidentally and has been the unforeseen death of a stranger. If you are the owner of a funeral parlor, or a nurse or surgeon, or a soldier of fortune, or if you are intimate with or related to the corpse in any way, or if you scrupulously maintain an adolescent indifference to everyone else on earth (*"Ma mère est morte hier"* Blam! blam! blam!), then things might be different.

But my mother is trying not to step into that other world, where she has no business going.

But on the ranch she is miles from anyone. And she must wait for my father to arrive, or for his foreman, Juanito, to come by, or for the ambulance she's phoned for an hour ago. An almost peasant abundance and radiance inhabits her face, flushed now from her labors, while white droplets of water shine on the singular black hairs sprouting around the dead priest's nipples. Elsewhere his chest is hairless, white, serene, and unlovely.

Of course she feels it's her duty to wait here, beside him. Even leaving him for a moment to go inside and call seemed to her the brief violation of some deep but unspoken taboo, although, yes, for a split second she did feel, recradling the phone, the thrill of a pure indifference.

And so, she waits.

But my father is still hammering the tines of a springtooth cultivator into position, then tightening the five nuts fast to their bolts on each of the thirty tines. One hundred fifty nuts that have been leased to rust all winter. It will be hours, and besides, he's in the almond orchard on the north forty, seven miles away. And Juanito is irrigating vines, trying to get each trickle of water running at the same rate down each furrow. But they never do. In all the years he has been here, it has never flowed exactly right—one furrow's flooding the vines at the end of a row by four in the afternoon, while another will have to bask in moonlight. He turns a valve sixteen degrees to the left in one of the small standpipes at the end of a row, but no; it's wrong; he opens it again until the water splashes over the small, round concrete walls that resemble an unimaginative child's castle on a beach, if the sand were a cement gray.

And the ambulance? Although the switchboard operator is only temporary help, and although she doesn't for a moment believe that a priest has drowned in anyone's pool, and thinks it is only the prank of a lonely farmwife, she does take down the message. Only she gets the address wrong. Instead of 10818 South Mendocino Avenue, she has written 1018 South Mendocino, which, if it existed, would be a sand bar with the limb of an old oak stretching across an eddy in the King's River and carved with hearts and the initials of lovers, and even of their enemies, in a fantastic, livid embroidery of what has passed. She replaces the phone and stares into the small mirror on her desk. She decides to pluck out a little more, but only a little more, hair from each eyebrow. Then she thinks no, maybe she shouldn't after all.

By now the ice has completely melted in the untouched tea, and the silence of the ranch seems to emanate from my mother as she sits there.

And it is in this moment that she first notices the thin line of red ants—most of them no larger than the *1* in a page of type—a line that has come out of the cracks in the smooth patio stone like an infinite, silent, single-minded divinity. As they approach the body, their Host, she shoos them away, but they can't hear a word of it. It's as if they listen on a different frequency. She scrapes a few of them back with one foot, but they simply advance again as if the white flesh of the priest had been part of some revelation or prophecy in the one, unprintably holy text they all know and have not read.

My mother tries to sweep them away with a broom, but now there are too many.

It won't work.

She has to get the hose and spray them, flood them back on a cold tide.

There goes a tiny Noah on a grass blade.

But why do they persist in this? Is it the cold, obscene infinity of their Queen's eggs, a Queen vast, sticky, inert, with a heart that has nothing in it but a cold wind?

How do they do it?

By now, someone knows. But for ants there is no Ark, no Virgin Queen, no past of any kind, nor future either. They live wholly in the present, and they complete it thoughtlessly, and are a little of what Heidegger saw a glimmer of, and are the little Maoists of a perfect state, in a perfect time, when alienation and labor have been erased, and when flames have erased the chicken sheds of La Colonia and Hell's Hole.

And when the last memory of them has been erased, then ants will overwhelm everything, from the stored certificates of our births and deaths to the thin, dry, translucent gray sheen on a fingernail.

5. ANGLOS.

If your name were Ramon or Coronado or Xavier, or if they simply called you Dead Rat (pronounced Debtrat, *y rapido*), and if you had just stepped onto the high rung of a ladder to pick early Santa Rosa plums, and if you happened to peer out, over the trees and into the pool, you would not know exactly what to do because you would believe that you had just seen a woman hosing down a patio while a dead man lay beside her. And each time you glanced over at them again, he would be slightly bluer in hue, and, as the afternoon wore on, he would slowly become paler and bluer until he seemed mottled, like a trout. But as you worked, your bucket would keep filling with plums and, in a while, it would no longer seem to be any of your business. You would feel silly inquiring into it, especially after an hour had passed and you had said nothing, done nothing. Not that the dead man was more dead now than he had been earlier (although that was something to reconsider, whether death itself didn't mature with time)—but . . . the fact that time kept passing in this way, in the quiet of the trees, seemed to intimate to you that it was none of your business after all, that Anglos were not, in fact, any of your business. After all, you didn't ride under a green canvas tarp in a stolen truck all the way from Los Mochis to Fresno just to get involved with some dead guy and a woman with a hose, did you? Ask the vacant spiderweb about it. Ask the sound of plums rolling into the wooden field boxes dark as charcoal with time.

6. TIME.

It was Time, Time Itself that frightened my mother. Time that waters the vines, and that would finally allow the springtooth's thirty tedious tines to blend together so that the dirt sang once again through its one cello, and Time that would also delay the ambulance (and tempt the operator to a longer coffee break the second time my mother called, and the third time also), and would delay Juanito who is by now trying to close off a broken furrow before it begins to flood two acres which are not even ours, but Kurokawa's, our neighbor's; Time, incontestable Time is what she imagines will begin, any moment now, to play its remorseless game in the empty, summer vacated halls of the dead body beside her, just as it did in the body of a border collie on the road's shoulder, though in a young man it will be different, she thinks—too familiar and too strange all at once as it stiffens his neck so that he inclines his head to one side as if he's hearing confessions through the little screened slot in the dark, or loosens and then contracts the abdomen and bowels, or locks a knee while the other leg flutter-kicks, or casually crosses his legs, or stretches an arm out leisurely, only to retract, just as inscrutably, whatever question it had been lifted to answer about Augustine or Aquinas.

And although nothing like this had begun to happen yet, it was just this world that she did not wish to step into.

Finally she couldn't bear waiting for it any more and went quietly through the hot, unshaded yard into the barn and got a rope—long, thick, dishwater-blond hemp—and first tied his ankles together, then his arms, and then, out of fear, she coiled what was left of it around and around this wide-eyed pardoner of all earthly desire and necessity—yes, coiled him up in it until he looked like nothing so much as he did a mummy from some unadorned, bankrupt kingdom. Unadorned, that is, except for those striped trunks gleaming through it all like a barber's pole in a sandstorm, or an ice cream parlor hidden by the fallen debris of some explosion, or the red headbands of the Khmer Rouge as they entered Phnom Penh on tanks.

You see? If you sit beside that corpse long enough with her, that other world opens so effortlessly you do not even know it is there until you've stepped into it.

She was hosing the ants back once again when she heard the tires of the ambulance slow and stop on the gravel drive, and almost at the same moment (as these things happen), she saw my father's face blossoming between the ivy-festooned, golden oaks which joined their limbs together to form a sort of archway, and in that moment she looked at the dropped, still gushing hose, at the ants, at the blue-lipped, perishable mummy of a priest coiled in the rope, and then, taking a deep breath, she began to rehearse an explanation of it all.

No one doubted her word. No one had ever doubted her word. Not there.

In San Francisco, during the depression, she could barely manage to hold a job as a secretary, having lied that she knew typing and shorthand to get it.

Here, she was sovereign.

And why not? The years followed in their inexorably reconciling pattern of vines in winter bonfires and the summery silence of one young orchard after another, and children (polio in one daughter and a cure for that polio), and grandchildren, and the thick, muffled, full leafed, maturing privacy of it all, which is its only dignity.

7. THE WORD BENEATH THE WORD.

This is a true story. Even the address is correct. A priest did drown in our pool, but it happened so long ago, before I was born, that no one spoke of it. My mother was alone when it happened, and she did haul him out and try to resuscitate him.

But I added the ants. I added the long vigil of my mother and the mummy she made from the coiled rope. In fact, in those moments at least, I am the only one waiting beside that dead bachelor, waiting and refusing, with a hose, with a rope, to enter the other world.

But why did I have to wait so long beside the dead body of someone I could never have known? And where did everyone go?

The word beneath the word, my mother disappearing into myself as I waited beside the body, is a word composed of nothing at all except a small refusal, but it is an infinite refusal.

8.

Still, why have I admitted all this? Because, although the altering of facts and the justification of any fabrication because it is "art" is permitted everywhere now, it is not permitted on the East Side of the San Joaquin Valley, not without the restoration of fact. And there are some taboos that I am unwilling to transgress, no matter what the consequences.

There is of course no Sedan of Death and no ferris wheel. Nor was there ever a passing, bankrupt carnival. But the dark row of walnut trees, and the hum of the engine beneath it, are real, and still there, the motor running even as I write this.

The chicken sheds of Hell's Hole and La Colonia have been demolished, and replaced with the plywood of cheap tract homes.

Roma Wine went out of business long ago. But in a bad year for raisins they and other wineries bought grapes from us and other growers for twenty dollars a ton because the cheapest way to sweeten a cheap sauterne or tokay is to mix in tons of Thompson Seedless grapes.

Twenty dollars a ton.

Which, I suppose, kept bums from freezing to death in boxcars or in vacant doorways for a while, although it would in itself eventually lead them, slowly in its arm, to the most final chills of all.

And the water? Was it really that cold?—you might ask.

Colder.

Rudolfo A. Anaya

Children of the Desert

H e had worked the oil fields of south Texas for as long as he could remember. Abandoned as a child, he was passed from family to family until he was old enough to work. He grew up living and breathing the desert, but never trusting it. He sometimes drove into the desert alone, not looking for anything in particular, perhaps testing some inner fear he felt of the vast landscape. Sometimes he would find sun-bleached bones, and he would feel compelled to take one back to his trailer.

Once he had seen the bodies of two Mexicans the sheriff had brought in. They had died of heat exposure in the desert. Their mouths were stuffed with sand, sand that in their last feverish moments they thought was water.

He could not forget the image of the two wetbacks, and after that he developed the habit of hiding plastic milk containers full of water along the desert trails he knew. The desert was merciless; without water a man would die of thirst.

He kept to himself, but once a year at Christmas time he went to Juarez. He took the long drive across the desert to drink and visit the brothels. It was a week in which he went crazy, drinking to excess and spending his money on the prostitutes.

When his money was gone he headed back to the oil town, his physical yearning satisfied, but the deeper communion he had sought in the women remained unfulfilled.

One Christmas he stopped to clean up and eat at a trucker's cafe on the outskirts of El Paso. The waitress at his table was a young woman, not especially pretty, but flirtatious. She wore bright red lipstick which contrasted with her white skin. She drew him into conversation.

He was self-conscious, but he smiled and told her he was going home. He talked about the oil town, the aluminum trailers clustered together in the desert. He had a job, he had a truck, and he lived alone.

"A man without water will die in that desert," he said, and held his breath. Would she understand?

"The desert's all we got." She nodded, looking out the window, beyond the trucks and cars of the gas station to the desert which stretched into Mexico. "It's both mother and father. Lover and brother." She was like him, an abandoned child of the desert. He looked at her and felt troubled. Why did she pay attention to him? What did she want?

She wanted to go with him. Would he take her? He had never shared his space with anyone. Only during the week in Juarez, and then he went crazy and could not remember what he had done. The women he slept with were a blur. After that week of debauchery he felt empty, like the unsatisfied desert.

Now a new emotion crept into his loneliness. He thought the feeling came with the sweet smell of her perfume, her red lips and blue eyes. She squinted in the bright sun as she looked at him. Her skin was white, and beneath her blouse he saw the rise and fall of her breasts. He wanted to touch her.

"I can't take you," he mumbled.

"Why not?" she asked. "I can take care of your place, wash your clothes, sew, cook. You said you ain't got a woman."

No, he didn't have a woman. Did he need one? He needed something, someone.

"Get in." He nodded.

"You won't be sorry," she said. She ran back into the cafe and returned with a small, worn suitcase. "All I got's in here." She smiled.

He had never been able to say much more than a few words to any woman, but as they drove across the desert he opened up to her. He told her about his work on the oil rigs and about the small aluminum trailer he had in the oil town. He told her how once a year he went to Juarez and became a different person, but he would give that up for her.

She had no family, so they guessed they belonged together. She was happy with the trailer, she was happy to belong.

He was happy too, now he whistled on the way to work. He gave up the old habit of hiding the containers full of water, and he began to forget where the precious water lay hidden.

The other workers joked about him. The older men said they had never seen him so happy, and it must be because he was getting it regular now. Get your young wife pregnant, they said, otherwise she might start running around. They knew the women of the oil town were lonely. There was nothing for them to do in the desert, and each woman spent a lot of time alone. Sometimes three or four of them gathered together to talk or exchange recipes or to play cards. Usually they drank, and then they cursed their life in the lonely and merciless desert.

The men didn't want their wives to form these groups. On those days dinner wasn't ready, they argued and fought. It was better to have the women stay at home, alone, not getting fancy ideas from the neighbor ladies, each man thought. In preserving that false peace each woman was driven deeper into loneliness.

He thought about a baby, but he didn't mention it to her. The child would be an extension of something that happened when they made love. That was what he felt, and it provided a small measure of contentment.

He wondered if she thought of a child. She said nothing, she seemed happy. There was no sign of pregnancy, and he grew more intense, driving deeper into her flesh to deposit his fluid of life, water he hid in her desert. But she, like the desert, was never satisfied. She took pleasure from his emptying in her, but he had nothing to show for his possession. She lay in bed when he was done, glowing with the sweat of their love.

She is the desert, he thought, she thrives on the heat and sweat.

"I love the heat," she had told him once, and what she said mystified him. The heat of the desert was death. The men with sand stuffed in their mouths, the bleached bones of those who died there.

He remembered the earrings he had found in the sand. The glitter of gold and the red rubies had caught his attention. Someone had lost her way, a woman. The sheriff found dead people out there all the time. Mexicans coming across to look for work, looking for a better life. The promised land.

He had not told her of the earrings. He felt them in his pocket. Would he give them to her someday?

"Come here." She smiled and drew him to bed to make love, her words like the cry of the doves when they came to drink water. Her movements beneath him were urgent, searching for her relief. He was still thinking of the earrings when he tasted sand in his mouth.

He felt the hair rise along his back, he drew away. She moaned and smiled, awash in the convulsion that swept over her. Sweat glistened on her breasts and stomach. She kept her eyes closed as she caressed herself, slowly running her hands between her breasts, along her flat stomach.

"Hotter than hell," he said, and lighted a cigarette.

She was still out there, in the space the orgasm created. The soft sounds she made irritated him.

"You sound like a cat," he said.

"It's just cause you make me feel so good," she answered. "When you're on me," she said, "a bubble forms right here, between us. I can feel it. I hold you tight so the bubble won't escape. Here. Feel."

He felt sand.

She held on to him even after he was spent. She held tight even when he was choking for air. The desert swept over him and covered his mouth with sand. At that moment he always cried out. Why did fear and pleasure come together?

"You're crazy," he said.

"I can feel it," she said.

He looked out the window at the hot, burning land. Mirages formed in the distance, green trees and the blue shimmer of water. An oasis. Hell, he knew there wasn't water out there. A mirage. Nothing. Death. Like the bubble, sucking you in.

"Crazy woman," he repeated. There she was covered with sweat and rubbing herself, in dreamland, and the trailer was hot as an oven.

"It's hotter than hell," he shouted, got up and flipped on the air conditioner.

"I like it hot," she answered.

He looked at her. She was caressing the spot where she said the bubble formed. Her nails were red against her white skin. Her breasts were full, round, crowned with pink nipples.

Sweat dripped from his armpits, ran in trickles down his ribs. He thought of the pile of bones around the side of the trailer, bones he had collected over the years.

"What do you think about when you feel that bubble?" he asked.

"It's a secret." She smiled.

A secret, he thought. A fucking secret. The men were right, a young wife shouldn't be running around with the other women. Getting ideas. He knew she went into town with them, drove the seventy miles just to sit in the cool movie house. Hell, they probably went drinking.

"I don't want you hanging around with the women. Damn floozies."

She looked at him. "They're not floozies."

"You do what I say!" he shouted, and kicked the small table near him. The red plastic flowers crashed to the floor.

"Get rid of your crazy ideas," he said in anger, and fell down on her, to crush away the secret of the bubble. But he couldn't do it. The irritation he felt made him impotent.

"You're hurting me," she said, and struggled away.

He stood over her, trying to catch his breath, trying to understand what was happening. Her toenails were painted red. Red like the fruit of the cactus. Her lips were red, the curtains were red, the dress was red, even the plastic flowers were red. And the earrings were red. He stumbled to the sink to splash water on his face.

"You okay?" she asked.

The water was like sand. His hands trembled.

"You like it here, because of the bubble," he said.

"We both like it here," she answered. "Didn't I tell you, we're children of the desert."

He looked out the window over the sink. There was nothing. Nothing. Only heat and sand. He had forgotten where he hid the water, or where he had found the earrings. Now he had nothing. He was at the mercy of the desert.

"There is no bubble!" he shouted at her, struck out. The slap caught her flush across the mouth. Blood oozed from her lips.

"There is," she insisted, fighting back the pain. "It's here, between us. It's the most beautiful feeling on earth. There's no harm in it!"

———

Her cry rang in his ears long after he left the trailer. In the desert he could hear the sound of her voice, see the red of her lips. He drove deep into the desert, away from her. But now being alone frightened him. He lost his way, panic swept over him like a suffocating sandstorm.

He had never before been lost. He stopped at an arroyo he thought he knew and tore into the sand until his hands bled, but he couldn't find any of his water containers. He remembered the men with their mouths full of sand, their eyes eaten out by the vultures. In that moment of fear, his mother spoke to him, her red lips taunting him. He saw her clearly, the gold earrings dangling.

Finally, when he found his way back, he was exhausted and trembling. A terrible fear made him shiver. He drank all night and the following day.

He used her roughly in a brutal attempt to destroy the images which haunted him. "No more bubble!" he insisted when he was done. "It's gone!" he shouted triumphantly.

But what was that pocket of air he had killed? The child he had wished for? The secret she hid from him? His failure to understand? And why had he seen his mother in the desert? The questions haunted him.

She withdrew into herself, cowering in fear. He had become a man she did not know. He used her, but now there was only the suffering. The bed became a bed of sand. The more frantic his need, the more silent and withdrawn she became.

He went across the border to Agua Arenosa, to the whore house. He drank and went to the prostitutes until he was exhausted. When his money was gone he argued and fought, and the cantinero threw him out in the street.

He sat in the dust, a bitter taste in his mouth. Around him the town was deserted. Dervish dust swirled down the street, the wind cried like a mourning woman.

He was lost in that wailing wind. Sand stung his eyes, he tasted it in his mouth.

He turned to an old woman who sat by the door of the cantina. Old and wrinkled and dirty, she was called into the cantina only to test the men before they went to the whores. He reached out and grabbed her.

"Demonio!" she cried in terror and struggled to pull away. *"Deja me ir, diablo!"*

"No! No! I won't hurt you!" he cried. "I won't hurt you. I only want to know! Inside! *Aqui!"* he shouted and pointed to his chest, the place where emptiness gnawed at his heart.

His cry was one of torment. The old woman grew calm. She had seen eyes like his before. The devil of the desert was in the man. He had seen death, or he was about to die.

"Aqui," she said. *"Corazon."*

Heart? His heart was dry. He had opened his heart and the desert had swept in.

"Mira, hijo," the woman said kindly. She drew a line on the dirt. She spit to one side and a ball of mud formed from the dirt and the spittle. *"Hombre,"* she said.

She spit to the other side. *"Mujer,"* she said.

Then she spit on the line, and a perfect ball of wet earth formed. *"Semilla,"* she smiled.

She pushed the two balls towards the one in the middle, and the three dissolved into one.

"Amor," she said and moved away.

The seed was love. It lay between the man and the woman. It belonged to both. It was like a child growing in the belly, or like the bubble she caressed.

Even in the sand the seed of love could grow. He reached into his pocket and found the gold earrings with the red rubies. He looked at them, feeling the great burden of the past. Whatever was out there in the desert would haunt him no more, and he threw the earrings as far as he could. For a moment they glistened in the sun then disappeared into the sand.

He drove home, careening down the road, a speck in the vast bowl of desert and sky. He drove fast, full of a new urgency to see her. Near the trailer he crossed an arroyo, the front tires caught in the sand, the truck flipped over and he was thrown out.

For some time he lay unconscious, then awoke to feel a sharp pain in his lungs. When he spit he saw the red stain of blood. But he could not rest until he saw her and told her what he had discovered.

Holding his side he ran to the trailer, calling her name. She was not there when he arrived. The trailer was empty.

He slumped to the ground by the door. The pain was sharp in his chest, he could not breathe, but he felt a calmness. Around him the desert was a space opening and receding. Her bubble. A space to hold a seed. He looked across the silent sand and understood.

Leslie Johnson

Back in Aberdeen

Today is the day, Vance has decided, that he will get his stepdaughter to like him. He has it planned: Sunday brunch in a nice restaurant, an afternoon drive through the desert, a leisurely walk at some scenic spot. Just the two of them, all day. And no matter how sullen Inez, his stepdaughter, appears, Vance will persevere. Perhaps as they're strolling past giant saguaros or blossoming prickly pears, he will pause and glance thoughtfully down at his stomach, as he sometimes does before making a sales pitch, and then, looking up at Inez, reveal something meaningful about his life, something personal. Eventually, she'll open up to him, maybe even cry a little, maybe apologize for giving him the silent treatment these last few months.

But at the moment, Inez is in her bedroom, refusing to come

out. Sandy, her mother and Vance's new wife, has gone in after her. Vance is standing in the hallway by the closed door, trying to listen. "Something for nothing," he hears Sandy say, but the rest is muffled. Both Sandy and Inez have very soft voices. Vance found that appealing about Sandy when they first met: her low, breathy voice. But lately he finds himself telling her to speak up a little, enunciate. He gets tired of leaning forward to hear better.

Whatever they're saying in there, Vance wishes they'd get it said. He wishes Sandy and Inez would just yell at each other, get it all out, the way people in families do.

He leaves the hallway, walks to the dining room and through the sliding glass door to the outside patio, which is his favorite part of the house. He paid extra for its terracotta tiles when he bought the place. Sandy has hung hummingbird feeders along the sides of the veranda, and although they've seen no birds yet, it's a cute idea, Vance thinks, since they live on Hummingbird Drive, a newly developed stretch in North Phoenix.

Vance steps across the yard's soft bermuda grass and plucks a tangerine from one of his trees before settling into a padded lounge chair on the patio. He bites the soft, tart skin of the fruit, forgetting for a minute, or at least not caring much, that Sandy and Inez are battling inside. He throws a chunk of rind into the mouth of a large Indian pot set for decoration by the wall.

He's lived in Phoenix for five years now, not so long really, but as he leans back in his chair, popping sections of citrus in his mouth, dressed in white slacks and a golf shirt, warm in February, his old life in Aberdeen, South Dakota, seems like distant history. "The old Vance might still be walking some cold Aberdeen street," he told Sandy the first day they met, on a trip to the Grand Canyon for single adults, "but he's not a guy I'd care to share a beer with."

Even though Aberdeen seems far away and his birthday next month will be his fifty-fourth, Vance himself does not feel older. Not really. He feels comfortable, which to Vance is the best way to feel. He often tells his salesmen at Sun Casuals to imagine taking off a scratchy flannel shirt, one that cuts under the arms and squeezes at the neck, and slipping into a nice smooth cotton-poly blend. "That's how I want every customer to feel," he'll say, waving at a long rack of men's sport shirts in cool, shimmering shades of peach, mint green, lemon yellow, "Comfortable."

His stores are making money. He has a nice home, and four months ago he married Sandy. She's forty-two, blond, nice looking. And he looks fine beside her, he feels. His gray hair, waved back from his forehead, is still thick. He's a large man, always has been, but he's not really fat. A masculine build, Sandy says. She's easy-going like he is. She laughs at just about anything, and almost always they have a good time. Things are going well.

Except for Inez. She stares at him with her little black eyes. She hates him, at least that's how it seems. She's sixteen, and Vance knows that teenagers are supposed to be difficult. And he expected it might take some time for the three of them to get used to each other. But he thought Inez would at least like him. He's always been known as a likeable guy.

He's tried to win her over. He had one of the bedrooms fixed up just for her, with a flowered bedspread and her own telephone. If nothing else, Vance thought Inez would appreciate the house, which is much larger than the rented condo where Sandy and Inez lived before. Vance's house is spacious, uncluttered, "southwestern contemporary" his decorator calls it. Thick tan carpets cover the floors, and pictures that look like Indian sand paintings hang here and there on the white walls. But the day she moved in, Inez just dropped her bags and shrugged, as though she'd checked into a Travel Lodge.

Vance tries to be friendly. He offers to drive her to school and take her to the movies, but she always says no, and when he leaves envelopes with twenty-dollar bills inside on top of her dresser, she never thanks him.

Sandy says Inez has always been quiet, sort of a strange kid. She says not to worry, that Inez will come around on her own with time.

But it's been almost four months, and Inez still won't talk to him. He'll be pruning his citrus trees or mixing himself a margarita

at the kitchen counter and suddenly get a creepy feeling, like someone breathing on the back of his neck, and when he turns around,
it's Inez, standing behind him as still as a wax statue, staring at him
with those black eyes. Some days, although he wouldn't say this to
Sandy, he can hardly stand to have Inez in the house.

He is about to get up and pick another tangerine when he hears
the glass door slide on its runner.

It's Sandy, still wearing her pink kimono and rubber thongs.
She smiles and leans against the door, half of her body pressing the
glass. "Okay," she says. "Everything's okay. Everything's all set."

"Sweetie." Vance stands, smiling back at her.

Behind Sandy, Inez waits, looking at the ceiling, clutching a
large green purse across her stomach.

After four months, Vance is still surprised when he sees them
beside each other: they barely look related, much less like mother
and daughter. Sandy is blond and pale, watery blue eyes and almost
invisible brows. She's tall and tends to slouch, her hips pushed to
one side, but her posture looks relaxed rather than weary. And
smiling, she's always smiling—her top lip stretched above her wide
front teeth.

But Inez, she's something else, standing there so straight, her
lips clamped together in a thin line. She's dark, with black hair and
tan skin and serious eyebrows. She's not like the other kids Vance
sees sometimes in front of the high school, with their spiked hair
and tight clothes. Inez always wears loose jeans and a pressed cotton shirt, her hair in a neat ponytail, just like today.

"You two," Vance says, stepping inside. "There you are. I almost forgot about you two."

Sandy hugs him and through the cool silk of her robe, her
body feels warm and solid. Inez stares at them, her eyebrows drawn
above her narrow nose.

Vance slaps his stomach. "News flash. I'm hungry as hell. I'm
ready for that brunch." To Sandy he says, "I don't know when
we're getting back, Sweetie. This afternoon sometime."

Sandy shifts her weight from one hip to another, smiling. "Whatever."

That's a favorite word of hers—"whatever"—and she seems to say it sincerely, as if just about anything is really okay with her.

She follows them to the front porch. "Okay," she calls as Vance opens the car door for Inez. "Okay, have a really super time."

They drive along in silence. Now and then Inez sighs. She stares at the dashboard, twirling her ponytail with one hand and holding the purse on her lap with the other.

Such a large purse, Vance notices. Bright green, stuffed full, lumpy, the size of a travel bag. What could she have in there, he wonders. Sandy has all sorts of little bottles and tubes she always carries, but in a much smaller bag, and Inez doesn't seem to use makeup anyway.

Vance reaches toward the radio, but just before his finger hits the button, Inez says, "My mom told me you want to get to really know me. She says you want to be like a dad to me."

Surprised, Vance turns his head toward her—she's still looking at the dashboard, but her right hand is fiddling with something in her purse—and almost runs a red light. As he steps on the brakes, Inez pulls something from her bag.

She reaches over and holds a wallet-sized snapshot in a plastic cover above the steering wheel. The man in the photo is wearing blue jeans and no shirt. His skin is light brown; his black hair hangs to his shoulders. His arms are raised, as though greeting a crowd. Even through the grainy plastic, the arms look sinewy, his bare ribs sharp. The man isn't smiling, but his chin is lifted and he seems pleased with himself. Almost immediately Vance knows the man is Roger Rodriguez, Sandy's first husband.

The light turns green; someone honks from behind. Inez snatches the picture away, and it disappears into her big purse. *"That's* my father," she says.

Rodriguez has been dead for six years, and Vance knows little else about him, except that he worked for the mines in Ajo. Sandy doesn't like to talk about him much. "This little glob in his blood, this little aneurysm it's called, just killed him. I couldn't believe it," she told him once. She shook her head slowly. "He was a nice guy, really nice. I just can't believe I was married to him."

Vance glances at Inez, at her hands folded on top of her green purse. He drives on, past shopping complexes and a golf course. Why should the picture shock him? True, the man in the snapshot could be Vance's opposite. A Mexican mine worker with long hair and blue jeans, skinny and tough. Funny, Vance thinks, that Sandy would wind up with someone like himself now: big-bellied, middle-aged, a man with white shoes and a shiny pink golf shirt.

Funny, but not so surprising, he supposes. After all, his last wife, Trish, was a thin redhead, a chain smoker, hyperactive, always busy with her hands. Her hands were always cold, he remembers, so she always kept them moving, knitting those blankets that were piled up everywhere around their house in Aberdeen. Not like Sandy, so calm and agreeable. Sometimes he notices Sandy just sitting somewhere, on the sofa or the edge of the bed, not doing anything at all. The two women couldn't be more different, and he married them both.

Actually, Vance was married another time, too, although just briefly. Her name was Joan. She had dark hair and a long neck, and she modeled for a department store. They were both nineteen. When she got pregnant they married, but then she didn't have the baby after all, she decided not to, and they divorced a few months later. She moved to Chicago. Now it seems to Vance that the whole thing with Joan never really happened.

But anyway, he tells himself, people end up with all different kinds of companions in one lifetime. It's quite common, really. Still, he wants to ask Inez to show him that picture again. He wants another look at that Rodriguez.

Instead, he turns on Scottsdale Road and then into the parking lot of Hacienda Inn.

In the restaurant they're greeted by a smiling hostess wearing an embroidered smock and orange flowers pinned behind one ear. She leads them to a long buffet table flanked by potted palms and illuminated by golden lights overhead. The food on the table looks shiny and intensely colored: mounds of bright yellow eggs and orange enchiladas in warming trays, pastries dollopped with glistening jelly, tortillas covered with sour cream and red salsa.

"What're they going to put out for the rest of you folks," Vance says in a loud voice. The others in line nod and chuckle as he slaps his stomach. Vance knows people appreciate a big man who can laugh at himself.

Barely lifting her feet, Inez trudges along in front of him, the right side of her body weighed down by the big purse slung over her shoulder. She won't let him put anything on her plate when he tries. Finally, she selects a few wedges of cantaloupe and some grapes from the huge fruit salad at the end of the buffet.

At their table, beneath a large oil painting of a desert sunrise, Inez sits across from Vance, and in the chair between them carefully settles her purse.

As she slowly slices her cantaloupe into small pieces, Vance watches her face. Closely set eyes, thin cheeks. Vance is used to watching faces. During his salesman days in Aberdeen, it was sort of a hobby of his. Almost always he could tell when a customer was turning the corner, coming around his way—it was the skin at the temple going soft, the eyeballs loosening up in the sockets. The jaw would drop just a little, the flesh at the mouth turn rubbery.

But Inez keeps her mouth in a tight dark line, her pointed chin pushed forward.

Vance polishes off an enchilada in three big bites. "Good thing I'm in men's wear," he says. "After this I might need a bigger pair of pants."

"You know, you refer to weight a lot," Inez says, still slicing the melon, eyes on her plate.

"Well, hell, I've got a lot of weight to refer to."

Vance laughs, and when Inez smiles a little, turning up the corners of her closed mouth, he laughs a bit more, pleased.

But then she lifts her chin, looking right at him. "Too much junk food," she says. "You better cut down."

She keeps smiling, but now Vance can tell it's a sneer, the kind another salesman might give you when he's sabotaging your commission.

He knows what she's talking about. He sets down his fork. "The Cheese Nips," he says. "Give it to me straight, Sweetheart. You mean cut down on the Cheese Nips."

Inez shrugs. She begins picking sugar packets from a ceramic dish on the table, arranging them in a line between their plates. On the front of each packet is a tiny Arizona scene—the Grand Canyon, Petrified Forest, Montezuma's Castle.

Vance shifts in his chair. He knew this would come up sooner or later. It happened a couple of months ago. One day at Sun Casuals, Vance's alterationist, usually the cheery type, started crying in his office. She's a middle-aged housewife who works for him part-time; she does alterations because she wants to, she's told him, not because she has to. But that day she suddenly stopped at Vance's desk, dropping zippers and mending tape on his paperwork, and burst into tears. When he managed to calm her down, she agreed a cocktail would help, but not at a bar where people would see her red eyes. So Vance took her to his house. He figured Sandy would be there, and the three of them could sit on the patio.

But Sandy wasn't home, so Vance poured a Scotch for the two of them at the kitchen table. After they finished, the woman opened her leather cigarette case and tapped out a joint. Vance stared as she held it between two of her pink fingernails and lit the end, inhaling deeply. Wiping a spot of lipstick from the joint, she passed it to Vance, and he smoked with her. She said she knew it wasn't her life, but she couldn't help it, she was terribly depressed about her son dropping out of medical school.

Then before Vance knew it, the woman took off her shirt, just peeled it right over her head. Her plump breasts were squeezed together by a blue brassiere; she had a suntanned chest and a roll of white flesh above her skirt. She pointed at her breasts with both thumbs and said, "Tell me I'm not in for some cruel years."

She started laughing, and Vance laughed too. He found a box of Cheese Nips in the kitchen cabinet and they ate from the box. Vance was hungry; he spilled the crackers out on the table and ate by the handful. He wasn't worried about a thing, but then the alterationist hiccupped and pointed, and when Vance turned around there was Inez standing at the kitchen door. "I came home for lunch," she said in her quiet voice; she stood there a minute and then ran out. A moment before, it all seemed like nothing to Vance, but he knew how it looked: the woman in her brassiere, half a joint in an empty Scotch glass, Cheese Nips all over the table.

"Listen, Sweetheart," he says now. With the edge of his hand he sweeps the sugar packets to one side. "I told you how I feel about that. I feel like a big old clod about that."

Inez gives him her thin smile. "Don't worry. I haven't told my mother."

Vance shakes his head. Smoking a joint with a topless alterationist means nothing, really, in the scheme of his life. And he knows Sandy probably wouldn't care much about it either, although he hasn't bothered to tell her what happened.

"It's not your mother," he says. "It's you. That's who I'm worried about."

Which is true. But why should he worry? Actually, all Inez does is ignore him. He can't seem to help it, though. When he comes home in the evening and sees Inez dusting the television screen or straightening magazines, his neck tightens. If she blasted her stereo, stayed out late, or even threw tantrums, Vance could deal with it. In fact, he'd appreciate it. What irks him is the way she walks so carefully through the halls, her hands at her sides, the way she stares at him with no expression, the way she whispers things in Sandy's ear.

"Oh," Inez says. "Don't worry about *me.*"

She reaches toward her purse on the chair between them and

runs her hand over its front pocket. Vance thinks she might open it and take something out, another photograph, but she just rests her hand on top.

"Sweetheart, I want to tell you," Vance says, watching her tan fingers on the green cloth, "I'm real glad you showed me that picture of your dad. I know you were just a little girl when he passed on."

Inez doesn't look at him. She draws her hand back to her lap and sits still, but Vance can see her breathing more strongly, her small nostrils widening. He can still get through to her, he thinks. He can feel it. He says, "I'm real glad you showed me that picture. Because I know you still miss your dad. I sure do know how you can miss people even after they're gone a long time."

Inez nods, just once. She picks up a sugar packet, turns it over and over in her fingers, then studies the little picture on front—the Painted Desert, Vance sees.

"It was summer when he died," she says. "It was hot."

She tosses the packet aside and shrugs. "I can tell you about it. I don't care. It was hot, and my dad was working on our car. We had a blue Ford. I made him a glass of limeade. What's weird is he didn't even ask for it, I just fixed him a glass with ice. I took it out to him and he was under the car, and his feet and legs were like sticking out. There was some tools and stuff around his feet. Some wrenches. Small ones and a big one, and some rags."

She strokes her ponytail and looks past Vance, the whites of her eyes enlarged.

"Sweetheart," Vance says, and puts his hand over hers. Her fingers and knuckles feel small beneath his.

"I was standing by the back door holding the glass of limeade, and it was slippery on the outside from the ice. I was looking at my dad's feet. He had his black All-Stars on. Then my hand like opened up and the glass crashed right on the cement. I was only ten, you know, but I could tell something was wrong, from the way his feet looked. My hand opened up and the glass dropped."

Beneath his hand, her fingers lift and her nails press against his calluses. A connection, Vance thinks, and pictures green liquid and ice spreading across a hot, oil-stained driveway.

But then quickly, almost before he realizes it, Inez slips her hand out from under his. She narrows her eyes. "I don't care about the woman in the blue bra," she says. She pushes her chair back from the table. "And if you don't mind, Vance, don't call me Sweetheart."

Vance feels the space under his palm where Inez's hand was just a moment before. He looks at the bright orange sun in the painting above him. With his napkin he dabs perspiration from the back of his neck. Then, seeing the smiling hostess with flowers in her hair, he waves at her like a friend. "Check," he calls. "Check!"

Back in the car, Inez won't talk anymore. She holds her purse on her lap and stares at the dashboard again. Vance feels defeat, throbbing heat spreading from the base of his skull. Back in Aberdeen, even on the coldest days sometimes he'd step outside and scoop some snow in his glove and hold it for a minute behind his neck. For instance, when Trish would start one of her cleaning frenzies, crying about the grease smudges.

But that was Aberdeen, and this is Phoenix, where there's no snow, just warm sand. He doesn't get headaches here, hardly ever. Just now, sitting in the parking lot with Inez. Vance thinks it's almost funny, really, the way he's working to impress this teenager. With her mother, it's no effort: Sandy agrees with everything, laughs at every joke, even before he gets to the punchline sometimes.

He forces a laugh himself now, turning the key in the ignition. "So, *Inez*," he says. "Let's do something you want to do, Inez. You name it."

"I don't know." She keeps her eyes glued to the dash.

But Vance isn't giving up, not yet. "Okay, Inez. Let me ask you directly. What? I'm a bad guy? I marry your mom, make her happy, try to make things nice for the three of us? That's what you have against me?"

Nothing. Same frozen face, thin lips and narrowed eyes. She's holding the end of her ponytail between her fingertips.

"What?" Vance says. "The Cheese Nips incident? That's what you have against me? That's *it?*"

Inez opens her mouth, but then clamps it shut again.

"Oh, right. I forgot. You don't care about the woman in the blue bra."

Vance pulls out of the lot, but instead of heading toward home, he turns in the opposite direction. They'll have a scenic drive in the desert whether she wants to or not.

They pass condominiums and a large construction site with piles of red sand and pink cement blocks. Desert Shadows, the sign in front says, Soon to Be Your New Luxury Resort. As they drive, Inez stares at him, her black eyebrows furrowed. If he glances over, she turns her head away.

Vance takes the turn-off for Hole in the Rock, where there's a nice desert park with picnic tables and a man-made duck pond. He drives slowly along the curving road, which is one of his favorites. After just five minutes, he feels like he's really in the desert: for a while you can't even see any building, just sand drifts and mountains, palm and manzanita trees along the roadside, cholla and saguaro beyond.

Vance rolls down his window and breathes in the dry air. "Beautiful," he says. "Who couldn't like the desert in winter? Back in Aberdeen right now you've got two basic colors, your white and your gray. But look at this!" He stops the car—no one is coming behind him—and waves his arm out the window. "Look at that *blue* sky, those *red* rocky hills, those *yellow* flowers on those cactuses. Everything just looks so goddamned bright, don't you think?"

He leans across the car seat toward Inez, who sits perfectly still. "Don't you think? Don't you think the colors look goddamned bright?"

Inez repositions her purse on her stomach.

Vance drives on, past the pond where some kids throw chunks

of white bread at clumps of birds. A few families are eating at the shaded tables on the other side, but it's not too crowded and everyone's quiet. No motorcycles today, or church potlucks, or teenagers with oversized radios.

"Beautiful," Vance says. "This is a beautiful little area, don't you think?"

Around the next curve is a full view of Hole in the Rock. Vance drives to the base of the jagged butte, parks, and stares up at the round opening toward its top. Two people have climbed up and are standing in the hole, which to Vance looks about the size of his living room. Cast in shadow by the rock ceiling, they hold hands, silhouetted against a circle of clear sky.

"Think of it," Vance says. "A big old rock with a circle cut right out of it. How do you guess it got like that?"

He pauses. Inez shrugs slightly, which Vance figures is better than nothing. He says, "What do you think? Do you think the wind does that over years and years and years? Or is the hole there from when the desert used to be an ocean or something? You learn about that in science class?"

Inez clears her throat. "I've been here before," she says. "It's easy to climb up to the hole. You go around back. It's only the front side that's hard." Suddenly she opens her car door. "I'm going to climb."

Vance grabs her elbow, a flashing image in his mind of Inez running away through the desert toward the southern mountains, vanishing like a heat mirage, her tracks lost in windswept sand.

"Climb, there's an idea," he says. "That's a damn good idea." Still holding her elbow, he looks through the windshield at Hole in the Rock. He's driven here a number of times, but never gotten out of the car. The butte looks steep and slippery, planes of red rock glistening in the sun.

"You really want to come?" Inez pulls her arm from his grasp.

"Sure, what the hell. You said it was easy." Vance slaps his stomach. "I carry extra baggage, but I can still make the trip."

He laughs and jumps out the driver's side, jogs around the front of the car to show Inez that he's ready, willing. The two of them will climb Hole in the Rock. It will be something they've done together. They'll stand up there and look across the valley—the buildings, desert, distant mountains. One more time Vance will try to win her over, maybe say something about perspective and life.

Slowly Inez steps out of the car. She smooths down her hair from her forehead to her ponytail.

"You can't take that," Vance says, poking her purse, which she holds over her shoulder. "You can't hike with that big thing."

"We're not *hiking*. It's not that far."

"Come on." Vance tugs at the purse's strap. "Put it behind the seat. We'll lock up."

She sighs, but places it on the floorboard and slams the door. She pulls on the handle, checking the lock.

Without a word to Vance, she turns and walks quickly toward the butte, her arms and ponytail swinging. Vance keeps pace till they reach a path that curves around the side of the rock, where the slick soles of his shoes slide on loose dirt and crumbling stones. "Slow down," he calls, but Inez just keeps going, skipping lightly up the path in front of him, and then disappears around the corner of a large boulder.

Vance pushes on, trying to move more swiftly. The incline isn't too steep, but Vance feels his heart thump and a calf muscle cramp. He's gotten out of shape, it's true. At least Sandy isn't the exercising type either, something they have in common. But suddenly he gets a picture in his mind, a fast one, of Sandy's soft, pale body pressed against Rodriguez's, his hard, skinny one.

When Vance makes the turn by the boulder, Inez is waiting for him, sitting on top of a big flat rock. Crumpled beer cans are strewn on the ground here, "Eddie Z. Sucks" sprayed in blue paint on the stone beneath Inez's feet. Used charcoal lies in a makeshift campfire a couple of yards away. On this side of the butte, the rock is cracked into chunky formations like building blocks, the color of drying mud.

"The path ends here," Inez says. "You have to climb over rocks the rest of the way."

She sits cross-legged, her thin arms resting on her knees. She's smiling a little, that same closed-mouth sneer, maybe laughing at him, Vance thinks, at the way he's panting already, probably red in the face, only halfway up.

"You better wait here," she says. "You don't look so great. You look hot, but it's not even hot outside."

Vance walks to the tall rock where Inez sits and leans against it. He feels sweat accumulating under his polyester shirt. He could be home on his patio, drinking margaritas. Sandy is probably out there right now, just sitting there in her kimono and plastic thongs.

"When I was your age I could've jumped right on up there," he says. He looks up at Inez, her sharp brown face and narrow shoulders, and a wave of anger swells under his lungs. "I'll tell you, when I was your age, I was getting ready to get married. Just a couple of years older, anyway. That was back in Aberdeen. I sure as hell didn't know I'd end up here. My own two stores. With a new family."

Inez runs her ponytail slowly through one hand, still smiling.

"Listen, Sweetheart," Vance says. "There used to be dinosaurs here, right? Look over there"—he points across the desert to a range of scrubby hills—"See those fences? Those tall fences? That's to keep in a bunch of big-horn sheep. That's where they preserve them. They'll be gone someday anyway, though. Extinct. Right?" He scuffs the toe of his shoe in the dusty sand. "If you looked around here you could find arrowheads. From the Indians. And fossils."

Inez is still fingering her ponytail. Vance would like to pull it, a quick jab, to see her eyebrows jump, her mouth open.

"You see my point? You see? Life just rolls by. I'm an old guy now. You'll wake up one morning and be my age."

Inez folds her hands on one knee. "Deep, Vance," she says. "Very deep."

"Well, damn it." Vance kicks at a stone. "You can laugh, but

I'm not trying to be deep. I'm trying to have a nice time with your mother. I'm trying to get you to stop staring at me in my own living room like I'm a big jerk."

Inez stands up on the rock, throwing her shadow over Vance. For a while they both wait. "Okay, I'll stop staring," she says. She points at Hole in the Rock. "I'm going up. I'm going the rest of the way."

"Fine." Vance looks up at the dark crevice; from this angle the opening in the butte looks smaller. "You go on ahead."

She steps to the next highest stone. "Inez," he calls after her, and she turns around. "Listen, Inez. I'll tell your mom about what happened with the Cheese Nips. That woman who works for me. Okay? I'll tell her right when we get home. Just so you won't be worrying about it."

Inez reaches with one hand to her ponytail and pulls the rubberband from her hair. She shakes her head, letting her hair fall around her shoulders. She stands on the boulder, her feet set widely apart, shaking her head, and to Vance her dark hair looks the way Joan's used to look, and Inez seems older all of a sudden.

"I haven't been worrying about it, Vance," she says, and she isn't yelling but her voice sounds loud and strong. "My mother acts the way she acts, but she's not stupid. She knows how things are. She won't care about that woman in the blue bra, and neither do I. I just don't like you, Vance."

She spins on her heel, spraying gravel, but then stops and looks down at him again. "And about what you said in the restaurant. About missing people. If you really missed anyone, you wouldn't be here. You'd be back in that town. That town you're from."

"Aberdeen." Vance says. He watches as Inez leaps from rock to rock.

He takes his time working his way back down the path, stepping carefully around broken glass and sandy holes that could house scorpions. The tops of his white shoes are creased with red dirt; he'll have to get them polished.

He waits until he's reached the car again before he turns

around and looks up at Hole in the Rock. The couple holding hands is gone; there is only Inez's silhouette against the circle of bright blue sky. She stands with her feet apart, her arms lifted slightly, her hair blown to one side from a breeze that must circle and gain force in the rock's opening. Each day, Vance thinks, the wind must wear the rock away a little more and make that hole a little bigger. If he came back in twenty years, forty years, could he tell the difference? He figures you don't notice change that happens like that, a tiny bit every day. *Deep, Vance, very deep.* He laughs a little to himself.

He gets in the car and rests his forehead on the padded steering wheel. He should have climbed the rest of the way with Inez. He should have stood there with her in the circle. He could have said, *my first wife had dark hair and a long neck and real soft skin. She had dreams about walking on ice and the ice would break and she'd fall into a different world where everyone already knew her. People in her dream would say "Hi there, Joan!" just like they already knew all about her. She'd wake me up at night to tell me. She'd put her head on my stomach with her feet hanging over the edge of the bed. Right from the start, I never knew what to say to her. I guess she was too good for me.*

He lifts his head from the steering wheel. Inez is gone from the circle in the butte. Soon this will all be over and he can go home and drink margaritas with Sandy on the patio. He'll tell her about smoking a joint with the alterationist. Probably she'll let her mouth go slack for a minute, running her hand through her curly hair, then laugh in the way that she does, with her top lip stretched over her big front teeth. "Oh, whatever," she'll probably say. And for some reason Vance thinks of shaking her by the shoulders, hard, as though waking her from sleep. What if he told her he slept with the alterationist? Would she cry, throw something? Just say, "oh, whatever"? Vance isn't sure.

Trish, now she was predictable. She'd scream at anything, then cry, till finally she'd say she was through. He'd rub her feet; they'd have a drink. Except for after the last fight, when things went too far.

Before long, he supposes, Sandy will be predictable too. More or less, she already is. Maybe tonight, if they drink enough margaritas, when they're in bed with the television flickering, the sound low, he'll whisper in her ear—"Rodriguez," he'll whisper, "tell me about that Rodriguez."

He wants to see that picture, just quickly, one more time. He reaches behind the car seat for Inez's purse. It's heavy, as though filled with stones. He drops it on the front seat and lifts the top flap of green fabric. Inside are brown paper bags, stuffed full and taped shut, wads of cloth, papers rolled like scrolls and tied with string. Vance rummages through and finds an envelope of photographs, but none is of Rodriguez, they're of other people, kids, probably from Inez's last school. He looks out the car window, but she's nowhere in sight; he turns the purse upside down and dumps everything on the seat: a small bald doll in an orange dress, aspirin bottles wrapped in masking tape, a diaphragm in its blue plastic case. Finally he finds more photographs in one of the brown paper bags, but just as he starts thumbing through them, he sees Inez walking briskly toward the car, frowning as if she senses something's wrong. Veins throb at the back of Vance's neck. He starts stuffing the purse as fast as he can, but it's too late, he can tell; Inez is running toward him, her elbows flapping like a child's, her hair whipping back and forth across her face, her mouth open wide. Vance reaches for the lock on the car door and pushes it down, as though this will help him, as though the window isn't glass that anyone can look right through and see what he's doing inside.

Thomas Fox Averill

The Man Who Ran with Deer

Harry and Mavis marry late, just when they think marriage will never happen to them. And just when they think they will never have children, Mavis becomes pregnant. For three months, Mavis has terrible morning sickness. Harry is cautious of her moods, her sudden nausea, her new distance from him. She is a different creature. He wishes sometimes for their life before the pregnancy.

In the fourth month, Mavis finally feels better. She begins to show. Harry remains shy. He acts as though he has just met her. In the morning, he watches Mavis rise and put on her clothes. The slight swell of her womb embarrasses him. When she sees him looking, she hurries to the bathroom. Perhaps they are too old for the unexpected, Harry thinks. He cannot talk. Mavis does not speak her feelings, either. They learn how easily quietness sets in.

Then, one morning, they sit as usual at the breakfast table. The first chores are done. Butter slowly melts into hot oatmeal. Scrambled eggs and coffee steam between them. Mavis looks out the window, across the draw, into the thirty-acre pasture rimmed by woods. They enjoy watching the dawn. This is their one time to relax, until evening, when the sun sets and they go to their bed.

Suddenly, Mavis jumps up out of her chair. "Harry," she says, "they've come back. But look." She points.

Harry looks. In the distance, where the pasture turns to trees, he sees the deer, a buck and two does, before he sees what looks like a man, naked, slightly stooped, moving among them. "What the heck," he says.

"It's a man," says Mavis. She crosses her arms over her chest and stares. "It's a man with them," she says again.

"What the heck," Harry says. He starts for the door.

"No," says Mavis. "You'll scare them away."

"I'll be quiet," Harry says, and leaves the house.

Outside, the sun rises into the woods, turning sky, trees and pasture red, then bronze. Harry's cattle still nudge each other in the barn. Their one rooster decides to crow. Harry moves slowly across the graveled drive, through his waiting machinery, to the edge of the draw. He looks back at the house, expecting to see Mavis, but every window glares back at him with the reflection of the rising sun. When he looks back into the pasture, the deer and the man stand alert. They stare at Harry, then move, more gently than shadows, back into the woods. For a long moment, Harry watches the place where they disappeared. Then he goes back inside.

Breakfast is cold. "You frightened them away," says Mavis. "Who knows when they'll be back."

"That was a man with them," says Harry. "After breakfast I'm going to look for tracks."

Mavis says nothing, until, breakfast quickly eaten, Harry goes to the closet for his gun. "You don't hunt," says Mavis.

"Protection," Harry says. "If I see them, up close . . . If I get close to the man . . . If that man is crazy or something . . ." Harry doesn't know what he might do, but the gun makes him feel better.

"You've never shot a deer," says Mavis. "You've never shot a living thing."

Harry nods out the door. He once killed a deer, when he was a young man, before he knew Mavis. When he married and took over the home place, he quit hunting. He lets her think what she thinks.

Harry climbs slowly through the draw up into the pasture and heads straight for the spot where he remembers seeing the man and the deer. By the time he reaches the edge of the woods, the sun is a brilliant yellow. Morning has separated the trees from their shadows, light from dark. Although he sees the tracks of deer, Harry cannot find evidence of the man, either in the grass or in the soft earth around the oak and hickory trees. He wonders if he and Mavis really saw what they thought they saw.

He moves on into the woods, as silently as he can. After ten paces he realizes he is holding his breath. The day is still cool among the trees, and Harry walks until he reaches the barbed wire fence that separates his from his neighbor's property. He doubles back along the fence line, avoiding the few crisp early leaves, the few clumps of brittle grass, the few fallen twigs that might reveal his presence. He stops sometimes and stares hard in every direction, his head erect, his nose in the air.

After he walks the full half mile through the timber line to the road, seeing only what is familiar, Harry turns and starts back to the house. He cuts diagonally through ten acres of head-high corn, checking the ears. They are nicely formed, but he knows better than to call them money in the bank. By the time he is at the back of his barn, the August morning has declared itself as summer. He is sweating through his work shirt when he reaches the house.

"Nothing," he tells Mavis. "There's nothing out there." She is sitting at the table exactly where he left her.

"We saw them," she says. "We saw him with them."

"There's nothing there now," he says. "I didn't see a thing." He puts his gun in the closet. Still, Mavis does not move. She stares out the window. When Harry starts to clear away the dishes, she rises and starts her day.

For three days they watch and wait for what they might see. Harry does not mind the silence. Their mornings are a kind of meditation as they stare out across the pasture. The sun turns the tree leaves from black to silver to gold to green, their trunks from charcoal to fire to the color of upright earth.

Neither Harry nor Mavis can say exactly when the deer appear on the fourth day. One moment, the two of them sit, watching out the window. The next moment the deer are on the land, without movement, as though a shroud has been lifted from around them, as though something has lifted in Harry and Mavis. And before they exclaim on the sight, or on how their breaths both quicken before each one sighs, the man appears, too, slightly hunched, naked, hair the color of doe-skin. The deer graze, the buck occasionally lifting his head erect to listen and smell, anticipating danger. The naked man stands very still, as calm as though he is asleep.

Harry pushes himself up from the table. Mavis puts her finger to her lips, as though any sound, even so far away as from their house, might scatter these animals into the woods. "I'm going," he says.

"Do you see him, too?" asks Mavis.

"Of course I see him," Harry says. "I'm going around the back way, behind the barn and around." He moves quickly to the closet, as though he can only make up his mind as he speaks.

"Not the gun," says Mavis. "You don't need it."

"Never know," says Harry as he leans in and grabs the gun from the corner.

Mavis does not look at him. She hasn't seen him since the deer appeared. She sits transfixed, instead, in her kitchen chair.

Harry leaves without looking back at her, or the house. He walks the way his father taught him years before, the gun tucked loosely under his arm, its weight leaning against his forearm, the barrel pointing down. He has made sure the safety is on. He hurries through the barn, cuts across the corn field, finds himself among brush and rock, then in the cool of the woods. He does not stop to look or listen until he judges himself to be a hundred yards from where the deer and the man were when he and Mavis saw them. He hopes they are still there.

As he nears the rim of the pasture, he is almost on tiptoe. The gentle sawing of crickets disguises the sound of his feet even from himself. He hears nothing but morning: a small throb of wakefulness, a low hum, as though someone is blowing a stream of breath into a huge jar. As he reaches an open space between trees, and finds his way into it to look towards dawn and deer, several birds scold him and fly away, hammering the air with their fright. When he looks where he wants to look, nothing is there.

He walks the edge of his pasture anyway, stepping boldly now, until he reaches the spot where the deer and the man must have been. This time, he finds many signs: grass folded gently by the weight of large creatures; the ragged edges of nibbled brome; deer feces—small black pellets as round and distinct as marbles. He turns away to begin his walk straight back to the house and steps into another feces, brown, indistinct, as awkward as a stain. The smell reaches his nostrils at the same time as his realization that this is the sign of the man, and that it is very fresh, and that perhaps Mavis . . . He doesn't like to think about Mavis sitting at the breakfast table, watching this naked man do his business in the pasture. He scrapes his boot against clumps of grass and starts back to the house. Down in the draw he lets his foot wander into the creek. His boot is clean by the time he reaches home.

"You didn't even get close," Mavis says. "I saw you come out of the woods. They were long gone by then."

"I never could get close to deer," Harry says.

"He sure gets close to them," says Mavis. "They all just bounded off together. Even the man was beautiful to watch. Graceful when he moved. Like a dancer."

Harry looks at Mavis. Her voice sounds the way it might if she were describing a dream: slightly distant, focused on the inside of her mind. He doesn't mention the dropping he has wiped and soaked off his boot. She doesn't mention it either. Behind on the day, they go off to their separate chores.

Late summer has its own rhythm of days, as dawn moves more slowly into the sky, as corn swells and stiffens in the fields, as brome reaches up for a last cutting, as tree leaves gather an abundance of light and heat before Fall. Harry and Mavis sit each morning watching for the deer, and the man.

For the first time in his life, Harry is intensely aware of things so small they have no names, and he has no way of talking about them with Mavis. They are things like the peculiar slant of light across an abandoned bird's nest so that the molted feathers glimmer like the lace trimming of a beautiful gown. Or the way sunset fills the barn with cracks of light so intense he feels it might explode. Or his discovery of how each plot of earth, each plant, each piece of board, stone and brick is perforated, ready to rip away, separate, dissolve, given enough time.

Harry thinks constantly about the man who runs with the deer. Each morning he and Mavis watch through their breakfast, but Harry also watches through the rest of the day. At odd moments, he pauses from his work and stares in all directions, his nose in the air, his ears alert for any sound. He tells himself he is looking for the deer, and the man, but he feels as though *they* are watching him, and he is trying to discover them doing it. As he moves through the daily work of the farm, he thinks of the creatures, and where they might be.

He and Mavis do not talk about it, except when the deer and man appear around breakfast, every week or so. Then Harry hurries out the door to see if he can get close. Sometimes he finds evidence: more human droppings; once, a footprint, smaller than he expects, in the soft earth after a rain; another time a stripped ear of corn, thoroughly eaten to the cob in a way no raccoon would have the patience for.

Harry brings what news he can, though Mavis is not curious for his details. She is content to sight the deer and the man, to watch them move out of, then back into, the woods, and disappear. As her womb swells, she seems to nest herself in her kitchen chair. Harry has quit taking his gun; he feels awkward with it resting in his arms.

One crisp morning on the edge of Fall, Harry is out in the woods after he and Mavis have sighted the deer and the man. He traces a noiseless path towards the lip of the pasture where the man and deer have appeared. As he nears the open space where he wants to look out, he bends down and removes his boots. He wants the silence of human skin on earth. He edges forward, his feet stiffening with cold. He wonders again, as he has all through the cooling season, how the man keeps warm.

At the edge of the woods, Harry stations himself behind a hickory tree. He hugs its shaggy bark and leans his head around to see what he can see. For the first time, he is rewarded. There, fifty yards away, stand the buck, the two does, and the man. Harry has seen deer before, but never this close. He has seen naked men, too, but never this far away, never with deer, in his pasture. The man is slightly bent. His hair is shaggy. He has a tangled beard. He moves when the deer move; settles into his stoop when the deer graze the grass.

Harry watches quietly, not trying to move closer. He wonders if Mavis is watching for him, if she sees how close he has stalked them without frightening the animals away. The moment he has the thought, the deer move again, towards the woods. The man moves with them. Harry sees the white tail of the deer. The man has extraordinary body hair. Thick and brown, it cascades down his back, across his buttocks, and trails down his legs. The deer continue into the woods, slowly withdrawing, their movements fluid, full of grace. The man moves, too, slowly, raising his feet up and placing them with the same cautious sureness, the same mincing elegance. As both man and deer disappear, Harry's toes, curled into the earth, begin to hurt. He lets go of the hickory tree. As quietly and gracefully as possible, he moves to the spot where he saw them last.

He sees them again. They are only a short distance into the woods, where another draw of the creek begins. A small spring trickles through limestone, there, and gooseberries and pawpaws flourish. Harry hunches forward and tries to glide towards them between trees. For the first time, he is not hiding from them. He wants the man to see him. But what he sees makes him stop short, take refuge behind a cover of bushes. The man, thin and wiry as a hungry animal, approaches one of the does. He puts his arms up, towards her shoulders. He holds her against him and moves into her. Though Harry cannot see well, he recognizes the act, has seen it many times among his cattle, horses, chickens, dogs and cats. The man shudders, and moves away. The deer walk calmly down the draw, their hooves smushing in the soft earth, or sounding a hollow percussion against rock. Harry does not hear the man retreat. Harry does not try to follow them. He wishes for his boots, his kitchen, his breakfast, for Mavis.

When he returns, Mavis still sits by the window. "You got close this time," she says, not looking up. "I'll go with you next time."

"No," he says.

"I will," she insists.

"Well, I'm not going again," he says, but he doesn't tell her why.

When they don't see the deer or the man for over two weeks, Harry is relieved, Mavis disappointed. He feels haunted by the image of the man copulating with the beast. On the mornings he and Mavis speak at the breakfast table, he asks, "Why would a man want to run with deer?" or, "Won't he quit soon, get someplace warm?" or "You haven't told the neighbors about him, have you?" Mavis doesn't answer. She is still fascinated. Harry hates to see her sitting there so eager to spot this naked man.

But it's worse when they finally see the creatures again, and Mavis stands up and puts on her brown jacket. She cannot zip it over the swell of her pregnancy. "Come on," she says.

"No," says Harry, "I've traipsed through the woods enough. Seen all I want to see."

"Okay," she says, "I've walked the place by myself before." She is out the door before Harry can argue with her, before he realizes he must go with her, that deer would never hurt her, but the man could, if he saw her alone. He goes to the closet for a jacket and his gun, then leaves the house, quietly. She'll be mad if he frightens the animals.

By the time he walks through the barn to the edge of the corn field, Mavis is just disappearing into the edge of the woods. Harry feels odd, gun in hand, following Mavis without her knowledge, but he can't call out, or whistle. And then soon, he doesn't want to disturb the morning: a clear blue bowl of sky shot through with the last of the night's stars, a pale sliver of moon slowly disappearing in the gathering light, a delicate crunch of frost underfoot. Harry moves deliberately into his own frosted breath. The morning is so quiet Harry can stand still and hear Mavis walk, a hundred yards away, through the woods. She will frighten the deer and come home, he thinks. He follows after her.

He takes the cow path through the trees, moving, calmly and steadily, towards the places where Mavis has been. He can feel her lingering presence, as though they are in water and she has left a wake. Birds and insects begin to sound the morning air. Trees stretch into a rising morning breeze. Harry sees Mavis again, among some brush, at the edge of the pasture. Perhaps she is watching the deer and the man. Perhaps she is waiting for him. She stands very still, regarding the open space like a meditation.

Harry decides to get as close to Mavis as he can, without her seeing him. He leans his gun against a tree, takes off his boots, and continues towards her. It is all he can do to keep from shouting, bursting into laughter, clapping his hands. Hunched forward slightly, his breathing shallow and intense, his vision keen, his ears alert, he stalks his wife. From tree to hiding tree, he moves, pauses, moves again. He can think of nothing but coming upon her, maybe even reaching up to touch her, all without her knowing.

So he is surprised when, behind him, he hears movement, loud, awkward. He turns to see the deer, and behind them the man, drifting through the woods towards the fence line. Harry stands his full height to watch them disappear. Just before they do, the man who runs with the deer turns and looks back, his black eyes glistening as he moves a searching head. Harry cannot tell if the man sees anything but the backdrop of the woods he moves through.

Harry hears a sound. He sees the deer tense, then start away. The naked man shakes his head and follows. Harry looks towards the sound. Mavis is so close she can almost touch him. She smiles, then bursts out laughing. "I sneaked up on you," she says. "You didn't even see me coming."

Harry puts his finger to his lips. "Shhh, don't let him hear you. You don't know what he might do."

She is still smiling. "What could he do?" she asks. "He runs away, like the deer." Her voice is louder than he is used to, giddy, the way it was when he courted her.

"He's not a deer," Harry insists.

Mavis looks at Harry, laughs at his stern face. "Where are your boots?" she asks. She puts toe to heel and kicks off one shoe, then the other. "Let's walk," she says, and takes his hand.

They move together towards the pasture, where the day has begun. When they see how bright it is on the grass, they stay on the pasture's edge, in shadow.

"Look," says Mavis, and she points to the house. Harry looks where she looks. The house shimmers with morning light; the drive circles it and snakes away towards town through a line of carefully planted trees; the garden beside it is still in neat rows, wilting tomato vines yielding up their last ripe tomatoes, as red as rising suns. The house is surrounded by machinery and buildings, everything that contains work and livelihood, everything that makes their life possible. Harry sees it all as though he is above it, with the knowledge of so many steps through the barnyard, so many times of turning the garden plot, so many years of riding the machinery, planting the trees, laying up wood, corn, hay, wheat. Harry and Mavis stand there looking, and Harry feels an uncommon joy. He imagines two people, sitting at the breakfast table, looking out, trying hard to spot deer. Instead, they see Harry and Mavis, just at the edge of the woods, holding hands.

Antonya Nelson

Mud Season

That first night in the city where her daughter had died, Lois
dreamt she was standing in the English countryside.
Though she'd never been to England, everything looked
just as it should. Green hills dipped back on themselves as
far as she could see, stilled waves in a grassy ocean. In this dream,
Lois could fly, and she sailed above the ground, taking in the hills
and the fine yellow light of sunset, which was so bright she couldn't
look at it directly; rather, she had to watch covertly, staring ahead
of her while noting it in the periphery.

Suddenly she began rocketing skyward, fast enough to see the
world changing below her, slow enough to appreciate the expand-
ing color of the blue sky. Soon she saw a new world, England
turning from a borderless countryside into an island all its own.

Marvelous. Still, there was that intense light to the west. Perhaps it was not the sun after all, she thought. Perhaps that was the atomic explosion that would end the world. But, no—its light was yellow and white, painful to the eye but restorative to the skin. Lois knew that if she didn't waken she would continue upward, shooting into some other, dark galaxy. She hesitated, atmosphere thinning around her, before she fought her way from sleep.

She and her husband Alan were staying at a bed and breakfast place in Durango, Colorado. Their youngest daughter, Gwen, had been killed on a mountain pass outside town—not more than a ten-minute drive from where they were—five months earlier. Lois and Alan had come to see the site, at last.

Lois looked out their window into the muddy landscape. A boy on a bicycle came slowly meandering down the street, twisting the handlebars from one side to the other, seemingly in order to maintain the slowest speed possible, stalling. He wore bright primary colors, red shirt, yellow cycling pants, blue plastic boots. He wobbled lazily through a puddle while Lois watched, and thereafter left an endless dreamy curve of S's after him.

"What's his name?" Alan shouted to Lois from the shower. "I've forgotten this S.O.B.'s name."

"Pittman," Lois said, dropping the curtain. She spoke only loud enough for her husband to hear her voice and not the word.

"What's it?"

Lois walked into the steam of the bathroom putting an earring in. She pulled the shower curtain completely open and enunciated quite clearly. "Pitt man." She gave her husband's body a thoughtful appraisal. Do I love you? she wondered. He was small as a preteenage boy, skin still almost tight over muscle, but not attractive. The sense of promising vitality beneath the surface was gone. Lois's own body had relaxed into its years. Lois hadn't really felt comfortable with herself until she'd had children; since then, somehow, her joints and flesh had suited her better. Men's bodies, she thought now, looking at Alan's flaccid penis, never got the chance to ripen—just to age. It was her theory that this was the reason he'd had affairs in the last few years.

Later, over breakfast, Lois confessed that she wasn't sure she wanted to see the site. Her heart had begun beating audibly in her ears, louder as the hour drew near. "Maybe you could go without me."

Alan was pretending to read the paper. He wrote a syndicated column and this paper was open to his small picture and byline. *About Which,* Lois read, upside down. They were running his old pieces while he was away. A little flare of impatience went up in her; Lois thought it would have been more honest to simply let the column go for a week.

"Going will make you feel as if it's done with," Alan said. Maybe he didn't realize he was mimicking their counselor. Or maybe he didn't think Lois would know, since their sessions were separate. Could he possibly believe Dr. Frank came up with completely fresh advice for each of them?

"Actually, I think I'll have this vivid mental image," Lois said, slowly, pinning the feeling. "I think I'll be better able to imagine Gwen flying off the mountain . . ."

Alan turned sharply away. He was contemptuous, staring angrily out the window at the falling snow. What was it, this time? Her word choice? He felt bad for her, for both of them, but he could barely stand to be around her anymore. It sometimes seemed hopeless, their marriage. It had seemed that way before Gwen's death, but now it was fated to continue for a while longer, on a different path.

"I'll be okay," she said, waiting until he turned back to the paper before she opened her own section.

Lois believed in human-interest stories in the newspaper the way she believed in dreams. She was susceptible to both, drawn to their messages, which she took almost entirely at face value. What did a dream of flying over England mean? It meant she wished to fly over England, to see the earth from a distance. As for the newspaper, her husband's column included stories about his youth, things he saw in a passing car or while standing in the grocery line. He liked to make a point, shaping the tidbits he witnessed into an emotional essay. But over the years, Lois realized those columns were awfully overwritten. All the daily pieces were. No one seemed capable of controlling tone. Everything was so unmanageable it all rang false. She believed in straight facts. They spoke for themselves.

These stories sought her out. When she sat in the sun-room in the morning, paper spread on the glass table before her, she had only to slowly turn the pages. Soon, the boldface proclamations would rivet her. *Three Sailors Wed Lottery Winner.* Little stories from out of state, stories that might get far too much attention if they were local but which only received a cursory paragraph or two of lucid facts if they happened elsewhere. *Baby found alive under El tracks.* The baby was abandoned, then found after surviving on its own for at least twelve hours. Amazing. Heart-stirring, and without any pomp. *Nurse playing hero may have killed 10.* A nurse injected patients with lethal drugs, then revived them in order to be a hero. What could be clearer? Why comment further?

Her husband made use of these stories, but only to elucidate some point more specific to himself. Lois imagined if he'd read about the nurse injecting patients, he would write about a culture that required heroics and heroes to garner attention. The everyday heroism of nursing was not enough; life-saving was now necessary in order to receive commendation. That would be the first part of his column—Lois could see it as if it were before her on the page— the next part would be about something comparable in himself. Lois tried to think what. How had he made himself perversely important in his life?

She admired that he seemed completely able to confess his flaws. All of the nation knew his failures and shortcomings, his sins against himself and others. What bothered her was that, in confessing them, good Catholic he'd once been, he somehow felt absolved.

"Alan," she said. "Did you read about this male nurse?"

He had finished reading the paper and was now working the puzzles, his bifocals balanced on his nose. He looked at her through the top part of the lenses expectantly, if a little impatiently, which meant he hadn't. After she'd told him about it, he grunted.

"What does that make you think?" she asked.

"It makes me wonder how the hospital explained away those deaths." He licked his pencil tip and went back to work.

Lois nodded to herself.

But in a moment, Alan looked up once more. "It also reminds me of that report that said most serial killers, when asked what profession they'd most like to pursue, answered cop. Remember the ambulance driver who was a mass murderer? Killed prostitutes and then picked the bodies up later the same night?"

Lois did. Alan had speculated on the desire to be a policeman, a surgeon, any occupation that involved day-in, day-out exposure to carnage. He wrote about soaking a cat in gasoline when he was younger, setting it on fire. He'd won an award for that column. It was a brave essay, Lois knew, though it had made their children cry to read it.

"I had the strangest dream," she began. "I took off like a rocket. Usually when I dream of flying I go horizontally, like an airplane. But this morning I was heading up, up and away." Alan was working another puzzle. This one was the one where a sentence was given in code. Each letter stood for another. "Why do you like that puzzle, do you think?" she asked him.

"Couldn't tell you," Alan answered, without raising his eyes. He had been whistling the rhythm of the missing words and discovered the solution in the process. Rapidly, he filled in the last blanks and swung the paper in Lois's direction so she could read the nonsense sentence. *Life of crime can oftentime pay overtime.*

"And then I saw a boy on a bicycle," Lois said to herself.

"That whatshisname is going to be here soon," Alan said, rising and running his thumbs between belt and trim tummy. "I believe I'll brush my teeth."

Sheriff Pittman met them in the bed and breakfast house foyer. He was kind and slow with them, which made Lois a bit awkward. He had children of his own, she understood. They drove out of town, up the winding mountain road, listening to police static and sudden bursts of dispatched, sputtering numbers on the radio. Lois tried to guess what the numbers stood for, which ones meant robberies, which ones meant fatalities. The sheriff clicked his end of the radio after each one, answering in his own code. The scenery—snow filling the deep and high crevices of granite peaks and turning them somehow more than three-dimensional—made Lois feel unbalanced and she noticed she was holding on to the vinyl of Sheriff Pittman's back seat. Their waiter at breakfast had told them this snow was unusual, as it was mud season: the end of the ski season, and before the summer tourists arrived. He did not know why they were there, and Lois was grateful for his obvious disdain of people so out of touch as to visit Durango during mud season. She basked in it, the normality of his smugness.

Riding along, she was tempted to tell Alan about something else she'd read at breakfast. A woman had written Dr. Lamb to say she was sick of her husband's habit of eating his own hair. Except she phrased it like this: he finds the coarse hair on his body, pulls it out, chews it up and swallows it. Lois wondered if anyone she knew had a habit as shocking. The atavism of it thrilled her. What would Alan make of it?

But Sheriff Pittman was pulling over, very cautiously, next to a yellow diamond warning sign. The sign showed a black arrow bent at a forty-five-degree angle. Underneath, it read 25 m.p.h. Alan, who was sitting in the front seat, had stared out the passenger window the whole trip, not noticing the sheriff's glances now and then in his direction. Lois had tried smiling into the rearview mirror to let Pittman know they appreciated his taking care with them, but she had never quite caught his eye; after all, she told herself, he was a man, and he was identifying more with Alan than with her. Now, Alan remained for a moment in the car as the other two got out.

Lois had prepared herself to draw in breath, to have her equilibrium abandon her entirely, her heartbeat become so furious her body pulsed, but nothing happened. It was a beautiful place, and she stepped right into it. She was not frightened as she walked over to the edge and looked down. What had she expected? Gwen's body was in Missouri, buried in the same cemetery with her grandparents and great aunts. There was gravel and then the drop, which Lois saw was gentler than she'd pictured. A squirrel hustled by, holding a nut in its mouth. At the bottom was no black void where the world had reclaimed Gwen; up here, no white cross.

She could see how it pained Sheriff Pittman to show them the spot. He cleared his throat. "There were skid marks," he said, swiping his cowboy boot heel across the crumbly asphalt. "Torn brush and the bent aspen saplings."

Gwen had toppled like a toy the thousand feet. It was Pittman's pain that touched Lois; he certainly must have children of his own. He must have seen every one of them, in his mind, make the same horrifying miscalculation, slide and fall. For herself, Lois had been imagining that fall for months now; it seemed she had been anticipating such a fall since the day she'd brought her first baby home from the hospital. She'd looked at the world from then on as a place full of forty-five-degree angles and cliffs. It surprised her that seeing the actual spot—*here,* she told herself, *right here*—somehow lessened its power. Even the gray sky and wet snow failed to make the turn ominous. An Airstreamer in the far lane rounded it like a ponderous metal elephant. And behind it was the boy on the bicycle. She recognized his yellow pants. Now he bent forward, pedaling hard, a smile—or, more probably, a grimace from the hard work—on his face. Lois lifted her hand in a wave, and felt her whole self lift just a bit. She wished she knew his name to call out.

Alan turned to look behind him at what she was waving at. He scowled at her. "I've seen enough," he said. He hadn't even come to the edge. Pittman, between them, stood with his arms dangling, as if he might draw, also watching Lois. She resisted, the way she had in the car, asking Alan why he didn't want to look over. Their states of mind were at such odds these days that she did not trust his understanding her—something that, once, she would have taken for granted—and she did not want him to turn away from her, as he had at breakfast. So she allowed herself another private glance down. Wildflowers would grow. More squirrels would appear. She hadn't wanted to come, it was true, but now she was glad she had. There was nothing—not the skid marks, not the broken aspen, not the crumpled machine—to indicate what had occurred. This place had healed.

Gwen had missed weeks of class in Boulder, her parents discovered later. They received notes of condolence from several of her professors. The man who taught her Social Problems and American Values course had called one afternoon (teacher's hours, Lois had thought, long-distance in the afternoon). He introduced himself and then seemed at a loss. Lois heard, in his silence, the things that could have been between him and Gwen. If Lois had learned nothing else in her life, she had learned to trust what was not said.

"When did you last see her?" she asked him, quiet Peter Somebody or Other, desperate that he not hang up.

"Let me think."

Lois could hear him breathing. He remembered, she could tell, and was trying to put it some way that was presentable to Gwen's mother. They'd been lovers, Lois understood. She wanted to tell him it wasn't his fault. He was tangling with all the little parts—his loyalty to Gwen, his loss, his not knowing Lois at all.

"I saw her at the Union," he chose to say. "She was getting a salad and paying a parking ticket." And then he was silent again. "I don't really know why I called," he said after a moment.

"Thank you, anyway," Lois said. "Even if you don't know, I

appreciate it." She was crying, but she thought she could sit for a long time saying nothing with this man.

"It's useless," he finally said, "but what I feel like is that if I could take some of your pain, I would."

"You probably have enough already," she said. "Thank you, though."

Lois did not tell Alan. She could have secrets, could she not? Alan, fortunately, was gone all day; otherwise, he would have answered the call. She imagined him wanting to reach through the telephone receiver, across all those miles of cable, and strangle Peter Whoever. He would have demanded answers: Why was she in Durango? Where had she gotten a motorcycle, for God's sake? Alan had kept up an annual vigilant campaign against motorcycles, writing column after column about their dangers. They were second only to handguns on his list of consumer evils. It was registered in Gwen's name; she'd owned it for over a year without ever having told them. Alan wanted someone to blame, and Peter, sad and silent, would have sufficed.

Lois had come to admire her daughter's life, secret from the family. She imagined Peter as a kind and older man. Gwen's belongings had been carefully packaged and sent to them, two large boxes that arrived UPS one day when Alan was away. Lois had read the return address, Gwen's dorm, and felt for an instant that she'd been offered a reprieve. Packages from her daughter.

The boxes were full of both familiar and unfamiliar items. Lois picked them up one by one to investigate. She couldn't tell which hurt her more to see: those things that were the past, or those that were the present? The ceramic rabbit Gwen had had since she was little, cotton balls for a tail? Or the mysterious sky-blue case that snapped open to reveal a diaphragm?

It was not long after Gwen's belongings had come back that Lois stopped wanting to leave the house. Maybe she was waiting for another phone call? She had started any number of days with the intention of going somewhere—the Nelson, the plaza—and had made it through all the preparatory stages, but once she opened the front door she was lost. The world wowed her; leafless trees appeared somehow to be sapping her of energy. It took all her willpower to shut the door behind her and walk to the garage—there was no spark left to actually make her drive away.

Instead, she'd allow herself to be drawn back inside, where she'd gather all the linen napkins in the house to launder them. Their size and texture made for perfect ironing and folding. She was in love with the starchy warmth of these napkins fresh from the dryer. Countless times she comforted herself by sorting them, folding them into perfect squares, her hands flattening, smoothing, stacking, making order out of chaos.

Lois told Dr. Frank about it. It was an "am I crazy?" kind of question. Dr. Frank had pointed to the enormous potted begonia in her window. "That's its third pot," she said. "Every time it gets root-bound, it throws itself to the floor and breaks its pot. When that happens, I just have to get it another one. Bigger, of course."

"You think I'm outgrowing my house?" Lois asked. "Like a hermit crab?"

Dr. Frank laughed. "Really, kind of the reverse. You're turning back toward that smaller world. It's healthy, I think. The point is, you seem to be helping yourself by doing what feels right. Warm napkins? They sound lovely."

"They are lovely," Lois said.

If Peter had called again, she would have had something to tell him.

Sheriff Pittman invited them to his house for supper. His wife, he informed them, had been very sorry to hear of their tragedy.

"Quaintly small town, isn't it?" Alan said to Lois, after they'd declined (at Alan's insistence) and Pittman had driven off. Briefly, Lois pictured a column for *About Which*, eating supper with Durango's sheriff and his wife. The tone would be flat, affectless, but affecting nonetheless.

"He's a good person," Lois said, though she, too, was relieved they were eating alone. She enjoyed the thought of oblivious strangers, like the boy at breakfast, serving her.

They stood at the inn's entrance and looked up and down the street. It would have been a good time to nap, to pass the two hours before dinner with mindlessness, but they could not sleep. Instead, they walked.

It was Alan who had wanted to come here. Lois had never believed it necessary to see where Gwen had died. She hadn't wanted to see the body either. Alan tried, without success, to make her agree to an open casket ceremony, sure, Lois knew, that he was acting in her best interest. He'd had just enough counseling to know there were things, unpleasant, resistible, one had to do to recover. This trip was in the same vein. He considered traveling, by any means, a dangerous business and he avoided it whenever possible, so Lois knew he felt he had to be here, had to do this. They'd driven to avoid flying, taking a southern route to miss the highest passes. He'd been very nervous (that is, short-tempered) the whole way. Though he'd thought this trip essential, Lois had agreed only because she wanted him, them, to be cured, to be strong enough to overcome such tremendous odds. The counselor had told Lois that most marriages did not survive the death of a child. Dr. Frank also suggested that Gwen might have committed suicide. She said this as if she were offering consolation instead of complication. Lois had made her promise not to tell Alan either thing, believing that she could successfully circumvent them, but that he could not.

The two of them wandered the older section of town, Lois peeking into shop windows out of habit. Soon she realized she didn't even know what she was looking at, could not remember whether the place they'd just passed sold antiques or car parts. She put her arm through Alan's for balance, smiling but scared.

He did not pat her hand, as he once would have. His love was confused, she knew. It tore him this way, that way, distracted him. His latest affair had been longer and more serious than the previous ones, ending only a year ago. He and Lois had still been mend-

ANTONYA NELSON

ing the terrible wounds their marriage had suffered when Gwen
was killed. It was like stepping from the foreignness of another
country into the alienness of another world. Their grief took hold
of them like a merciless wild animal.

And Lois understood that he felt responsible somehow, that
he'd pulled his love from the structure of their family and let the
edifice slide. His ego allowed him that feeling; he considered himself a cornerstone. He had yet to write about it, and perhaps he
never would. It cheered her to think there were some things, however rare, he could not purge.

Now, Lois felt they were riding some wheel together, that on
the far rungs of this wheel they could not touch, could not even
know one another. They could only suffer. Eventually she hoped
they would work their way toward the center, toward love, where
they could be together once more. Alan's affair had created the
wheel; Gwen's death enlarged it. They had more distance to come,
it seemed, though she believed, finally, that there was no way off for
either of them.

Alan stopped suddenly and somehow made Lois drop her arm
from his. "I don't think it's too much to want to know why," he
said, irritably. "Do you?" He looked hard into her eyes. He was
looking to see if she was sane.

"Yes," she told him. It was far too much. That was the whole
point. "Look there!" she said suddenly. "That's the third time
today I've seen that boy on the bicycle. See his yellow pants? He's
like some friendly poltergeist . . ." No, that wasn't it. "Or something."

Alan glanced where she indicated, then slowly turned back to
her, his eyebrows and forehead drawn downward in a V. But Lois
barely noticed, she was so happy to see the boy again.

They sat on opposite sides of a plastic booth in a fast-food restaurant eating chili from Styrofoam cups. Of course this was better
than being at Sheriff Pittman's, where the only thing everyone had
in common was a death. Better to be here, which could have been

138

downtown Kansas City in winter, snow turning into slush as night fell, headlights and muddy cars passing outside the window, where large cheerful pictures of hamburgers, french fries, and chocolate ice cream hung.

"You think Durango carries the *Times?*" Alan asked her. They hadn't spoken for a long time and Lois's thoughts were far away from the newspaper business. Sometimes, when she and Alan were close, they seemed to think along the same lines and when one of them spoke, it was precisely what the other had been thinking, two minds in a winding relay race, passing the baton. Not so, today.

"Surely," she said, shifting her thoughts to match his. Reading the paper, she knew, was his way of coping with empty time, idle hands.

She wondered what sort of story the Durango paper had run about Gwen. It had never occurred to her before that there would have been a story, but of course there must. The story in the *Star* had been front-page news, since Alan worked for them. They'd run a photo of Gwen from one of the awards dinners her father had been honored at several years earlier. She'd been clapping, big teeth exposed in a beautiful smile, her sister and brother flanking her at the table. The editor had wanted to run a column Alan had written about Gwen, and asked Alan to choose one, but, in looking them over, Alan had realized how many of them were about her foibles as a safe driver. The story ran alone.

But what had been in this paper, Lois wondered? Perhaps a two-paragraph piece, facts only.

"This was a good idea," Alan proclaimed suddenly, their thoughts having gone different ways once more.

Lois considered it. "I don't think we'll know for a while," she offered, disagreeing.

He scowled, standing with his plastic brown tray full of trash. "I meant dinner," he said. On the way out, he threw everything in his hands away, tray and all.

———

At the inn, which had once been the home of a Durango doctor during mining times, Lois and Alan sat on their twin beds staring at the fireplace as if there were a fire in it. There was wood in the grate, newspaper beneath it, long matches in a cup on the mantel. Still, neither of them moved toward lighting it. Lois was thinking of Alan's mistress again, imagining their making love. She was tired and these images came to her when she was too exhausted to fight them. Her friends had rallied round her when Alan was discovered, but then had fallen away when he'd come home again, happier, Lois supposed, to believe him irretrievable. To put Alan and his mistress from her mind, she tried to remember flying from the night before, the light and the freedom and the frightening unknown. It had been exhilarating, but now there was no fuel left in the memory.

Eventually they turned out the lamp, both in their own beds. It was only nine o'clock. The snow had stopped and they could hear a dog, barking in an otherwise still night. Lois attempted to put a good image before her, Gwen walking to class, one of the other children hanging Christmas tree ornaments, the table set for a formal dinner—crystal, linen—their own dog, barking in their own yard, a colorful, simple boy on a bicycle, but superimposed over them all were those other awful images.

By morning both she and Alan were in her bed, wrapped together among the sheets and blankets as if they'd wrestled all night for leverage.

They left town before sunrise, taking a different route, at Lois's request, than the one they'd arrived on. This one would lead them over Monarch Pass. It felt good to Lois to be leaving Durango. Somehow, in the clear melted light of morning, she was comforted in having seen the place, in no longer having to hang on to her imagined site. She couldn't really even recall the accident she had played over and over in her mind. It had disappeared, and a new one, one that included the place Sheriff Pittman had shown them, had yet to come to her. She would fight against its arrival, she decided, sitting beside Alan in the granite-blue of this Colorado morning. If she fought the image hard enough, all day long every day, it would not be able to come in. For a second she could see Gwen's throat, twisted unnaturally, exposed, her youngest, most difficult daughter tumbling down a hillside, new aspens crushed beneath her . . . but she stopped herself, made herself remember only color, blue and red and yellow, and then focus on the scenery outside the car. A fence, the gateposts of a ranch, cows—steam coming from their mouths—clustering at a barn entrance.

When they hit the deer, Lois saw only fur and a single eye before the windshield broke. Its glass rained down on them like pebbles. The deer slid off the hood, leaving a broad smear of blood.

"Is it a mother deer?" Lois whispered to her husband. In a flash she thought of fawns and of full udders, the terrible ache of needing warm milk and needing to provide it.

Her husband remained in his seat, staring straight ahead of him, his hands bouncing lightly on the steering wheel, then harder, until the dashboard rocked. He turned on her, his face a horror, red, monstrous. Through his clenched teeth he spat, "Didn't you see antlers? Are you so blind and *stupid* not to have seen antlers? *Mother* deer do not have points. That's *father* deer."

And just as suddenly he fell against her. He cried without tears, male crying. She did not know what to do at first, his head against her chest, butting into her again and again, the hard guttural sobbing. It would have been easier to handle in the dark. Even the day they'd heard of Gwen's death, he'd been late at work and she had sat on the back steps waiting for him, her arm around the dog, unwilling to enter the house. When he'd come home, they'd sat there together until it grew dark and then they'd been able to comfort one another.

She tried to soothe him now, running her hand through his hair. The worst had to be over. This would be the last bad thing. She imagined the deer, which she could not see, in front of their car. Perhaps it was alive? But she had no resources; she could not make herself leave her husband to go find out. She pictured its fur as she smoothed her palm over Alan's head. The fur would be sprouting in whorls at its haunches and throat. Its underbelly would be white. There was only so much you could do with one pair of hands, she justified.

"There can't be any more bad luck," she told Alan, in a firm whisper, using a tone of voice she'd once used to promise her children their house would not be robbed, their parents would not die. "We've reached our limits." Alan nodded adamantly into her breasts. "This trip is the end of it," she went on. "*Fin.* Goodbye."

Not a single car passed. What odds, Lois thought, Alan finally quiet on her lap. The only car on this highway and this deer could not avoid getting hit. Alan would see a column in it, but to her it seemed like a mathematical problem, the kind she used to try to help her children with. In a landscape with only two moving objects in it, how long will it take for them to collide?

Forest rangers on their way to work found them ten minutes later. One of them was young and impatient, shaking his head at their out-of-state license plate, angry with them for having hit the deer. Lois found herself nodding in agreement with his assessment. Careless of them, yes, traveling too fast. They should have known to expect wildlife at sunrise, in the spring, indeed. The other ranger was like Sheriff Pittman, a man who saw them through eyes screened with sympathy and recognition. Perhaps he saw that more than this accident had claimed these two people, both of whom still sat in their broken car, unable to go on.

Kent Meyers

Wind Rower

1. THE NEIGHBOR

I was up on my silo attaching blower pipes, and I happened to look across the field and saw Philip Hanson's windrower, that new one with the hydrostatic drive, going around and around. At top speed. Seemed crazy to me, but I figured that Pete Hanson was just having some fun the way kids do. So I went on bolting on the pipes, but every once in a while I'd look up, and there'd be that windrower, spinning in the middle of the field. After a while no way could I make sense of it. So when I finished getting the last pipe bolted in place, I climbed down and got in my pickup to go look.

I should have been more suspicious. I mean, I'd seen that thunderhead come out of the west. I was going to put on those blower pipes earlier, even, but decided to wait till that cloud had passed.

Didn't want to be up there during a storm. So I should have been thinking. Sometimes what's obvious is just too scary, maybe, to think about. Or maybe because it's so obvious, you don't think about it, your mind gets going too fast and starts to make things up, and then it gets going faster and makes more things up, and you have all these explanations, and none are the right ones, but you're spending so much time seeing how they could be right that you just ignore the real one.

So even when I got over there and saw what was happening, I didn't think he was dead. I sat on the road for a while, with the pickup idling and watched. Something was wrong, but I couldn't tell what, and you kind of hate to just go driving across someone else's hay unless there's a clear and good reason. But the thing kept whipping around out there. I could hear the engine sound rising and falling as it came around. And then this feeling came to me, real sick-like, and I knew somehow that things were worse than just wrong.

It was like when I was a kid and I used to trap pocket gophers, take the legs to the extension agent for the bounty. I'd always carry a stick with me, and after I uncovered the trap, if there was a gopher in it, I'd slam it on the head, put it out of its misery. Well, this one time, and I'd never done this before, I didn't uncover the trap, I just pulled up on the chain, figuring that I'd just pull everything up and if there was a gopher he'd come on up with the trap, and I'd ding him on the head.

Well, I heard a funny sound as I was pulling. Like if a cat got its foot stuck in mud and pulled it out. A small, sucking sound. That's what I heard, something like that. And right away I felt kind of sick. Like I'd just done something terrible, but I didn't know what, and there was nothing I could do about it, it was way too late. I stopped pulling and just stood there with the chain in my hand, and I wanted to push the trap back into the ground, just push it back in, the way it had been, and either walk away and not know anything, or else start all over. I even started to lower the chain, but of course it just folded, there was no way I could push down the trap even if it had made sense. So finally I just gave it a yank, pulled it clear up out of there, and kind of jumped back away from it, you know how a person will do that.

The trap came up jingling, rusty and spewing dirt. And sure enough, it was sprung. But there wasn't no gopher in it. Just a leg, like a little, clawed hand. All nasty and bleeding and torn. Fresh blood. From being pulled clear out of the socket. The gopher just hadn't come up. Too much weight of dirt pressing down. I stood there and held that chain. And watched blood gather and drop. Drop, drop, drop on the ground.

Sitting there in my pickup, that's how I felt again. That very way. Finally I just backed down the road till I came to Hanson's driveway, and I drove on in and found Linda. I told her something bad had happened. I was that sure. Then I called the fire number.

2. The Fire Chief

Lord, I didn't hardly know how to respond to this one. People here don't make prank calls. But I've got to admit I thought it was some kind of joke at first. I only got to be fire chief four months ago—the youngest one ever in Pallum. It's only a volunteer force, but still, no twenty-eight-year-old has ever been chief. I trained and worked real hard for this job. I studied a lot. I know the procedures better than anyone. I've never been to college, but that's because I wanted to stay here. My wife and I are thinking of having kids pretty soon, and this is a good place to raise kids. So that's why I'm here, still. By choice, not because I'm less than smart, or a screw-up.

But I figured right away that someone was testing me. I figured even it could be someone else on the force, trying to see how the kid was handling the job. "A windrower out of control," I said. "What's it doing? Chewing through fences?"

I probably shouldn't have said that last thing. But I was serious enough, just in case. And the guy came back: "No, it's spinning circles. At full throttle."

"Is there somebody on it?" I asked. Right away I thought that was a dumb question, but there was a pause, like the caller was debating how to answer, and then I figured I had him, this was a prank.

But then, real quiet, murmured into the phone like he wanted only me to hear and there was maybe someone close by, he said: "Something's happened. I don't know what. Maybe he's unconscious. I don't know. But someone's got to stop the thing."

That's when my heart started pumping. From the way he was uncertain. To tell the truth, I couldn't even imagine what he was talking about. Sure I knew what a windrower was, but I was never a farmer, and I couldn't really see the problem. I couldn't visualize it. He said it was out of control, but that didn't really sink in, I guess. How could it?

Procedure says, assume the worst: if you're going to respond to a call, go with everything you got. But this wasn't a fire. I didn't know what it was. It was more than a kitten in a tree, that old story, but I didn't know how much more. The machine wasn't going anyplace. It didn't seem like a major emergency to me. I'm not saying I wasn't concerned about whoever was on it. I was concerned, real concerned. But I figured I could probably handle it alone.

Maybe I screwed up. And if I did I'm saying right here that it was my fault, and I accept that. That's part of the job of being chief. But given the information I had I couldn't see getting twenty men away from their jobs and roar out to the Hanson field with five trucks and nothing to do with them. Besides that, the town council is always telling me to keep costs down as much as possible. And people've told me I did good, that in my position they would have done the same thing. They really have. A lot of people have said that to me.

Anyway, I just figured I'd go out alone. I could always radio back for help. I got out there—it was five or six miles from town, a good distance—and I could see the trouble from the road. Sure enough, the machine was out there, spinning away, with three people standing watching it, two of them real close—Linda and Philip Hanson—and the other, their neighbor Tom Jerrold, kind of away. I pulled off the road down into the ditch and went bouncing across the hay, over the windrows. Jerrold saw me coming and turned and waited, not waving me on or anything.

I drove right up to him and got out, not too fast, not wanting to seem hurried or panicky. The machine was just howling and whining. "Fill me in," I yelled, standing next to Jerrold and looking at the thing whipping around. But he looked at me like I was nuts or something, and I got real uncomfortable. It's like that a lot, being young. People don't believe you know what you're doing. I just looked back at him, though.

"You got trucks coming?" he yelled.

"No," I yelled back. "There's no fire, is there?"

"Jesus Christ!" He spit, and it gobbed up on an alfalfa plant, one that hadn't been cut, and rolled real slow down the stem. Disgusting, I thought. Then he shouted: "How do you plan on stopping that thing?"

"I got to take a look at the situation first," I yelled.

All of a sudden Jerrold grabs me by my shirt and comes in real close to me, his face all unshaven and smelling of sweat and silage. I felt for sure I was going to be smacked, and I was getting ready to fight back. I'd had some martial arts classes over in Oak Falls—just about took the test for my brown belt, in fact—and I know how to take care of myself. But I got to admit, Lord! he was strong. Big old fists like anvils on my shirt. I mean, I'm jerking away, jerking hard, and I'm not moving at all, I'm not hardly straightening his elbows. He just keeps on drawing me in, like I'm at the end of a tow cable and he's the winch.

And then all of a sudden I realize he's not angry at all, he's got something entirely else on his mind. He's looking past me, over my shoulder. And then, right in my ear, real quiet, under the scream of the machine, he says: "Get an ambulance out here. That boy's in tough shape up there. He might even be dead."

Then he stops but keeps right on holding me, and I get real uncomfortable with it. Real uncomfortable. But he had me tightened and screwed down with those arms of his, unless I wanted to rip my shirt pulling away. Then, no louder than before, he says: "That's the boy's mother over there. And father. It took the both of us to keep her from running right into that thing and killing herself. She was on her way when I tackled her."

Then he lets me go. I look up at the machine, howling around in a haze of dust and smoke, grinding, groaning, pounding into the ground, and I imagine Linda running right toward it, all desperate and her hair streaming out behind her, and Philip too dazed to even know what she's doing, but she's going right into that thing, and then Jerrold comes from somewhere and tackles her, hard, just rams her down into the ground, and her breath grunts out of her, whoof, but there's no sound because the machine is so loud, it's like everything is silent, and I see her head kind of bend back, then whipslam into the stubble, and she's fighting, she's hitting at Jerrold, and he's got those iron arms of his like steel cables wrapping her, but even then she's getting away, slippery and tough as a cat, and then Philip comes over real slow and dazed yet and just grabs her and sits on her, and he's stronger than Jerrold, even, not wiry though, just solid like a rock, and finally she just quits moving, and all the while, above them there on the ground, the windrower is whip, whip, whipping around, the sound of it rising and falling as it swings.

It gives me a real funny feeling to picture all this, but I don't let on. I straighten out the front of my shirt, then reach through the window of my pickup and call for an ambulance. But I still can't see what good a fire truck is going to do, I just can't see it, so I don't ask for one, leastways until I can survey the situation a little more thoroughly.

I put down the radio and turn back to the problem. First though, I look at the parents. Linda is watching me, expecting me to do something, and she's crying, not doing anything about it, not even trying to wipe the tears away. Philip is watching the windrower, and holding her so tight she's just pressed against his chest, but he's so still it don't seem natural, like he's frozen or turned into wood.

I decide they're far enough away from the machine for safety. You're always supposed to keep people back away from things, to allow for safety and freedom of movement, non-interference. I got to admit it was something of a relief that I didn't have to go over and ask them to move back some.

I study the windrower, and I start to see how it'd be possible to get the thing stopped. It's really ripping around, but I start to feel this rhythm, and I see how you could wait for the engine to go by and then sprint for the center. You couldn't just go charging in there, but if you timed it right, it could be done. And once you're in the center, of course, you could even walk, take your time, and climb the ladder and pull back the stick and shut the thing off and bring the boy down. The more I look at it the more it seems possible, and I even start to wonder why Jerrold or Hanson hasn't already done it.

But then I go closer, and Lord! a real strange feeling comes on me. I mean, I got plenty of guts. I was a football star in high school, not because I was big but because I'd go after anybody. I'd come out of games all bruised and bleeding, but I didn't care. And some guys, for instance, when they climb that big ladder truck and hang ninety feet in the air with nothing under them, they can't take it, they turn white, and once a guy even puked. But none of that ever bothered me.

But this . . . I mean, this'd give granite the shivers. For one thing, from closer up I can see the boy better, and I have to agree with Jerrold. He looks dead. He's a tall kid, he played basketball, and he's slumped over the machine's control stick, and he's absolutely not moving up there. He's turning, of course. His face comes around every few seconds, all white and blank-looking, and almost upside-down he's bent so far over. And his clothes are all scorched and I can see this black skin, burned and bubbly, along his right shoulder. But the worst is his hair. Curled up like charred fur on his scalp.

I got to admit I hadn't never actually seen a dead person before. I mean, out of a casket. I've been on enough fire calls, but they're always barns or grass fires or haystacks. I don't know how to say this without sounding, what? Sadistic? 'Cause it's just the opposite, really. But every time a call comes in, I kind of hope it'll be someone trapped in a building. I mean, I don't hope it, of course. Of course I don't hope it. I'd just like to save someone sometime. I'd really like to, to be the one to save somebody. But there's never the chance.

Sometimes when we're pumping water full blast on another haystack, I wonder why we don't just let it burn. The water's ruining it bad as the fire. But we pump away, we all pretend there isn't nothing more important in the world than getting that fire out. And afterwards people will tell us what good work we did. But I'll go home sometimes and just feel kind of empty. Like . . . is this all there is to it? Is this all there's ever going to be?

But right in front of me now is someone to be saved. I mean, I got to assume he's alive. The trouble is, I don't really believe it, though I try to—not the way that white face, upside-down, goes past me every few seconds, eyes just swinging over me like a searchlight at an airport would. And the other trouble is . . . well, like I said, it'd be possible to wait for the engine to swing by and then sprint for the center. But you got to picture this.

This whole machine is running, see, full-blast. The reel is turning, the spring-teeth on it like claws coming up and over, then ripping back down toward the sickle, and the sickle is just chattering away, those triangular blades a blur when the platform swings by, snicking back and forth, all green-stained and shiny, nasty-looking. I've heard of cats being cut in half by those sickles. And the boy's weight, you see, is pushing the stick far ahead as it'll go and all the way to the right, so that the right drive wheel is spinning backwards as fast as it'll go, and the left one forwards just as fast. The hydrostatics are just groaning keeping those wheels going. I mean, this thing is spinning around so fast you can hardly keep up with it. These things'll do, I've heard, twenty miles an hour or more straight ahead.

And the engine hanging over that big caster wheel in back—

it's bouncing into the air and slamming back down on the ground. I can feel it in my feet, right through the soles of my boots every time it does that. Thudding and sickening. Real heavy. It's as if you cast a capital letter "T" in iron, about fourteen feet long and about two tons, and put lugged wheels on the ends of the crossbar and knives and saws and cutting things knocking against each other inside the crossbar, and then set those wheels going in opposite directions, fast. And the vertical bar has the engine, see, hanging over a caster wheel, and blasting out gasoline fumes and noise—if you can kind of picture that whipping around in its own dust, you got some idea of what this thing was like.

Still, I can see this line, you know—like running a football, how you can see your way through the tacklers sometimes. I can see how I could make it into the center, and like I said, once you're there, it's slow. The boy up there on the platform, he's coming around every couple seconds or so, but not fast. Kind of dream-like and peaceful, unconcerned-like. If you could just get past the out-side circles safe.

And I even prepare myself. I stand real close, so close that the heat of the exhaust blasts me every time it goes by. I look in there, and I visualize the line I'd have to follow. I get all tensed, and I tell myself, five more swings and I go. And then I count them down. Five. Four. Three. Two. One.

But my legs don't move. They're all tensed and ready, but they don't move. So I try again, a different number, seven this time, and count it down. But the more I count, the bigger the platform gets, and every time it goes by I see those sickle blades shimmering back and forth, all blurry and sharp. And I got boots on, and they're not made for running, they feel awful heavy. So I'm all tensed and ready again, but I get down to one and I don't go, I just stand there like I'm locked up tight, like my whole body has a charley-horse cramp.

So I try ten this time, but about halfway down the count I quit seeing the line entirely. I quit seeing myself following it. Instead, I see myself tripping and stumbling, or I see my boots moving real slow, like one of those slow-motion wildlife films, and I just can't speed them up. And I see the back of the platform coming around, and me running but I'm getting nowhere, and then the front is coming around, and I'm nowhere near the center yet, nowhere near, and then, Lord! I'm looking over my shoulder, and the whole gaping maw of the thing is right behind me, or I've stumbled and I'm laying in the hay, and the platform is growing, growing like the whole world on me. And when I'm down around number three I get to where I imagine those pointed sickle guards poking right into my ribs and the sickles slicing away at me, turning everything red, and cutting right into my bones. And at two I see it cutting me right off at the ankles, and me falling backwards, grabbed by the reel, and run through the auger and out through the hole in the back, and then mashed right into the ground by the drive wheels. And my feet sitting there by themselves.

And I don't even say the one. I just go all untensed and let the engine go by. And I look up, and the boy's face is moving past me again, just moving on by, not caring what I do or don't do. I let it swing by, and just turn and walk away.

Linda is watching me. I catch her eye but I don't hold it. I look at Philip, but it's like his eyes have turned to stones, not seeing anything. Then Linda starts to go down to her knees, like they're melting and she's sinking right into the ground. She sinks that way, real slow, then all of a sudden drops. She's holding her face on the machine, on her knees in the stubble, and her hands are kind of fluttering in front of her, like they're picking flowers, but there're no flowers there. I can hardly stand to watch her, but I can't not watch either.

She sinks even further, she bends at the waist, and just kind of wilts, and her face goes down into the stubble, with her hair falling all around it. She sinks until she's curled up the way a baby sleeps, only her body is shaking, rising and falling. Philip is standing there, he has one hand reached out toward her. Then he sinks, too, with his hand still reached out, coming closer and closer to her. And finally he's kneeling beside her, and his hand is on her back, and it's moving in little circles there, but everything else about Philip is still again. His face is like a blank, dark window just before a brick hits it. And that one hand going around in little circles on her back.

I feel like a jerk. I feel like I'm the one just certified it: too bad, he's dead. I go up to Jerrold. I feel like crying. But I don't let on. I get real close so I don't have to yell. "We'll just have to let it run out of gas," I say. If he wanted to hit me, I wouldn't care. And then I feel his arm around my shoulder, tight as a vise. And it's kind of comforting, really.

And really, I kind of forget what happened after that. It took an hour and a half more for the thing to run out of gas. The ambulance came, and someone managed to get Philip and Linda in there and lying down. Other people showed up, Linda's sister for one, who I was awful relieved to see. And we all just stood around and waited.

A lot later I thought I could have called a boom truck out and had myself lifted over to the boy. Or I could have run my pickup right into the thing and stopped it that way, smashed things up quite a bit, of course. And maybe, even, I could have made it in there, running. But he had to be dead, didn't he? Right away, soon as that bolt hit him. He had to be. I mean, he never moved a bit the whole while.

Jerrold's the only one who saved a life. And I don't even think he knows it. That's what's so crazy. And she didn't even want to be saved.

3. THE MOTHER

I try to make sense of this. But there's no sense to be made. I stand in my kitchen. I have sheer curtains on the windows. In the breeze they move like veils of water white and falling, white and falling. We took a trip to the mountains once. We found a little waterfall. It came from a crack in the rocks and fell a long, long ways. There were people all around, gathered on the road. We stopped anyway. They were all snapping pictures. Philip got out the camera and started to snap pictures, too. Peter was eight, and I kept my hand on his shoulder. The road was curving and busy, and I was afraid he would go running across to look at the water more closely.

But he just stood there. He let my hand rest on his shoulder. I wanted to put it around him and hug him and stand like that, watching. But he was at that age when that would have embarrassed him, and I was afraid that if I tried he would shake me off entirely. So I let my hand just rest on his shoulder. It must have seemed natural to him. He didn't know how much I was restraining myself. How much my heart was wrenched. He was wondering at the falls. And I missed them because I wanted so much to share them completely with him.

I wanted so much. And I missed them. But they must have been falling dreamily. They must have been all spumy and white. Because he stood there for the longest time and then asked: "Are they falling up or falling down?" And maybe I saw how the water flaked in the wind. Maybe I saw how it had turned to a sheet that maybe was moving and maybe was not. But I answered, "Down, of course. Things always fall down."

"Even water?"

"Even water."

Again I wanted to hug him. I wanted to kneel beside him and hug him right there. All I was aware of was how much I was holding back. So that I could keep this least touch of my hand on his shoulder.

Cameras were clicking all over. They were like bugs in the breeze, loud, clacking bugs.

"Do you think if you had a rowboat and rowed real hard you could row to the top?" he asked me.

And maybe I saw how the water seemed solid, as bright as marble and as sure. Maybe I saw how it looked like you could drive an oar or a pole right into it and get a good grip, and push. But I answered: "No. There's nothing there, really."

And I almost gripped his shoulder, almost tightened my hold. I felt my muscles begin it. But I stopped them and just imagined them doing it. I imagined the tips of my fingers pressing deep till they felt his marvelous bones. I just imagined it, and he never moved. He stayed with the falls.

"Not even if the wind blew you up?"

"No. Not even then."

Then Philip came back, and he said: "Beautiful, isn't it? We got some great pictures. What do you think, Pete?"

And still he didn't move. He just kept looking at the falls, and he said: "I feel the water on my face. Do you feel the water on your face?"

And maybe I felt how the wind was softly laden with it, how the wind was cool and wet, filled with the spray that maybe was rising and maybe was falling. But I answered: "We better go now. We have a long ways to go yet today."

He goes around and around. In my mind yet, around and around. I see his white face, as cold and solid as marble, come around and around and around.

I remember my hand on his shoulder. How I went no further because I wanted to so badly. I was afraid he would shake me off.

So what if he had? There would have been a moment, a single moment before he knew what was happening, before he could break away. And in that moment I would have known the spume and the spray and my boy. I would have felt the world on my face.

Robert Day

My Father Swims His Horse at Last

In fact Verbena was not my father's horse but my mother's horse, and by the time my father got around to swimming her across the Big Pond a few years ago, both Verbena and my father were getting old—"long in the tooth, long in the tooth" as my father was fond of saying in his repetitive way and with his lifelong affection for things wizen and cranky, a kind of self-affection now that I think of it. Given my father's spectacular case of procrastination—something he also cherished—it was remarkable that the swim took place at all.

"I'm going to swim the horse this year," my father would say in his annual early-autumn phone calls to me. "You come back and I'll teach you a few things about swimming horses you might need to know—even if you are a vice president of some business that makes its money off the raw red backs of the workingman." My father was a dusty and battered High Plains Populist, probably one or two beyond the last of a dead breed, and his concern for the raw red backs of the workingman permeated his life—as did his hostility toward business vice presidents.

"I am not a vice president," I'd say, something my father knew very well. I sell mortgage insurance. Badly, as it has turned out. Still, my father didn't approve of my enterprise—no matter how poorly I did it, nor with what little conviction. After I graduated from college he had wanted me to return to the farm to raise the low-dollar steers we'd buy at auction in the spring only to sell off in the fall, never making very much money in the process—not that making money ever seemed the point to my father. But more than work, I think he wanted me around for talk.

"Tell me what profit is?" my father once asked me in his rhetorical way over supper when I was growing up. Before I could answer he said: "It's time turned into money. Now what do you think of a system of human endeavor that does that: turns time into money?" As a young boy I usually didn't know what to think of my father's opinions.

"What madness is it?" he went on, his John Brown beard jumping with a frustration it has taken me a very long time to appreciate: "What madness is it?" he said. "Tell me, son. Tell me. What madness is it?"

I could not, of course, tell my father what madness it was. But I did vaguely understand, even then, that the phrase was to be one of the several refrains of our lives: *What madness is it?* The use and beauty of work. Where is Sockless Jerry Simpson (a Populist, like my father) when we need him? Language is where life is. Time. Your poor dead mother. Time.

"Time," my father continued when, after a few minutes and with some walking about the kitchen, he had calmed down. "Time. Contemplate it, son. Muse on it. Watch it stretch out before you like a long afternoon down by the Big Pond. Look at the Russian olives on the dam wave back and forth through it. Time: See how gossamer a thing it is." Here my father paused and drifted into a detached look he got, the skin below his eyes bunching up and the point of his beard dropping toward his chest: It seemed as if he was looking through me to find Mother, and when he'd fail, his head would shiver slightly and that would start him talking again: "Do you know what 'gossamer' means?" he said.

"No." I said.

"Well, it isn't something you'd want to turn into money, now is it?"

Some sons learn to agree with their fathers when they are angry; I learned to agree with my father when for a moment he grew distant.

But my father was not distant the last time he called about swimming the horse; he was buoyant.

"You coming back to watch me swim the Big Pond with the horse or don't you think you can learn anything from your father anymore?" I sensed a grin behind the gathering hair of his winter beard, a beard he would not trim between the first of September and the first of May.

"I'll be there," I said. "I'll learn what I can about swimming a horse."

"You'll learn more about life from swimming a horse than you can from clipping coupons or figuring interest on your C.D.'s," he said.

"I don't clip coupons," I said. "Or have C.D.'s."

"No, but I'll bet your bank has neon signs that advertise its money-market rates," he said.

"It does," I said. "You have those in Hays as well."

"I expect we do," he said. "That's what we need: the perpetual instruction of the youth about interest rates: 'Six-point-three-nine percent with yield of seven-point-two percent.' Material madness."

"It's pretty harmless given today's youth," I said.

"It's not harmless to rot their minds so nothing of use or beauty can grow," he said; I could tell the grin was going and my father was about to go 'around the bend in the river,' a phrase my mother apparently used to describe my father's quick turns of mood on matters political.

"Better the young should read Jack London," my father went on. "Study *The Iron Heel*. That's use and beauty in a book. Peruse the *U.S. Farm News*, 'Peace, Parity and Power to the People.' Let the youth memorize that."

"We live in a capitalist country," I said.

"Don't tell me about it," he said. "The least the robber-barons can do is not afflict the general population with the interest rates some steak-and-potato vice president is getting on his money-belt wad."

"They eat pasta salad these days," I said. "And the banks are just trying to tell the public the facts." My defense was only half-hearted; I am—to a larger extent than I've ever told him—my father's boy.

"I don't want to know anything banks want me to know," he said. "It's pollution of the eyes and the eyes are the portals to the soul. Why cobble up a good soul with dirty money? Do you know what 'portals' means?"

"Yes," I said.

"It's about time," my father said.

It was conversation that reminded me once again that to my father the mortal enemy was the "vice president"—in whatever form he appeared, whatever madness he consecrated. I have a feeling that the printed complaint forms I've spotted these past few weeks on the counters of the business around Hays are a silent, although misguided, tribute to my father's forty-year war against "executive fat," as he was given to calling it then.

"When you see the vice president in his three-piece Du Pont plastic suit," my father said to the manager behind the counter at the Stockman's Supply a few years ago when we had come into town to get—among other items—some feed to lure Verbena into the corral, "tell him for me they waste our money wrapping these salt licks in paper that advertises we ought to buy more salt licks. I know how many salt licks I need. Don't cut down trees in Oregon just to be absurd."

The manager, like most store managers who knew my father, stared at the counter and studied the sales slip.

"And don't quote your horse-feed prices for fifty pounds just to make me think it's a bargain when you've raised it ten cents," my father went on. "It's a hundredweight that names the price. Not fifty. Use language to cheat the public and you'll pay a price you don't know exists."

"We had an increase at the home office," I remember the manager said as a last-line defense, forgetting it was best to remain silent in face of my father's jumping beard.

"Well, don't pass it on to your customers," my father said. "That's madness of the second order."

"We have to," said the manager.

"No you don't," said my father. "Wear out your shoes and grow a garden. It will be good for you. Shoot rabbits in the fall. Tell the vice president to eat soup and save soap slivers. We do. Take a bath twice a week; bathe every day in hot water and your skin will peel off your bones. A little frugality would be healthy for the establishment fat. In the meantime you can keep your horse feed until the price comes down." As I recall that was one of the first times we didn't get around to swimming the pond with Verbena.

Over the years it never occurred to me that we would ever swim Verbena—nor did I understand my father's fascination for insisting we should. The swim seemed the essence of something destined never to be accomplished, a kind of ultimate "I'm going to." I do remember, however, when the plan got fixed in my father's mind.

"The internal combustion engine is a bad idea," he said to me one summer afternoon as I was shooting baskets at the goal in our farmyard.

"Yes," I said.

"Don't agree with your father just because he's short," he said.

"O.K.," I said.

"We're not going anywhere on the farm in the truck any-more," he said. "We're going to use the horse."

"O.K.," I said. "What about taking trash to the dump?"

"We'll use the truck for the dump," he said.

"What about fishing?" I said.

"We'll use the truck for fishing," he said. My father had a way of compromising immediately. "But we'll use the horse to check the cattle and look at the fences."

"We don't look at fences," I said.

"We're going to start looking at fences," my father said. "On horseback."

"O.K.," I said.

As a short man, in order for my father to get in the saddle it was necessary for him to use the stump of a cottonwood just out-side a shed we called the Electric Company. He would never let me watch him swing into the saddle; instead he'd dream up some chore for me to do while he led Verbena out of the corral and across the yard. When I'd come back from wherever I'd been sent, there would be my father—full in the saddle—and Verbena would be twisting her head in the air against the bit. Small cyclones of dust would rise around her prancing feet.

"Did you see her buck?" my father would say.

"No," I'd say. "I was in the toolshed. Here's your hoof pick."

"Don't need it now," my father'd say. "You should have seen her buck. She always bucks when you first get on her; it's what gets your heart started." Then my father would send me off to the north end of the yard to open the gate into the pasture and out he and Verbena would ride to check fences and peer at our homely steers.

It could all have been done much more quickly in our pickup but instead once a week or so from about the time I was in my early teens until I left for college, my father would ride Verbena out over the pastures and back. An hour adventure at most, after which he wouldn't say much—not even during the evening radio news when it was his habit to make a running commentary on the events of the world. But on one such evening not long before I went to college my father said:

"Someday I think I'll swim that horse across Big Pond."

"Why?" I said.

"Think what you could learn from that," he said. "Just think."

"What?" I said.

He looked at me over whatever he was reading and shook his head as if he had failed.

"Well," he said. "There's much to learn from swimming a horse—if you contemplate the prospect for a while."

"What?" I said.

"I don't know yet," he said. "I'm just beginning to think on it. You might do the same. You don't learn anything in this world unless you consider what there is to learn."

"Yes," I said. My father was given to being dismayed at his only son.

"We'll swim the horse next fall," he said. "When you come back from college for a weekend. It'll fatten up your education. I'm sure it will need it by then." It was indeed the very next fall that my father and I began a rather long tradition of not swimming his horse across Big Pond.

And it was with the knowledge that we would fail to accomplish the swim—a friendly knowledge now that I think of it—that even after college each fall I'd drive from Kansas City back to the farm, taking Friday and Monday off so I might spend the long weekend helping my father with the various chores that needed doing if we were going to "button up the place" so he could spend yet another winter out there—which of course he was always determined to do. For three days we'd split and stack stove wood for the Melrose Oak, tack up plastic sheets as storm windows, lower a small evergreen cut from the shelter belt down the chimney to scrape it clean, and lay square bales of straw around the house's foundation against the chance that the great blizzard of '86—my father's favorite historical storm—would reappear. All this and the great horse swim of Big Pond to boot.

Saturday mornings we would pile into our sturdy Studebaker pickup and, with our coffee mugs spilling onto our jeans and my father's bag of unshelled sunflower seeds dribbling onto the floor-boards, prowl the west pastures looking for Verbena—a rather hefty roan of a mare who, as she got older, seemed to feed further and further from the house, so that our trip to catch her usually covered most of our pastures.

I remember the look she'd give us when we'd pop over some rise and find her browsing peacefully on the late grass coming up in one of the draws that grows wet with the springs that seep out in the autumn: *you guys again,* her shaggy visage seemed to say, for even by early October she had grown the remarkable winter wooly coat that was her hallmark, and by which my father judged—badly, it always seemed to me—the depth and duration of the High Plains blizzards that he imagined would come roaring down on him out of the Januarys and Februarys in the Dakotas above us.

"Two weeks of snow before the New Year," my father'd say, rolling down his window and looking at the mare while his coffee mug steamed a small balloon onto his side of the old windshield.

"It didn't turn out that way last year," I'd say.

"No two years are alike," my father'd say as a way of putting his past predictions behind him. "You've got to learn to read the coat. Look at that shag; look at how the halter is getting buried in the hair. That's a nasty winter right there in a horse's head." My father never read mild weather in Verbena's coat; indeed, some falls he'd contemplate encircling the house with the huge round bales of prairie hay he had cut off the pastures as winter feed for whatever stock he might be keeping through the winter.

"She always gets a good shag on her," I'd say. Like the cattle trails to our water tank, these conversations were well worn.

"Cold after the first blizzard," my father would go on. "Bitter cold. And wind. Blowing snow for a week. I won't be able to see the Electric Company."

"Maybe it won't be that bad," I'd say.

"Worse," my father'd say, as he'd point his beard defiantly toward the north. "So bad the television will rattle on about 'wind-chill factors' and tell me not to go to the horse tank in my boxer shorts."

"They're being helpful," I'd say.

"Why doesn't the television tell me about Spain, if they want to be helpful," he'd say. "The radio used to tell me about Spain. The *U.S. Farm News* told me about Spain. But no, it took the television two days to tell me Franco was dead. Franco! What a scoundrel! Dead for two days and I didn't know to celebrate."

"Nobody cares about Franco in Western Kansas," I'd say.

"Well, they ought to," my father would go on. "You've got to learn something about life besides the price of wheat. Why would the television tell me the windchill factor and not tell me that Franco was dead?"

"I don't know," I'd say. "I don't know." It was my own all-purpose refrain that I'd use—even as a small boy—to change the direction of the conversation, not that in retrospect I give the technique high marks.

"Do you know what Brendan Behan said about Franco?" my father'd say.

"No," I'd say.

About this time Verbena would have edged her way to the truck for the grain we'd put in a bucket in the back; somehow she seemed to know the quality of my father's rant and knew it meant food: that, and a harmless walk back to the yard where she'd be fed again, perhaps saddled, but of course not ridden. On balance it must have seemed a good bargain to the old horse. And as chance would have it, she seemed to always stop my father short of telling me what Brendan Behan had once said about the "Generalissimo Franco."

"Catch that horse and put a lead on her before she bolts over the Saline Breaks," my father would whoop when, in the middle of his diatribe about Franco and television, he'd hear Verbena rattling around in the feed bucket in the back of the truck.

"She's not going anywhere," I'd say.

"She'll be in Nebraska by morning if you don't jump quick." Jumping quick had been my job since boyhood.

What I'd read in the shag of Verbena's head as I snapped a lead to her halter was that the old mare had no intention of bolting any breaks on her way to Nebraska and the blizzards lurking in the depth of her coat.

"Now you'll learn what there is to swimming a horse," my father would say as I'd get back in the truck. "You'll learn something more than the useful in life. You'll learn something to talk about when you're old and long in the tooth like that horse."

"I expect I will," I'd say.

"And talk about it at length," he'd say. "You're too quiet a boy for the good of the country. You've got to learn to scream bloody-murder when the four-door Cadillac of capitalism is about to make road kill of your bony hide."

"I'll speak about it at length," I'd say. Good, my father'd say, and put the truck in gear for the ride back to the yard, Verbena trotting behind.

But no matter how easy it might be to catch Verbena, nor with what efficiency my father and I would get together the tack from various sheds and storerooms, year after year we never got around to swimming her. Oh, we'd get close: some Octobers we'd even get as far as the Big Pond itself. And five years ago my father had the idea we should celebrate our impending accomplishment by grilling some steaks in a pit fire on the south point that poked itself out into the pond.

"Ceremony," I remember my father saying on this occasion, "is a drama we can all write for ourselves." We were cutting cottonwood logs for the fire. Verbena was tethered to a tree, her saddle cinched tight.

"We've got plenty of wood," I said. We had enough for a high-school bonfire; my father was as excessive as he was frugal.

"Cut some more," my father said. "I'll want to dry off by the blaze when I come out of that pond, and so will you."

"We've got enough for that," I said.

"Not for both a blaze and a bed of coals for the steaks, we don't," he said. "And then we'll want some fire in the hole to talk by. Don't you want to look across the flames and see your father's face when he tells you what you've learned from swimming a horse?"

"Of course," I said; we cut more wood.

In fact, looking back on it, I suspect it was all part of my father's dallying dance before the swim, and I guess in some dim way I knew that and I was glad for it. Perhaps I sensed we had gotten such a good start on the swim that year, I had half a fear we might pull it off, and what the name of that fear was I have never been quite sure. But in the end we spent our time in a kind of slow-motion puttering: first with the pit, then with the fire, and several times with the horse (my father walked over to Verbena to say something to her and then came away still talking—but to whom I couldn't be sure). Once, pretty late in the afternoon, he walked around to the dam and through the double line of Russian olives that grew up on each side. I watched him as he looked back at me over the pond. I remember he didn't wave; he just stood there a moment, looking my way. And then he walked back around. In the end evening came on and the muskrats began to etch their V's onto the flat water and my father said:

"It's gotten away from us again, now hasn't it, son? We've run out of daylight."

"I guess we have," I said.

My father went over to Verbena and unsaddled her and tossed the gear into the pickup.

"I can't teach you about swimming horses in the dark," he said. "It's a lesson of life. You need to see it clearly. You should have been shown long ago." My father looked out over the pond to the other side. "Time flies when you're having fun," he said. "I've never known what to do about that."

"We'll swim her next year," I said.

"Probably," said my father.

We cooked our steaks over the cottonwood coals and talked with the flame dancing in the pit. Verbena didn't go far, and as we ate we could hear her moving through the trees, grazing. Once, I thought I heard her at the pond taking water.

"Your mother never rode Verbena," my father said as the fire got low.

"I didn't know that," I said. It was getting difficult to see his face; I got up to get another log, but he held out his hand, palm down, to indicate he didn't want me to.

"Your mother wasn't political," he said. I didn't say anything; there was a moment of silence between us, and in the distance I thought I could hear the night flight of Sand Hill cranes.

"We'll get it done," my father said.

"O.K.," I said.

"Her world was flowers," he said.

"You never told me that," I said.

"We'll swim her horse," my father said.

"Agreed," I said.

But the truth becomes that in the years after that evening we cooked our steaks on the pond's bank, and listened to the old horse browse among the cottonwoods, we seemed to recede from the swim. The following year we only drove to the pasture and looked at Verbena while my father held forth on the rising cost of electricity—due, he felt (correctly, I suspect), to the new atomic power plant they had installed down the wires from the farm. A few years later we didn't even get out of the yard, and had Verbena not come up to the corrals on her own that weekend I might not have heard my father's dire prediction of yet another bad winter.

"We're not talking the blizzard of '86," he said as we stood by the horse just before I was to drive back down the highway. "But we are looking at the blizzard of 1912. Or '48. Do you remember the one in '48?"

"I was pretty young," I said.

"Couldn't get out for a month," he said. "You, me and your

mother. All buttoned up in here with rice and beans and pickles. Jerry Simpson would have been proud."

"Call me if you need help," I said.

"Maybe," he said, looking back at the old white house, "we should have put the big bales around me this year. At least lay them along the north side so I don't get drifted in."

"If you want to," I said. "I've got some time yet. The front-end loader is still on the tractor. It wouldn't take an hour." But he shook his head no, then said:

"You come back next year, and we'll swim that horse first off. Friday afternoon. Make your mother proud of us and teach you something at the same time."

"O.K.," I said.

"Keep track of what you learn," he said.

"What?" I said.

"Keep track of what you learn from swimming that horse so you can tell me what it is in the long run."

"We haven't done it yet," I said.

"We will," he said. "But you've got to get ready by thinking ahead. See the swim in your mind's eye. Watch the water part at her chest. Watch the cottonwood leaves coming down on the pond. Don't think of anything without seeing it in your mind's eye: that's the problem with you vice presidents. You don't watch what you're doing in your head. It's all dry columns and furniture-appliances."

"Furniture-appliances?" I asked. Generally I don't ask.

"Like dishwashing machines," he said. "God help us."

"I'll try to watch what I'm doing in my head," I told him.

"Good thinking," said my father. "Don't watch television, as it will rob you of the ability," he said.

"I know," I said.

As it has turned out, the following year my father would swim his horse at last.

"To swim a horse across water," my father said to me, "you do not have to take off the saddle. Water doesn't hurt the saddle; you'll need to neat's-foot oil it of course, but water itself doesn't hurt leather." I nodded.

It was Friday afternoon; I had come home as promised, escaping—my father pointed out in the first minutes after my arrival—the impending crash of various financial markets which in his opinion damn well deserved to tumble down: on top of me if I insisted on living off the backs of the working poor. We were sitting in the kitchen at the table. Outside it was a warm gold-and-blue day. Windless. When I was a boy it had been my job to neat's-foot oil all the leather we had between us: boots, saddles, an old rifle scabbard my father had bought at farm auction against the day he was going to get a rifle to shoot a deer.

"O.K.," I said. "Let's put 'oil leather' on the weekend list. I'll do that."

"Good thinking," said my father. He seemed dreamy, as if there were something he was trying to recall but couldn't. He fiddled with his beard; over the years it had grown two tufts to it, a kind of forked beard; and while it had gone gray it had not turned white: my father looked in old age like some wizened satyr, modestly pleased with himself, but a little lost.

"First off," he continued rather abruptly after a moment of silence and with no prompting from me, "you ride your horse directly into the water; don't let him turn away from the swim at hand." I realized my father always called horses "he" or "him" no matter what their sex; in this case Verbena had been a mare for nearly thirty years.

"Yes," I said.

Usually my father took the Friday afternoon of my visit to bring me up to date on the state of politics in the country: a kind of Who's Who of the nation's leading rascals, with refrains of "Where was Sockless Jerry Simpson when we needed him?" After that we'd make up a list of chores that needed doing, and often we'd get a start on them before evening. True, later at dinner it had become our custom to lay out once more the horse-swimming plans, but until this particular weekend that had never included any real instruction on how the swim was to be made.

"When you get your horse out into the water where he can swim by himself," my father said, now more calmly, "you slide off to the left and hold on to the saddle horn with your right hand. Do you understand?"

"Yes," I said.

"Don't fight the water," said my father. "A horse will tow you along peacefully if you don't thrash about and if you let your feet come up, which they will, boots and all."

"O.K.," I said.

"Notice you can swim a horse without being able to swim yourself," my father said, "and cross a river or a pond in spite of your deficiency." Both my father and I could swim.

"I understand," I said.

"Now when you get to the other side of the pond," my father continued, "let your horse find his feet, and then come out beside him, walking yourself. Don't get lazy and think you'll keep your boots from getting muddy by slipping into the saddle at the last minute and riding your horse out. Let him come out by himself; stand back and he'll shake."

"Yes," I said.

My father grew quiet: he had that distant look in his eyes. Over our house a hackberry tree had grown up over time and its branches were beginning to touch the tin roof. When a breeze came along you could hear the tree scrape, as it did while my father and I sat at the table for a moment in silence.

"You want me to cut that tree back this weekend?" I said.

"No," he said. He seemed to have lost track of himself.

"You want to get started on the chores yet this afternoon?" I said. "We can put some square bales around the house." He shook his head no, then:

"Why don't you shoot some baskets?" There hadn't been a basketball around the place in years.

"We got work to do," I said. "If you're going to make it through winter."

"We'll make it through the winter tomorrow," he said.

"O.K.," I said.

"You know why I'm short?" he said.

"No," I said.

"To live a long time," he said. "You don't see very many tall old men, now do you?" he said.

"No, I don't," I said. He pulled at the left fork of his beard.

"The Big Pond was the last project I saw through to the end," he said.

"There were others," I said.

"Not many," he said.

"It wasn't the point," I said.

"Shoot some baskets," he said. "Pretend you're Bill Russell. I want to read some radical paper. We'll eat turkey legs and rice at six."

"I'll cook," I said. "I've brought some things from town." I'd picked up a roast and some potatoes.

"Pizza?" he said.

"What," I said.

"You didn't bring pizza from town?" he said. "I won't have it on the farm. Imagine what it does to your colon. I want turkey legs and rice. They're in the icebox."

"O.K.," I said.

"I'm going to read," he said. He got up and went into Mother's room.

I spent the afternoon laying square bales around the base of the house; once I went out to the basketball goal and looked at it. The net was gone and the rim was rusted. But the Boston Garden looked much the same even though some bindweed was creeping in on the western edge of the parquet. I took an imaginary shot and made it.

Around sundown I came back to the house. I could smell the cottonwood smoke in the yard and knew that my father had fired up the Melrose Oak to boil his turkey legs. We had a fine dinner at the kitchen table and spent the evening talking about the time we'd lost the load of wood on Eighth Street. I was going to tell my father some of what I'd learned that day, but he put his finger to his lips and shook his head.

"Keep it in," he said as his finger bounced against the shag of his beard and mustache that in winter he'd let close in over his mouth. "Keep it in until it grows wings and talons and flies out of you by itself. It will soar. It will find me. It will have good eyes."

The next morning when I got up my father was out of the house. I poured myself some coffee and read the *Farm News*: the editorial letters were about the Middle East and parity. The quotations at the bottoms of the columns ran from Gandhi to Reagan. I thought my father might have gone to town.

"I've got the horse," he said as he came in a few minutes later.

"I could have helped," I said.

"It wasn't any trouble," he said. "I talked to her about Franco and she came right over."

"Do you want to swim her today?" I said.

"Was Jerry Simpson sockless?" my father said.

"Let's line out some chores first," I said.

"Let's not and say we did," said my father. The twin points of his beard were shaking with some kind of excitement I had not seen in him before.

"O.K.," I said.

We went outside; Verbena was saddled and tied to the chain latch on the bed of the pickup.

"You drive ahead," said my father. "The horse and I will come along."

"You sure you don't want to wait until it warms up?" I said. "Later this afternoon." It was a bluebird day, but cool. Besides, it was never very clear to me who was going to swim this horse— much less who was going to learn what from it; speaking for myself, I wanted a little warmth when I came out of the Big Pond.

"Get going," he said. "Do as your father says or I won't let you in my government when the revolution comes." He untied Verbena from the chain latch.

I got in the truck and drove it down to the pond. As I left the yard I checked the mirror and saw my father heading for the cottonwood stump by the Electric Company. When I got to the Big Pond there were teal in the west slew and they took off and circled once and then went over the hill. I drove to the dam and got out and lowered the tailgate and sat on it. Pretty soon I could see my father coming over the hill on Verbena; against the brown of buffalo-grass pasture he looked like something from a poster you'd find in a gallery.

"How is she?" I said when they got to the truck. I noticed for the first time that in recent years Verbena must have been growing a gathering of her random white hairs into a small cluster in the middle of her forehead.

"Old," my father said. "But full of piss and vinegar."

"She's as old as I am," I said. "Older than you if you count horse years."

"You should have seen her buck when I got on," my father said.

"You want me to swim her?" I said. I thought that might be best.

"What do you know about swimming a horse?" my father said.

"You just taught me," I said. "Last night up in the kitchen."

"That was talk," he said.

"You ever swim a horse?" I said.

"No," he said; he reined Verbena around in a circle. "Don't ask me questions you know the answer to. What madness is that?"

"Well," I said, "we're about even when it comes to swimming horses."

"No, we're not," my father said. On the point of land across the way a breeze came up and sent some cottonwood leaves in a shower over the pond. We both watched them as they settled on the water.

"You're right," I said. "Let's swim your horse."

Two days later, on Monday, when I am getting ready to go back to Kansas City, my father and I are standing in the front yard of the house. It is surrounded by huge round prairie-hay bales I have stacked to protect him against the impending winter.

"You wait and see," he says.

"For what?" I say.

"The yard will be full to the bales with snow and the television will babble on about the frozen dead out here."

"It won't be that bad," I say.

"Worse," he says.

"I think you'll make it," I say.

"Maybe," he says. He doesn't say anything for a moment, then: "I'm not going to watch television anymore."

"O.K.," I say.

"You don't sell water beds, do you?" he says.

"Mortgage insurance," I say. "Why?"

"They're selling water beds on television," he says. "Chairs that vibrate. Plastic do-hickeys that shoot sliced cucumbers into salads."

"What madness is it," I say.

"It's 1886 and I am Sockless Jerry Simpson," he says, looking up through the circle of hay bales at the blue roundness above us. "The frozen night is coming up my legs but I am looking for an eagle who is looking for me."

"What?" I say. I look at him to see if he is all right; my father stares back at me, but not as if he is looking for Mother.

"At least I don't have to ride around this country trying to find out where I am," he says. "I get to stay put. Historical cold."

I don't know what to say and we stand together in silence.

My father told me to drive the truck around to the point on the other side and watch him from there.

"You can't learn about swimming a horse without watching me do it head on," he said.

When I got to the point I could see that my father had dismounted and was patting Verbena on her rump. A small cloud of dust came off when he did that and floated away in the slight breeze. Then he ground-tied her and walked along the water's edge toward the dam. I couldn't tell what he was doing. The horse looked after him. In a moment he came back and I wondered how he would get into the saddle without his tree stump, but he seemed to spring onto the horse, jumping his foot into the backward facing stirrup and swinging himself into the saddle in a sure manner like a Western-movie cowboy.

Verbena was startled for a moment; she did a little crow-hop buck. My father made a circle to the left and then came straight at me into the pond. Verbena kept her head up and her nostrils were flared.

From where I was on the point I could see that once Verbena started swimming my father slid off her left side. The reins were draped over her neck and with his right hand he was holding on to the saddle horn. But his feet hadn't come up and he was slipping through the water at an angle; there was a slight wake at his neck and it was breaking into his beard. He seemed to be looking at some point just in front of himself.

"How you doing?" I shouted. He didn't answer. It was a long swim; perhaps the longest line you could take across Big Pond. Near the middle Verbena turned her head south to look down the slough and then back north again toward the dam; there was a little S to her wake at that point, but not much. By then the ripples of their swim were beginning to reach the pond's edges and I could see that the cottonwood leaves and small branches that had been floating on the water were bobbing slightly.

"How's it going?" I yelled. Again my father didn't answer. They kept coming at me. The teal I'd jumped earlier crested the ridge to the east of the pond and circled us once, then hustled back over the hill. Some wind sent another small storm of leaves adrift in the air and they sailed out over the pond, Verbena and my father.

"You O.K.?" I said again. No answer, only firm swimming straight ahead.

When my father found his feet at the pond's edge and stood up in the mud of the shallows with some wet leaves clinging to him and with water running out of the cuffs of his shirt and dripping from his beard he said:

"It didn't get away from us this time, now did it, son?"

"No," I said. "It didn't." Verbena shook and the spray of water made a lovely colored circle around her.

"Did you know your mother named this horse?" said my father, still standing with the horse in the water, and brushing off some of the leaves from his shirt.

"I didn't know that," I said.

"She named this horse for that batch of flowers we got at the end of the lane," my father said.

"I know those flowers," I said.

"So do I," my father said. "I'd pick some for your mother now and then to make up for my madness."

"Do you need help?" I said.

"Who knows?" he said.

In a moment he seemed to gather himself and walked out through the mud and up onto the bank. The horse shook again, and my father stomped his boots and water shot out of the seams at the soles.

"How was it?" I said.

"Your mother would have been proud of you," he said. "That's her in the head of the horse. The white coming out. That's your mother."

"I am snow," I said.

"I wonder where I'll wind up," he said. "I want to be a soaring bird; some great soaring bird with good eyes."

"Yes," I said. I tried to get my father to let me lead the horse back up to the house, but he wouldn't hear of it.

"Give me a boot lift into the saddle, son," he said. "It's about time I let you do something for me."

I followed them back in the truck. The sun was to the south and warm; it was the kind of warmth that cuts through the coolness and it warmed each one of us and we in turn warmed the surrounding air.

When we got to the house my father gave me the horse and went inside to change his clothes. That afternoon we started doing the chores we usually did to get him ready for winter, and that evening I brought the saddle and other gear in by the Melrose and gave them a good coat of neat's-foot oil while we talked. My father seemed subdued.

"What did you learn from swimming a horse?" he said at last.

"That it can be done," I said. After all these years I thought I'd try a little irony on my poor father; it didn't work.

"That's not all there was to learn," he said; there wasn't any rancor in his voice; his beard did not shake itself at me.

"How about you?" I said. "What did you learn?"

"I'd rather not say now that it's over," he said. Perhaps it was the flat way he spoke that made something like Verbena's shake when she came out of the pond go through my body. My father noticed it and his eyes widened for a moment.

"You're O.K.," he said.

"Yes," I said. We listened to the tree scrape on the roof. I felt as if I had come through some historical place and was on the other side: there the light was lively and open, bright as a High Plains summer morning. I could hear my father talking; he was speaking out of the light, and what he had to say was not in words, but in the chunks and particles of our life: boots and generators and language and hoops and straw and trucks and wood and sorry cattle. And me. Standing in the stream of lovely rubble I saw myself conceived.

"Do you remember your mother?" my father said.

"I don't remember the sound of her voice," I said.

"Neither do I," said my father. He looked at me as if to test his memory of who I was.

"Tell me about mortgage insurance," he said.

"You don't want to know," I said.

"You don't cheat the working poor, do you?" he said.

"No," I said.

"You don't think time's money, do you?"

"No, I don't," I said.

"Do you know what 'gossamer' means?" he said.

"Yes, I do," I said.

"Well, there's some hope in the world yet," he said.

"I may not be it," I said.

"You might be," he said. "I was."

That was Saturday night. We worked together two more days to button up: plastic storm windows, stove-black, wood, square bales, round bales.

"Answer a letter with a letter," my father finally says on Monday afternoon as we stand in the yard amid the bales. "Not with a phone call. Don't put money in Ma Bell's pocket. Don't call me on Father's Day or New Year's or Easter. Don't send me any of those stupid greeting cards. 'Greeting card.' What kind of language is that? It's nothing but a gimmick so the vice president can slip his hand into your pocket while you're under the spell of the great blue hump of sentimentality. If they don't get rich on the raw red backs of the working people they do it on the sentimentality of the middle class."

"I understand," I say.

"Do you read what I mail you?" he asks. "Have you read your Veblen? Have you read the *Little Blue Books?* I don't want to be sending this stuff into the void. The post office doesn't censor mail anymore; thank God we won that battle."

"We did," I say.

"Don't eat Velveeta cheese," my father says. "Or Ann Page bread."

"I won't," I say.

"Not even rats will eat white bread," he says. "That's why they made it in the first place, so mice and rats wouldn't poop in the flour."

"I think you're right," I say.

We shake hands and stand there in the circle of huge hay bales and look at the ridge they make around the house. Toward the east I can see the top of my basketball goal.

"You notice that white patch that's coming out on Verbena's head?" my father says after a moment.

"I told you I did," I say. He nods.

"Historical cold," my father says.

"It's a tough winter in the shag of the horse," I say.

"You're beginning to learn," he says.

"I guess I am," I say.

"The blizzard of 1886," says my father.

"I think you're right this time," I say.

"Keep me in mind," he says. He taps his head, then lays his hand on mine. I realize we have not touched each other much over the years. "See your father in your mind's eye," he says with his hand on my head.

"I can't do anything else," I say.

"You're learning," he says.

That winter was mild; but in the spring two blizzards back to back buried the place and my father was stuck for weeks. The phones were dead; the power lines were down. When the neighbors and I got him out by using a tractor to clear the lane, we found him in the yard amid the round bales sitting atop a saddled Verbena in the snowy sunshine.

"I would have made it out," he said to me as I came through the drifts. "But I didn't know why I should. This horse and I have been riding in circles once a day and talking to keep in practice."

"Keep in practice for what?" I said.

"Somebody's got to stay honest," he said.

After everyone left and I was alone with him, he told me he'd heard my mother's voice during the second blizzard.

"It's a delicate voice," he said. "With small blue petals in it."

"I know," I said.

Ron Tanner

Jackpot

I owe a lot to Tim Britten. He hired me to drive him all over the desert to search for mustangs. He wanted one dead or alive, he was so eager for a catch. Live ones are better, of course, but he didn't know the first thing about keeping animals. Neither did I. "You're my cowboy," he'd say, lifting one of my hands off the steering wheel. I've got big hands. "Grip's important," Tim said the first time we met. He stood there hanging on to my handshake like he was about to arm wrestle and yank me over, so I pulled a little my way and he smiled. I smiled back. Then his wife, Marlene, said, "Let me see," and Tim Britten handed me over, so I gripped her hand too. All of us had big hands. "You must work hard," she said.

The truth is, I'd been working hard on the slots for a few

months, I had the fever so bad. It was just after I'd been fired for dealing lousy in Reno because I couldn't remember all the cards. Dealing twenty-one from two decks all night wore me out. So I played blind, not counting cards, and I lost lots of the casino's money. It's always *their* money, no matter whose pocket it comes from. I almost swung work at other houses until I got blackballed for dicking with one of the coin-toss machines in Harrah's—I was shoving it, trying to topple silver into the twenty-dollar hole. The security guards took me to a back office and I thought they were going to punch me some, but they only snapped my photo and sent it all over town. They could have arrested me, but I wasn't worth it, they said. So I went east across the state, playing little casinos. I wasn't in the mood for work and I figured if I found trouble I'd head to Vegas where the casinos wouldn't ride me, they've got so many big-timers to worry about.

I wasn't eating right and I started drinking a little, mostly screwdrivers, because they're hard to ruin, and before I knew it I was crazy for the slots. It was looking at all those coins—especially dollars and halves—that got me, those machines swollen with silver. And I was winning. It's the worst bet in the casino, any amateur can tell you, but when you're winning at slots, there's nothing like it, because it's a real private thing, just you and the machine, and you can play as fast or as slow as you please. I'd work as many as four machines at a time, all night, until my hands were black from the coins and my fingers nearly numb and my shoulders hot with pain. But you can only keep a streak for a short spell. I slipped until I was playing nothing but nickels. By the time I saw Tim Britten's ad in the Elko *Courier*, I was down to one cardboard bucket of them—about thirty-six dollars—and I knew I had to get away for a while to cool off and dry out.

Tim asked no questions and I suspected I was the only one who'd answered his ad. He wasn't offering any money, just room and board and some shares in his horse ranch, which wasn't built yet. All he had was a trailer on cinder blocks about fifty miles south of Elko—we passed through Carlin, went over the first range, took a turn onto a dirt road, then I was lost. There was a black rocky range to one side and one far off to the other side that had a white streak across the middle, which Tim said was salt. Otherwise, there wasn't anything except waist-high weeds, sage mostly, and long stretches of dirt that rose and fell all around. I had met Tim in front of Aces High in Elko, after waiting around until the top of my head was itchy from sunburn. "You've got an intelligent look," Tim told me. "Doesn't he, Marlene?" "It's the glasses," she said, "they magnify his eyes." I was still wearing my casino outfit—white shirt and black pants with black shoes, what all casino workers wear, except mine hadn't been washed in weeks.

When we got to the "ranch," as Tim called it, he gave me a cowboy hat and some new blue jeans that were too tight and cowboy boots that were too big, and I began that day, driving straight across the desert, doing all kinds of damage to the plant life. Tim would always wear his sunglasses, well-pressed jeans, some long-sleeve cowboy shirt with snap pearl buttons, and a light-colored cowboy hat (seven gallons, he said). He was tall and slump-shouldered and seemed to have spent most of his life indoors, he was so pale. He had shadows under his eyes as if from lack of sleep, and it's true, he slept little, maybe a few hours at a time. He spent most of his nights sitting in a lawn chair out back behind the trailer with a rifle and a bag of potato chips and a flashlight as big as a club. The first few nights, I didn't know what he was up to, so I went out finally and asked him, long after Marlene had gone to bed, "What're you doing, Tim?" He grinned at me. "Waiting for the unexpected," he said.

"Isn't driving like this illegal in the desert?" I asked him in the beginning. The truck rattled over ruts and swayed, the shocks squeaking, as I steered up one slope and down another. The air was always chalky with dust.

Tim kept looking from side to side like he was afraid of missing something or like maybe we were being followed by state troopers or poachers, or I don't know what. "Great thing about Nevada is you don't have to worry about things like that," he said finally. "Look at this." He held out one hand like he was offering me everything I could see. "It's wide open," he said.

The truth is, driving like that across the desert was illegal—there were signs just off the main road that said so. And I'd seen something on the news a year ago that said chasing wild horses was illegal too. But these weren't the first illegal things I'd done.

There wasn't much to it except boredom. The desert stretched on and on and Tim Britten usually said nothing, his rifle aimed out the window. I would have asked him to drive some, only he couldn't. He had trouble coordinating the gas and the clutch, and he never watched where he was going, so he'd veer off, gunning the truck into a ditch or racing headlong into a butte. It was queer behavior for a mechanical genius, I thought. That's what he was, he said, a mechanical genius. An engineer, he said. Just the year before, he'd been helping an oil company look for deposits near Tonopah. That was the first he'd seen Nevada, because until then he'd spent most of his life in school. He was real book-smart. And he had a lot of ideas for inventions—the trailer was crowded with his drawings—but he didn't do anything with them. Besides some pressure-sensitive liquid sensor he'd made for the oil company, the only other Tim Britten invention that ever got completed, as far as I know, was fifty gallons of Even-Steven, an alcoholic drink distilled from pine nuts and nonfat dry milk.

Drinking Even-Stevens was how Tim and Marlene spent most of their time together. They'd drink until they got real quiet and sleepy, then they'd lie next to each other in a lawn chair and lick each other's hands. That's all they did. Lick, lick, lick. It made me prickly to watch them, so I tried to stay out of the way. But that wasn't easy, since the trailer was small and I wasn't about to go out walking, on account of the rattlers all around. Outside, there was nowhere to go, anyway, and nothing to look at except the ridge in the distance, and no shade except next to the silver propane tank at the side of the trailer. So I'd sit on the front steps, fanning myself with the hat Tim had given me. Sometimes Marlene's retarded collie, Frank, joined me, though I wasn't too fond of his company. He'd lick my hand every time I reached down to pet him. Then I'd get prickly again, thinking of Marlene and Tim. That's when I'd ask myself why I was staying on. But I had to admit that, despite the inconveniences—or because of them—I was losing the urge to gamble.

Marlene didn't join me and Tim on the hunt until Frank disappeared. She claimed the poachers had gotten him. "What poachers?" I asked. They both smiled at me like I was stupid. Tim said, "You've heard of poachers, Lawrence. They're people—" "Marauders," Marlene corrected. "Exactly," said Tim, "they're marauders who are always looking for a steal." Marlene shaded her eyes with one hand and scouted the distance. "They got Frank," she said. "Good old Frank," said Tim. I couldn't imagine why anybody would want Frank. But I didn't say so, because Marlene was sensitive and kind of nervous, always halfway between laughing and crying—you never knew how she'd take an opinion. The truth is, though, Frank was an ugly thing, an overweight collie with a too-narrow face and crossed eyes, his coat dusty and knotted and smelling like piss. He was always gagging whenever he ate because he ate too fast, like he was afraid someone was about to take his bowl away. And he couldn't bark. He could make a whispered grunt, but he couldn't bark, no matter how much Marlene coached him. "Talk to me," she'd say. "Tell me what's on your mind, Frank." Frank would look up at her like he was about to cry, his tongue dangling and his whiskers twitching. Then he'd jerk with effort, but all you'd hear would be a grunt. Marlene had had Frank for fifteen years and that was all she could make him do, but she didn't seem to mind. "He's like a brother," she said. I'd always see Frank lying under Marlene's lawn chair while she sunbathed out back.

Sunbathing was what Marlene did most of the time. She had a great tan, wearing bikinis to show it off, though I don't think Tim cared one way or the other. She and Tim had met in Tonopah at the Money Bucket, where Marlene was waitressing. She was in her forties and he wasn't out of his twenties. Marlene had been married once before to a gypsum miner. But he had died after falling down an unfenced mine shaft. They're all over the desert—shaft holes about five feet square. Because of all the brush you won't see them until you're right at the edge. Marlene said she was still in mourning when she met Tim. "But I couldn't stand to see him carried off by the rednecks he was working with," she said. "He was different, you could tell right off. Sensitive. Look at those little gray eyes." I did and Tim grinned at me. "So I stole him that night," Marlene said. I saw her wink at Tim. She said, "He told me about the wild horses he'd seen while scouting for oil, and that was that—we figured wild-horse ranching was for us, because we could be our own bosses and get the animals for free." "And acreage out here goes for next to nothing," Tim added. They had used Marlene's insurance money to buy the trailer (used) and lots of supplies, like canned hams and blocks of cheese food. "It's been like a vacation," Marlene said, "except for dealing with the chemical toilet."

When Marlene joined us on the hunt, she sat in a lawn chair that Tim had bolted to the flatbed. I would've got sick sprawled in the sun like that and jounced around all day long. But Marlene didn't seem to mind. She wanted to find Frank. Tim decided to make a long trip that would last overnight. He was real excited about it and took charge of loading the truck, while I ran errands for him. All I could think about was having to sleep with rattlers around and tarantulas crawling out of holes at night to creep like hairy hands across my face.

We started out the same old way, heading south, early in the morning when it was still cool and the sun was white behind some high clouds. The air was sweet with the smell of sage, but as the day went on and the sun burned through, all I could smell was dust and truck exhaust. This is what I call low desert, because as far as you can see there's nothing growing higher than human height. No cactus or anything like that. Every once in a while you'll see a tree in the dimple of some distant mountain. But those are rare.

We'd been driving for an hour or so when Tim yelled, "Stop! Stop!" I stamped on the brakes. Billows of dust overtook us and it was minutes before I could see what he was excited about. "That's a hoofprint," he said, hopping out of the truck. There was only one print, preserved in the hardened mud. "A pretty sight," Marlene said, placing her big brown hand over it. "It gives me chills—" She stood abruptly, half crying. Then she laughed. "This is so exciting!" she said. Tim wanted to dig it up as a souvenir, so he got out a pickax and took a swing, but he missed and shattered the print. "I don't know much about the desert," I said, "but seems to me that print could've been there for years." Tim was looking down at Marlene as she picked up the pieces of the print like they were a broken plate. "Where there's one, there's hundreds," he said. "It's just a matter of probability." That made me think of gambling and I started wondering if I'd taken a bigger risk than I'd realized coming out here with these two.

By the time we stopped for lunch, Tim was in the mood to shoot something. He said he didn't feel right if he didn't fire the rifle at least once a day. I watched Marlene spread a picnic blanket in the shade of a sandstone cliff, while Tim aimed his rifle at objects on the horizon, where everything was watery with ripples of heat. "Blam blam blam!" he said. Marlene said, "Here, take this," handing me a cheese sandwich, then one to Tim, but he wouldn't take it. Maybe it bothered him to see us eating cheap, because the money was getting low. They'd spent most of Marlene's money on propane and gasoline to keep things running.

Tim decided he'd shoot one of the swallows that were darting to and from their nests in the shade of the cliff. "They probably taste like squab," he said, aiming. I told him there wasn't enough meat on those little birds to feed a cat. He shrugged. "Anything's better than cheese." For a while I watched the rifle barrel stir the air as Tim followed the birds. Then I sat in the truck cab and looked at the map, though there was nothing to look at—no roads, no settlements, nothing much but open country, dry, dusty, and so hot the air seemed to buzz with meanness.

The report of Tim's rifle sounded like the pop of a paper bag. The recoil kicked him onto the blanket, where he rolled over a bag of potato chips Marlene was eating. "Look what you've done," she said, pushing him off the crushed chips. He got up and looked around for his kill, but the swallows were gone. "Here," Marlene told him, "put some chips on your sandwich—it tastes better that way."

Tim and Marlene usually started drinking Even-Stevens at lunchtime. Tim had brought several one-gallon thermoses of the stuff, tossing each drink down with a paper cup. I didn't drink any, mainly because it tasted awful, kind of like bourbon and buttermilk. But Tim and Marlene drank the stuff cup after cup. They didn't usually start licking each other until dinnertime. "I miss Frank," Marlene said. Her chin quivered.

"Good old Frank," said Tim, pouring himself another Even-Steven.

The sun was almost directly overhead, stealing shade from the cliff. Marlene stretched out on the lawn chair in the back of the truck. I told her too much sun would ruin her skin.

"Do me a favor," she said. "Get me a drink." She wore little white cups over her eyes. A small pool of oil and sweat glistened in her navel.

"I'm going to make an airplane," said Tim, suddenly standing and emptying his paper cup. "A little one. I'll strap a camera to it and send it scouting ahead. It'll save a hell of a lot of gas."

"Does that mean we don't have much left?" I asked. We had two cans tied to the truck, but I hadn't checked what was left at the trailer.

"What would be really great is a video camera on the plane—everything remote control. Then we'd watch the thing over cocktails and crackers. Sound good?"

"You know how to live, Tim." Marlene smiled, her eyes still cupped. Her skin was gleaming.

"Before you work on any more stuff," I said, "you really ought to have the truck repaired." The clutch was chattering and the valves clacking like rocks in a can. "Did you bring the tool box?"

Tim shrugged and took another drink.

"It's dangerous being out here without tools," I said.

"We'll improvise," he said. "Like pioneers."

While Marlene and Tim finished one of the thermoses of Even-Steven, I counted the sagebrushes as far as I could see, pretending they were horses. Then I made bets with myself about how my count would change when I tried again. The numbers were never the same.

A few hours later, we stopped in a dry creek bed, a good place to camp, said Tim. He scanned the horizon with his rifle scope, then the binoculars. "Nothing moving but the heat," he said finally. A vulture circled in the distance, but Tim couldn't make out what had died. "Not big enough to be a horse." The truck ticked as if about to explode. I pissed on the hood, expecting it to sizzle, but it only steamed. Marlene was sleeping, slack-jawed.

"Is she all right?" I asked. "She looks awful oversunned."

"She loves it," said Tim. He poured himself another Even-Steven and sat in the shade of the truck.

I strung up the tarp and told Tim to wake Marlene so she could get some shade. He shook her. The sun cups fell from her eyes and she lolled her head back and forth, like she was drunk. "Ease up," she muttered. Tim patted her cheek. He said, "Come over here and lie down, Marlene." With his help she stumbled off the truck, then took off her bikini top and sat there like an old Indian, her breasts limp and withered. Tim offered her an Even-Steven, but she didn't seem to see it. "Dots," she said. "Goddamn dots all over the place."

"Too much sun," I said.

Tim wanted to scout around before sunset, so we left Marlene and hiked up a steep mound nearby. All was quiet except for the scratch of lizards scrambling over rocks. The sun was low, long shadows streaming from brush and boulders. A quarter mile away, the vulture sat hunkered over the dead animal. Tim took a couple of shots at it, but missed, and the bird lifted off with slow steady wing beats. Tim wanted to examine the dead animal, so we worked our way down, careful not to step where rattlers hide. What we found was a dog, or what might have been a dog. Ants and vultures had done their work on it and little was left but bones and bits of hair. It could have been a collie, but I didn't think it had Frank's colors. Tim knelt like a hunter reading clues. "No signs of foul play," he said, poking the remains with his rifle barrel. "It could have been a coyote," I said. Tim stood up and squinted at the sun. "I wouldn't mind bagging a coyote."

"They're just little dogs," I said. "You wouldn't want to shoot a little dog, Tim."

"I'd shoot Lassie if I had to, Lawrence. This is survival we're talking about."

"We have provisions."

"Cheese?"

"And bread and potato chips."

"What we need is meat. Pork chops and T-bones. That kind of thing. Or maybe rattlesnake."

"I like cheese just fine, Tim."

"They taste like chicken, you know," Tim said.

"I can live on cheese just fine, thanks," I said.

Tim said, "You're not talking like a cowboy, Lawrence." He started flipping over flat rocks with his rifle barrel. "Let's shoot a couple of rattlers and cook them on a spit like shish kebab."

"I don't want shish kebab," I said.

He kicked over a slab of rock the size of a place mat. "Here's one." He crouched for a better view. "Sleeping soundly. Coiled like a piece of garden hose." It was a rattler three feet long and as fat as a toothpaste tube.

I said, "Leave it alone, Tim."

Tim said, "Watch this guy's expression when I wake him."

"Don't," I said.

Tim prodded the snake with the barrel. The snake jerked its head back and was flicking its tongue, its rattles rattling. Tim pulled the rifle trigger but nothing happened. He pulled again. "Wait a minute," he said, like he was asking somebody to stop talking. He'd forgotten to reload. The snake hissed. "Just a minute." The rattler hit Tim's boot. Tim jumped back and the snake hit him again. I was so light-headed from fear I fell back into a clump of thistle. I saw Tim swing his rifle like a bat. Then he reloaded and shot the snake twice, sand and snake bits flying in all directions. "I think that did it," he said. After he had his breath back, he tied the two biggest snake pieces to his belt, where they dangled, oozing blood.

When we got back to camp, it was dark and Marlene was gone. I lit a lantern while Tim poured himself another Even-Steven. "Probably gone for a walk," he said.

"The desert's no place for a walk at night."

"Probably just taking a leak," Tim said.

I called out for her. She didn't answer. Tim started cleaning the snake, chopping and flailing with his bowie knife until his hands were covered with scales and guts. He was pounding the thing with the knife handle.

I sat on the tailgate of the pickup and watched the sky. It was a clear moonless night. I could smell the smell of suntan lotion from Marlene's vacant lawn chair. Tim didn't decide to go looking for her until he gave up cleaning the snake. We called and called, but she didn't answer. Tim swept the beam of his flashlight all around and to our surprise Marlene had been standing nearby the whole time, naked and silent, with a funny smile on her face.

"Hi, Marlene. You see what we got?" Tim held up the battered rattler.

"She's not looking too well," I said.

"How do you feel, Marlene?" Tim took off his hat like he was about to introduce himself.

"Could be sun poisoning or dehydration," I said.

"You hungry?" Tim asked her.

"She's out of sorts, Tim," I said.

"This is not like her," Tim said. "She's probably sick."

"Maybe we should get her to relax," I said.

"You want to relax, Marlene?" Tim said. He started walking to her and she started backing away. "It's me—Tim, Marlene?" Then he went for her and she took off, running.

Tim and I followed in the pickup, Tim bringing along the rifle because, he said, "you never know what's out there."

I'd never seen anyone run like Marlene. She was hurdling shrubs and rocks like a deer. We lost her finally because the truck couldn't make speed in the sand. I scanned a circle with the headlights, but Marlene was gone, so we stopped to listen. Tim opened another thermos of Even-Steven and this time drank straight from it.

"I should've winged her," he said, "just to slow her down a little."

"Shoot her?" I said.

"Just a nick." He pinched together a thumb and forefinger. "This much maybe," Tim said.

"You don't want to shoot your wife," I said.

He took another drink. "I never knew she could run like that," he said. He drank some more. "She's out there, creeping around," he said. "Turn on the lights."

I switched on the headlights and there, not twenty feet from the truck, was a mule—a black, gaunt, weather-beaten animal probably half stupid with hunger. It was startled to see us. Tim screamed, "A wild horse!" He propped the rifle on the dash as if to shoot through the windshield. "You ever see ears so big?"

The mule snorted, showing its dark teeth.

I said, "It's a mule, Tim."

Tim said, "Where's your lasso, Lawrence?"

I got a rope from the back of the truck. I'd never thrown a lasso in my life, but I promised Tim I'd give it a try if the mule would stand still for it. I tried and tried and missed each try, while Tim groaned and squirmed. "Come on, cowboy," Tim kept saying. The mule stood there staring like it had never seen people before. Maybe it hadn't. I got the rope around its neck finally after a lot of tosses.

"Hold him!" Tim screamed, jumping in his excitement. "Don't let go!" Tim tied one end of the rope around his waist. "We've got him now!" Tim screamed. He yanked the rope. The mule grew frantic, bucking until the rope was cutting my hands. "Hold tight, cowboy!" Tim screamed. I wanted to tell him to shut up, but I was hurting too bad. I could see that I had all my problems tugging at the end of that rope. So I let go. Tim screamed, "Hey!" and that was the last I saw of him. The mule dragged him off. A while later, somewhere out there, I heard a "Whoa!" but soon it was quiet except for the breeze that was stirring the sagebrush. I waited around for the longest time, but nobody came back. So I ate two cheese sandwiches, then fell asleep on Marlene's chair, the whole thing smelling like flowers because of her.

In the morning, I was still alone. I drove around looking for Tim and Marlene, and even the mule, but I could hardly stay awake, it was so boring. Besides, gas was getting low and I couldn't trust the truck, so I went back to the trailer, which I had some trouble finding. I kept looking for Tim and Marlene but had to stop by the week's end because the truck broke down finally and I didn't know how to fix it. I figured they'd come back one way or another. But now I'm not so sure. To my surprise, the one who came back was Frank, trotting around like he'd been only out for a walk. He's still an ugly dog and he still gags when he eats, but he's not bad company. He sits under the lawn chair while I take the sun every day. Sometimes I share a thermos of Even-Steven with him. Then I get up to take potshots at lizards, and Frank trots out ahead of me to grunt at noises I can't hear. That's about all we do nowadays. We've got enough supplies to last us for a while, so I'm looking at this as a vacation, a kind of jackpot I never thought I'd hit.

"Look at that," I say to Frank, waving a hand like I'm offering him the desert. The dog blinks at me and grunts.

I grunt back, letting him lick my hand.

Melissa Pritchard

How Love Is Found
When the Heart Is Lost

F
ilthy white Impala, stinking of sweet gardenia like a prom. Flopped on the vinyl front seat, Hallie feels light like murder on the heel of her face, pushes up to look in back. One rear window is cranked, she can see Bluebird, crosslegged on the rim of the gorge, a tiny monk, preternaturally contained for a child of five. Her entire nervous system clunks, oh but she refuses alarm, refuses any negative thing. Nothing to acknowledge but fabricated calm. Dumping her past, wind bailing it out the car windows, trashing roadsides from Cheyenne to here, nothing acknowledged but uncolored calm. Sometimes, doing one thing dangerous, sublimely out of character, the body steps in with a massive, hormonal calm.

———

Bluebird rubs a blue-black rabbit skin up/down up/down one chafed knee.

I could fly if I wanted.

How about a drive?

I hate the car.

Hallie flicks stones down the purplish cleft canyon, into gunky, taupe water flashing dully below, thinks about how much speed a thing gathers, falling.

Well. How about *you* drive?

Me?

Yeah. On my lap. We'll steer together.

The bridge is easy, the big, wingy car moseying. It is the other side, the land on the other side, that is hexed. The Impala starts horse-rodeo stuff, heaving, bucking, Hallie and Bluebird both bashing away at the steering wheel, stop it stop it stop it, get us to town then quit. The car waits for the south end of town before shimmying dead in the road. Three Hispanic men in a green pickup push it into the Pinch Penny Wash O Mat parking lot where it sits, a downed, chrome-tipped gull.

Must be time to do our laundry.

Hallie navigates with the passive oar of fate, believes there are few accidents. Synchronicity triumphs. Since leaving Cheyenne, they have been living out of the Impala; it is thoroughly trashed with Bluebird's Happy Meal boxes, Hallie's coffee cups and salad trays, a touring garbage heap. Right now, Hallie is pulling what dirty clothes she can find off the floor, out of the cracks of the back seat, yanking clothes like weeds, stuffing them in Bluebird's arms until her skinny chin rests on top like a stopper, a cork.

Ok, heave ho.

Hallie likes the theory laundromat owners are ectoplasmic. You sense their gray, elusive, irritable presence from handwritten signs taped to broken dryers and washers, in runny washroom signs over toilets, no napkins, Tampax, etc. She and Bluebird are the only ones in the Pinch Penny excepting a homely, wide dog, its freckled teats trawling the linoleum. Bluebird had to leave Pickles, her terrier; Hallie promising Rick could ship the dog after they were settled, but how can that happen if they're running away and he isn't supposed to find them? He isn't even Bluebird's father, but a mechanic, a coke head and a dirty drain on her money. The sex had been fantastic, initially cosmic, then a dirtier, faster drain on her heart, so bad she came to understand their relationship probably fell under the term Abuse though he'd mostly not struck her, only yelled, lied and had other girlfriends, wasn't that enough? She was afraid of him. Someday she'd figure out how she could let herself have great sex with such a lousy individual. Plus she'd keep an eye out for a dog similar to Pickles.

Hallie talks briefly into the pay phone, hangs up, stares intently into the floor, into bones most likely of Indians buried under the foundation of the laundromat, her hand on the receiver.

Shoot.

What, Moomers?

Damn. Darn.

Hallie runs the list through her head. Things seem past guidance, getting discouraging. Her insides feel like falling cake. Dead car, sixty-five dollars, the one personal friend she had counted on suddenly off to Nicaragua, part of a women's peace brigade. The linkage of events that was supposed to slide her out from under him had snapped. No job, no friend, crapped car. For a weak half-second, she considers going back—unhealthy familiarity, even abuse, sound safe right now.

It's ok, Moomers. Can we eat at Lota Burger? I see one right over there.

Nope, nope, final nope. No more junkfood troughs. You are going to eat a normal ham-and-egg breakfast, bacon and toast, juice and pancakes, whatever.

Then Hallie spots the mechanic's garage across the street, and within minutes, a guy named Roy (from the red, birthday cake script on his shirt pocket) has the Impala's hood up, fiddling in its sullen guts. Hallie has always experienced regrettable, extraordinary lust at the sight of men bending over opened hoods of cars.

Regrettable because that's how she'd got into such shit with Rick, the way he'd looked, fixing her car. Thank god this Roy person has no charm, no appeal whatsoever. Doesn't see her or Bluebird as much but objects to benefit him personally, chiefly financial.

Transmission's shot to hell.

So—

Three fifty to get it going or $50 for parts. These fifty-nines aren't worth diddly squat except parts.

Oh.

Foul news. Not true. Rick prized this car. To cover her ignorance, Hallie turns prim.

I'll consider it. Thank you.

You decide. Let me know. Slams the hood and walks back across the road. At least he didn't charge for his fatal diagnosis.

She holds tight to Bluebird's hand, thumb in the direction of town. One helpful attribute of children is their lack of perspective, their sweet, dumb trust.

Dreadlocks, Hallie explains, looking over at their driver. Right? My daughter needs to know about your hair (which is like some torn up, bright orange sink scrubber on top of flat, trout-colored eyes).

Ya, guesso.

A musician. Had to be. They shun speech as unrefined substance not to muck in. Bluebird's father had been a drummer, hyper, mute.

Five dollars you're a musician?

Yeah but no five dollars.

Veering the Volkswagen, he hits the curb, pulling in front of a man in a limp terry-cloth hat and plaid shorts videotaping an adobe doorway, his wife fanning herself with a map in the overhang of J.C. Penney's.

Town.

Swell. Thanks.

Hallie feels reckless with her puny cash, uninterested in aiming for mature, retentive behavior. When Bluebird starts jump-pleading in front of a toy store, she says, okok, *one* toy so long as it's not that, indicating the five-foot chili pepper windsock blowing from the store's vigaed porch.

Bluebird walks out wearing a tiara of paste diamonds, flicking a wand with glitter and gee-gaw, taking up the sidewalk with regal hogginess, chin hiked, body stiff. Halts before a souvenir drugstore on the plaza; it has a soda fountain. Here, brandishes the wand severely. An enormous green-black gorilla hunkers like a city zoo at one end of the counter, a newspaper propped in his shaggy paws; Bluebird wedges up next to him.

Here, Moomers.

Hallie drinks coffee, while her daughter sets gluey mosaics of pancake in front of the slumped gorilla.

What if he's real, Moomers?

Oh, he is. I'm quite sure he parties every night with loads of other gorillas.

A man next to them deftly flips the gorilla a toast crust, winks at Bluebird, peers myopically at Hallie. His hair is in two rag-woven braids, his face mildly pocked and fleshy, his black glasses taped in the corners. He says he's going over to the community pool, where there's free showers. She feels guided, pays both bills.

Bluebird pounces on a yellow Wuzzles suit in the Lost and Found, Hallie takes a plain black. The indoor pool is empty. They hike backwards down the chrome ladder into heavily chlorinated, wrist-hot water. Bluebird anchors her crown with two hands while Hallie knots the canvas straps of an orange life preserver on her chalky shoulderwings.

Jeez. He's got one leg. Vaughn's only got one leg.

Ssh, stop staring, Hallie whispers.

Do you swim every day?

No. His breasts shake, puffy, the nipples so female-pointy Hallie has this goofy urge to put her mouth down and suck. His glasses are missing, his hair in wet, black twigs to his waist.

Bluebird drifts face up in her orange vest, diamonds skidding light off the water. Hallie goes under, rising like a slow, white lump-fish. From the deep end, she watches Vaughn, one leg finning, two arms plugging, how he gets out pushing hard with his arms, jigging to a bench to rub at his stump, a man shining up a scarlet, squarish doorknob. She swims over to Bluebird, and they stand in the pool, watch Vaughn against the wall, moving into the dressing room.

Five dollars he's a war-hero, Hallie says.

They take turns under the lukewarm shower, rubbing their hair with pink gel from the Eurobath box on the tiled wall. Neither has bathed since leaving Cheyenne; Bluebird sits at Hallie's feet, by the drain, patting the stopped-up water and singing.

Vaughn is face down on a beige plot of chemically dead lawn, pink hollyhocks spindling up around him. Hallie's pretty sure he's drunk, was drunk at breakfast.

They cross the street to a park where Kit Carson lies obtrusively buried in one corner. There are swings, a slide, brown donkeys, yellow ducks and pink pigs on great silver coils. She and Vaughn sit on a bench, passing a quart of red Gallo, stewmeat wine, Hallie calls it, watching Bluebird, her face a little uppy sphere of brightness. Behind the bluish metal slide, Hallie sees a figure with black mangly hair high in a cottonwood tree, rolled into a thin blanket, a pale green cigar.

Vaughn, who's that?

Charlie. He lives in the park, hangs out in trees.

Does he think he's a bird?

No. Vaughn took the bottle. He is a bird.

A few minutes later, Vaughn climbs into an old truck with a friend and takes off. Bluebird has found a girl to play with, they crouch beneath the slide, building twig and stone houses. Hallie feels socketed to the bench, accumulating flaws as a mother. What's-his-name's still snagged in the tree, in his blanket, green, caught like a kite. There must be worse things people did than running off with

their kids when things got bad, running out of money, transporta-
tion and hopeful ideas. She'd gotten pregnant way too soon, that
was it. Too young.

They catch a ride back to the Pinch Penny. Hallie pays a dollar to
get their tangled, wet stuff out of the back room, shoves everything
into the dryer which has modern blue digital seconds ticking,
thumbs through a stack of Jehovah's Witness magazines, all there is
to look at. Bluebird headlocks the dog to her belly, its legs sag
listlessly.

So Hallie's got the grapefruit box of laundry sliding off her hip,
walking hobbled into a fiesta pink sunset, she can barely make out
the bulky figure hunched over the Impala's opened, white hood.
Hoping for the dour, greedy mechanic, even when she's right up
beside him, seeing exactly, inevitably, who it is.

He straightens, rubbing sly, clubby hands on a red rag.

Linkage, that's it. All that was wrong.

How'd you get here?

Oooh, who's overjoyed? He reaches down, squeezes Bluebird
on one shoulder. Hiya sportfan. Bluebird slowdrills, undrills, one
foot into nicked up cement ground.

Here. Gallantly hefting the laundry box from Hallie's hip,
kneeing open the door of the Impala, setting the box on the torn
seat.

Anybody hungry? I passed a place down the road, looks pretty
decent.

Taking the wheel, taking over again, thinking silence is back-
kin to forgiveness. Still, Hallie's thinking how Bluebird hasn't
eaten since the drugstore breakfast.

The Pueblo Restaurant is fluorescent lit, oxblood formica tables, turquoise plastic chairs, blobby green hearts of philodendron
snaking across the ceiling. They sit by the mud fireplace, a metal
fan on its ledge, a red and gold plaster Buddha, benign, incongru-
ous, stuck where fire's supposed to go. Bluebird and Hallie drink

cokes out of gold, pebbled glasses while he goes to the rest room. The waitress brings two beers, Hallie pointing where to set them, where he's sitting.

Are you glad he found you, Moomers?

Hardly.

But I like being with you. Just with you.

I like that too. Ohgod, Bluey, it's hard sometimes.

What.

Life. You know. Deciding what's best.

By the time Rick is at the cash register, paying, his wide, primitive back to her, she wants to be lying down with him, under him, this feeling, unwanted, resisted, beats out her caution and her anger.

He walks back, staring into her eyes the whole way across the grainy, bright room, a toothpick jutting from his white teeth, grinning, unsubtle. Half the time he reads her thoughts.

There's apartments right next door, twenty-one bucks a night. I got us one.

How did you find us?

Don't matter. How I got here, how I knew where you'd run to this time. Don't matter in any long or short run. It don't matter so don't ask.

Bluebird comes over, begging one more quarter to put in the glass machine that cracks out hard, shiny candies in fruit shapes. It ate my first one, she pouts.

He hands her two quarters, the whole time staring at Hallie like some cornball stunt he's absorbed from believing in movies.

Work's been good. I picked up an extra two hundred last week. That should help with the bills. And I replaced that pipe in the bathroom.

Waltzing her around. First waltz, then shove, that's his way. She ignores him, watching the cook behind the partition, fat, bland-cheeked, a chef's hat like a starched glacier on his head, polishing a frying pan, bringing it near his face, a woman with a hand mirror.

Rick swivels to check who she's seeing other than him. Damn I hate that, you looking at other men all the time.

I don't look at other men. I look at people.

Bullshit.

Bluebird comes back, bright pygmy bananas and oranges and limes clicking and rolling like the tropics on the black rabbit skin. She plops her head on Hallie's shoulder, yawning.

Ricky jogs, Bluebird on his shoulders, over to the apartment. Hallie holds two beers, one in either hand. When they get inside, Hallie sees two double beds, lifts Bluebird's crown off, kisses the ovaled heat of her head. Okay, Bluey, time to brush teeth and pee, get ready for bed.

When they come out of the bathroom, Rick's set up in his underwear in a plastic chair in front of the TV, the diamond crown tipped backwards, sliding off his big shaggy head. Bluebird shrieks, runs and jumps on his lap, thumb in mouth, hoping to stay up, watching TV on his lap.

Hallie's voice glints, nearly jealous.

Hey guys. Time for bed.

He won't kiss her, doesn't bother, just moves his fingers up her in a deliberate way that makes her bite her arm to keep quiet. Next moving his fingers out, teething and chewing a row of hickies on her neck, stopping to say he loves screwing her.

Love is confusing, love is sickness, Hallie thinks, the body tearing off one way, the mind another. He reaches an arm down, picks up the beer, drinks. The TV stays on the whole time, no sound, while he's doing stuff to her, calmly glancing over at the TV, watch it, watch her, watch it. Want some? Holding the bottle above her head. No. She's wondering about Vaughn, his one leg, how would it be, him climbing on top of both her and Ricky, a weight, buffalo-weight, and how would his blank leg space feel. He might have been her friend. At dinner, Bluebird had told about the gorilla, the Indian with one leg, and Rick had laughed. Yeah, your mom can reel in some weird trash.

And we saw this other man in the park who sits in trees and thinks he's a bird.

Fucking loony bird. Loony birds all over these days.

Hallie kicks him under the table. She hates for him to swear around her child.

Basement gray in the TV light, he's grabbing her butt, grinning at her, pinching it lightly, his eyes near-mean. So you're already out picking up Indians. Miss Wanna-Be.

Wanna-Be?

Wanna-Be-An-Indian.

Right. Where does it go?

Where does what go? He belches.

All the sweat, you know, after we make love.

Huh. Into the air I guess. Evaporation.

Five bucks it falls back down as rain. Our sweat comes down on people, their sweat comes down on us.

You're pretty crazy, you know that? And you do always look at other guys.

To stop the tears itching into her scalp, to reverse their slide, Hallie props on her elbows, stares at the crown on top of the TV, street-light giving it more false sparkles.

Calm was forming in her again, massive, fabricated, numbing. She walked into it like a picture, a picture of driving back to Cheyenne, the windows sealed up tight, the white Impala all sweetstinking like a high school dance. Ricky was going to buy that drugstore gorilla, he'd said that, falling asleep, and Hallie bet on how it would be, her and him in the back seat, down necking, Bluebird up front, peaceful as an adult in her diamond crown, switching radio stations, the gorilla taking charge, hands slow to react, dumb as any love, gigantic on the wheel.

Dagoberto Gilb

Ballad

The truth was that Cowboy Mike Duran had been getting miserably sick. So sick he'd finally let a doctor have his way. He'd allowed himself to be strapped to a soft bench, and he'd stared up into the wormy black patterns of the acoustical tiles. The laboratory was new and clean, crisp with the aroma of fresh plastic, alert with the intelligent stares of computer screens, their invisible grids always accommodating more and more fluorescent numbers and letters. As Mike Duran's skull penetrated this machine's cylinder, the radioactive hum he heard, and swore he felt, reminded him of television, and that made him think of Texas. Mike Duran thanked God for union benefits, because he knew this was not any office visit.

Mike wasn't surprised that the test didn't discover anything.

The doctor had wanted to find out what it was, but all he wanted was a prescription for pills. For Mike there was no mystery whatever—it was death, and that was not going to show up on an X ray, no matter where some doctor thought it might be. Of course this was not an opinion he offered openly. It was only that the sickness, the thoughts that came with it, convinced him of this overwhelming fact. Pills, strong ones, were the only hope that these thoughts would go away, despite that fact, though not immediately. At first they simply redirected the more specific pain in his head to an overall disgust and nausea. In other words, first he was sick, and then he was sick as he fought that off, and in either case he'd miss a day of work. Sometimes he'd take the pills—always much more than the recommended dose—and stay at the job. Usually when he did that it meant he'd lose the next workday anyway, because he'd have to recuperate from the combined exhaustion of work and overmedication. Sometimes he'd both take the pills and stay home, which often meant he'd lose two days. All of this had the obvious effect on his employment. He went through jobs. He'd get so unhappy or so unhealthy that, if he didn't get laid off, he'd quit. Which meant he was not always making money, which meant he felt pressured, which meant he'd worry, get angry about everything, and think that was why he got sick.

Nobody he worked with knew any of this. He only went to the union hall, signed the out-of-work list, and waited for the time to try again. In the trades, there were lots of reasons for a man to go through jobs, many good, many not so good. In either case, the discussion at the hall usually broke down like this: the job, according to a man who'd been there, was a bad one, run by assholes, designed by idiots, worked by suckasses; or, in the opinion of another man, the guy claiming that was such an incompetent he couldn't keep a job if the only thing he had to do in eight hours was sign a paycheck. It was often hard to know which was the truth, but reputation usually dictated which of those two views would rule the outlook at the hall, since every building that'd been started found men who'd stay to the end, who'd do it whether it was good work or not. Every job could be criticized, every job could be praised. But whichever the case, a man who was at the hall, who was out of work, had to give a reason for this, a convincing one whether a lie or the truth, because that was the nature of the men who chose the trades as the way to make their living.

Cowboy Mike's reputation was solid. He hadn't always been sick, and over the years he'd established himself at jobs so large that many men had come to know him and his sweaty, honest style of work. There was no reason for anyone not to believe that he was absolutely sincere when he blamed the union and the times. His claim was that the union had gotten so weak that just about anything could go at a jobsite and nobody'd say a word about it. Contractors didn't have to worry about safety, didn't have to treat a man with respect because the hall could, and would, always send another. He said he was tired of having some prick scream at him like he worked on four furry legs, and that he was tired of getting in arguments with morons who, as he put it, were so stupid that they thought everyone around them was stupider. Mike could go on, and often would, about what union was supposed to stand for, like dignity and security and craft, and about non-union. He liked to talk about Texas when he talked about non-union. How he used to work in Texas and was paid so little, how he'd have to have his own power tools at those jobs and how at this one some guy had plugged him into a 220-volt outlet, burned out his personal saw, which got him sent home without pay. He particularly liked to say this: non-union is you falling off the side of a building and the foreman running over screaming "You're fired!" before you hit the ground and workman's compensation goes into effect.

For him personally, it was more complicated than that. In his own local, Mike knew that the officers—and in particular the business agent, an alcoholic and the most powerful man at the hall—played favorites, and took money. Cowboy Mike knew these things because he knew men that told him how it worked for them. And he'd seen transactions with his own eyes. For all his talk to the men, Mike Duran did not consider himself either a fool or a hero.

Like anyone else, he wanted to survive. So in the morning and at the job dispatch window, he played up his knowledge to the BA, implying, never outright saying, he wanted in on it.

There were other details about Cowboy Mike Duran. Like, for instance, that he grew up without parents. His grandparents raised him, and there was no certainty that they were his blood. They never said so, and both were dead before he had the courage to ask them. He had no birth certificate. He knew of no other relatives. What he was told was that he was born in Texas, and growing up in an old, deteriorating neighborhood of Los Angeles, the state of Texas took on mythic proportions in his mind. Mike Duran, whose childhood was so confined by the smells and movements of old age, made his mother and father a knobless black-and-white television, and from that he learned his heritage, his personal approach to life. That was why, after his grandmother died, he took his only trip ever and ever since to Texas, first to El Paso, then up to Dallas, then down to San Antonio, the city where he met his wife. When he came back to LA married, he was driving a pickup with Texas plates, which he kept from then on registered there, and he was wearing a cowboy hat which, also from then on, he wore whenever he was behind the wheel. It was after this that he acquired the nickname Cowboy. And he liked that a lot.

Cowboy Mike Duran got into construction because he thought it was the only work that was still Western. He thought it wasn't much different than what cattlemen and trailer drivers, wildcatters and roughnecks did in the earlier days. They were drinking, brawling, whoring, hardworking men whose job tangled them up with the outdoors, men whose clothes were secondary to what was inside them, men whose independence was so dogged they'd do it alone if they had to, without cranes or dozers or backhoes, with two hands if it came down to getting the job done, and who afterwards would drive on without a second thought to the next job. Cowboy Mike Duran, in so many words, was about as committed to the union as he was to the belief that he was from Los Angeles.

He finally felt better and came those days when he was ready to go at it again, and came a day when the BA waved him over to the dispatch window to tell him, with a wink, that he was gonna like this one.

He wasn't lying. It was a site for a sixteen-story highrise on Sunset Boulevard, at the real center of Cowboy Mike Duran's existence, where billboards were as bright as lights and as big as banks, where pastel restaurants had names like poodles and atmospheres like clubs, where body-conscious men and women dressed like famous actors, or musicians, or producers, or just plain cool and rich. It matched everything Cowboy Mike ever wanted—here he could be admired, muscles veined with sweat, a real live Marlboro man across the street from where the largest cut-out one in the world never did more than hold that rope.

The job itself was like all the others. Three men, along with Mike, went out, and the three were laid off within the week. An old man, who was working on his thirtieth year toward a pension, got it because he was slow. A black guy got it because he didn't know the work, and the carpenter born in Mexico because he didn't speak English well enough. None of them were told this, of course. What they were told was that there wasn't enough work. It wasn't smart to say anything else, to open things up to lawsuits, just as it wasn't smart to hint at the deeper truth—that the guys who ran the job didn't like old men, most blacks, or Mexicans who weren't laborers. If Mike would have been laid off, he'd have been the first to say something about these injustices, but, especially from within the barricading of the jobsite, employed, he also could admit to the logic of their thinking: a good crew was one that liked each other, and a good crew got the work out. Construction operated on schedules, and missing them meant losing money. Why shouldn't a company have the right to let go of any man it thought would cost it profits? The same logic explained why those men were replaced by others not from the union hall, who were not even union until they got a card from the BA, who obviously thought that was good enough for him.

The steward on the job, the man who represented the union hall and union principles, who was the only one who could hear a complaint and take it over to a foreman or super without any fear of being fired, was called Bud. He doubled as the job foreman. He was brother of the superintendent, Charles W. Hobbs, whose name was that of the company, Charles W. Hobbs Construction. Besides these two, there was a son of Charles W., little Charles or Charlie, and there were the brothers Ben, Mack, and Preston. The Hobbs brothers were born in San Angelo, and each had trickled west to Los Angeles, one by one, for the work that oldest brother Charles W. was getting more and more of. Hobbs Construction was union only when the job required, and this one did because the rodbusters, from the United Brotherhood of Ironworkers, wouldn't work any job beside non-union men, period. There was no way Charles W. Hobbs could find a non-union crew of steel men who'd work a job this size.

The Hobbses liked Cowboy Mike, and not just because of the Texas background he claimed—less forcefully around them, of course. Cowboy Mike could work, and since he'd been on lots of highrises over the years, in most respects he knew more than anyone else on the job. That's why they let him work with anyone he wanted, doing whatever he wanted to do, though if a wall or deck or some columns really needed getting done, Bud or Charles W. would ask him, and Mike would have it ready for concrete on time.

Mike loved his work, and his outlook on life brightened each day that went by with him employed and healthy. He even made a special point of waving howdy to the BA when he stopped by and talked to Bud over at the corner of the jobsite when it'd reached street level. Mike figured the BA came around for a payoff. If he'd been sick, that'd be sure to fly him into a rage. But Cowboy Mike felt great, and didn't even care for a second that most—maybe all—of the crew took home two checks every week, one for hours that would be reported to the IRS, the other, from a separate account, for straight-time cash which wouldn't be reported by the company or the man who got it. This was something they'd never talked about to him directly, he figured because the BA was in on it and told them not to be too sure of Cowboy Mike yet.

His one check cashed, and that was enough for him. Besides, he was having fun. Because of the job's location, photographers were often around taking pictures, and one time Mike, a healthy-looking man, was asked if he wouldn't mind having some shots taken of him specifically. Of course Mike didn't mind.

The one he liked the most was the one with his shirt off, his cowboy hat on, standing with some of the guys drinking beer next to his pickup after work. That was the one he claimed was the best when it came out in *California* magazine, in a glossy photo essay titled "Men at Work." Along with a farmer, a steelworker, a butcher, and a firefighter, it was one of several pages of Mike Duran at the job. But naturally it was the one on the cover that made the biggest impression. Cowboy Mike Duran, his face as strong as any Indian's, his body as brown as wet earth, all muscle and hardhat, bags and hammer, a cord stretched out and a worm-drive skilsaw near him, became every man who banged at it, who built buildings.

Then the sickness began making its comeback. He tried to exorcise it with a good attitude and over-the-counter pills in front of a morning cup of coffee. At first that worked, which it always did. A whole week could go by. Gradually the pain got worse when he woke up in the morning. He'd take the stronger prescribed pill, and a handful of the others to the job. He'd maybe sweat more there, but in his sleep he was worrying. Certain kinds of dreams would tell him the sickness was in the shadow. He'd think it was too much sleep, so he'd stay up later and watch television. He'd think it was too little sleep. He'd drink more, he'd drink nothing. The pattern was a routine: Cowboy Mike Duran got sick bad and started missing a day or two of work every other week.

Either way, in the pain, or the relief from it through pills, Mike Duran would play back his childhood. His grandparents were old, and they were always worried. What they worried about was never too clear to him, and he never asked—he turned the television on. It was the only piece of furniture that was not chipped, whose varnish was not peeling away the same way he imagined his grandfather's skin was. He'd finally died when Mike was seven, or eight, he couldn't exactly remember. And then Mike's grandmother stopped talking in Spanish, for his benefit. Mike stopped listening at all. He made his own meals. Cans of soup, vegetables, fruit. He cooked hamburger meat. She made beans. If he didn't have the TV on, he'd sometimes stare at a knot in the slats of wood on the ceiling in the same room. He could stare at that knot until it came alive. One time he saw it as a black snake, coiled. He ran into his grandmother's room, found her in her bed, a woman so much weaker than he, and he stopped himself from telling her. He was in junior high then.

This sickness was like that snake. It slithered through him slowly, fearlessly, raising its head each time it came on some new detail from his present. Its venom was bitter—he'd take pills—and that detail would numb, twisting, a frenzy of ugly meaning, until it was overcome, when a calm, serene afterglow of remembrance would settle in. In those moments he would know himself with a clarity that he knew could only be death.

Hobbs Construction did employ carpenters that weren't relatives of Charles W., but, with the exception of Cowboy Mike, they were related to someone by friendship. Friends of family, however, were not family. Charles W. was the only one of them that couldn't be described as either dumb or lazy, and there was little doubt that his brothers' and son's working days would have been much less picturesque if the company didn't exist. These friends covered for them consistently, and gratefully, to all appearances. A healthy Cowboy Mike Duran would say he didn't care about that either— it wasn't his money, and the worse they were, the better he looked.

Since his picture had been on the cover of *California* magazine, Mike was given more slack than could usually be expected. It seemed everyone was more pleased to see him back than irritated that he hadn't showed up. That was the biggest payment he'd received for his fame. If everybody's fantasy was to be recognized on the cover of a magazine, it was no less so a working man's whose only achievement was doing what just about everyone took for granted, and it was the same for Mike too, except that his health had taken away some of the pleasure he imagined was also supposed to be his. He'd have thought his life would change somehow, in some big way. Instead, he didn't make more money, nobody called him to make a movie, women weren't throwing themselves in his way when he passed by. He still got sick. Nothing was like he expected.

He imagined that if it weren't for the sickness his life would be a whole lot different, that he'd be some other person. Maybe he wouldn't be union, maybe he'd be an independent like he always thought a man should be. If only things had gone as well as that trip he took to Texas. That had been the one thing in his life that'd turned out like he'd wanted it to, the way it was supposed to. He'd come back with a sense of place, of people, of land, of past. Everything since had been a disappointment, and he was sure it was because of the sickness. It wouldn't let him have the kind of stories he wanted to tell.

Sickness was what made him begin to resent watching the Hobbs boys not working, reminded him of the many times he'd seen men get their checks, how they were the ones who didn't know anybody, had no daddy or brother or uncle. He thought this particularly the day Bud, whose belly was so large he could eat his lunch off it, and who was the same age as Mike, asked Mike to walk this beam soffit to hold a grade stick so he and Charlie, who usually stood the stick up, could get a reading. Hobbs Construction was not the safest outfit he'd ever worked for by any stretch, but that was something he didn't care much about except on these days. He'd already taken three of the prescription pills and too many others and he was unsteady on hard ground, and right then fat Bud wanted him, not little Charles, to walk a twelve-inch beam soffit for twenty feet. Below, the scaffolding and x-bracing, stacked two high, wobbled sloppily, unsecured, unleveled. The soffit's plywood rested on two-by-fours on edge, because Hobbs Construction, which hadn't before worked a building this large, didn't want to spend money on more stable four-by-fours which wouldn't roll over if a man's step was wrong. On either side of the beam were open holes where elevators would be, four stories deep.

Cowboy Mike Duran couldn't tell anybody about his being sick, because he could not. He wouldn't tell anybody about taking too many pills, about weakness and fear. He didn't know how to talk about these things. So he stepped along the beam, a black shaft of death on each side of him, a blue Western sky above him. And when he did make it to the other end, he held that stick up as long as it took for dumb, fat Bud to read his mark, and he walked back across without complaining. But when Bud signaled and yelled for him to do it a second time—because he didn't think his gun had been set up right—Cowboy Mike Duran thought about the union, Texas, and death.

He tried to ignore that snake, and he'd moved a chair around the room so he wouldn't notice it. He moved the television. None of it did any good. He ate TV dinners with it above him. His whole childhood it was coiled above him. Once he stared into its jaws and let himself enter. It was dark and frightening, but then that went away, just as time did. Just as time did watching a movie on the television. Good guys, bad guys, guns, horses, right, wrong. The West.

Gladys Swan

The Old Hotel

1.

If you found your way out to the old hotel in the years following the Korean War, leaving the blacktop north of Deming and churning up dust for miles on the narrow dirt road that crossed the range, you'd have wondered that anybody still inhabited the place. It looked abandoned, like the shell of an older, more extravagant life. By then, one side of the porch that swept the whole front end had broken off and the columns were split as though they'd been struck by lightning. An effort had been made to give the exterior a new face, but the boards had soaked up the paint, eating up money and will and enthusiasm till finally you could see the line along the side where the effort was abandoned halfway down. It was an attempt to catch things before they hit the downside forever, but it was all patchwork, and no amount of it could turn things around. The whole place was sagging under the burden of weather and time, so that if you went inside, you'd have expected every door to hang crooked in its frame.

If you came looking for Jack Whedon, the owner, chances would be he was off somewhere "looking after his interests," as he put it, leaving the management to his wife, Penny, who kept things going in her own fashion, and their daughter, Jewel, who had to grow up there. Jack had been made a deal by old Jesse Harris, who'd have run things into the ground with his drinking if two wars and a change of style hadn't helped him along.

"Put some arm and back into the place and you've got yourself a gold mine." The old man had brought Jack back to Deming and was treating him to a few drinks after showing him around the place. "Why, you could make it into the showplace of the county. That hotel made a fortune in its heyday. On account of the springs. Folks all crippled up with arthritis and rheumatism walking away sprightly as a roadrunner." And now that the latest conflict was over and that great general was in the White House and the Communists were cleaned out of the government, the days of glory were coming back. Maybe Jack could turn the place into a fancy dude ranch. "What I wouldn't give to be young again," the old man said, "and watch the good times roll."

Jack took it all in, whiskey breath in his ear, as the old man leaned toward him and tapped the counter for emphasis. Jack had come from managing a restaurant and then a so-called nightclub, where the ranch hands came to drink and dance, but he didn't have much of a head for details and allowed himself to be overcharged by the wholesalers or cheated by the help. At the moment, he was standing at the lag end of opportunity, looking for an opening for his talents. He was intrigued with what he could do with a hotel in the middle of the desert: the great dining room and parlor across the front, the two extensive wings with balconied rooms that faced one another across the mesquite. A windmill to generate electricity and a well for water. And old stables—they'd even kept a milk cow—and sheds for the chickens. All of it watered into existence by the springs that bubbled up from deep in the rocky ground and fed the bathing pool. There was something grandiose in the isolation of the spot, the cactus-studded landscape stretching away to the blue imprint of mountains in one direction and twenty-five miles to the nearest town in the other.

"I'm thinking of taking over the Hot Springs Hotel," he told his wife that night. "Old Jesse is going to let me buy in."

"Let you! Why, he's been trying to unload that white elephant for as long as I can remember."

"It looks pretty run-down," he admitted. "But it's all solid underneath." It would be a challenge to scrape away the old paint, replace the rotten boards—tackle the hotel as if she were a ship that would take dominion of the desert once more. Think of what it would do for the country. Bring people out there to drink and dance, not only the townspeople but the folks down in Mimbres Valley. Give them something to do on weekends. Then when he and Penny got a little cash, they could really put the place in shape. They'd go after summer people and guide hunters in the fall.

"And work ourselves into old age and bankruptcy—whichever comes first. It would take a fortune."

"You've got to see the place to appreciate it. I know—at first I wouldn't have believed it myself." Besides, they didn't have to do everything at once. The place had a history in those old boards. There was local color, there was charm.

For a moment Penny Whedon was taken aback by this excess of imagination, for in the past Jack had never entertained more than the notion of stepping into a good spot and making a killing the next instant. But now that she'd nursed him through a couple of failures in which circumstances and other people seemed less to blame than his own stupidity and flaccid amiability, she wasn't about to give him any margin. Finally, after he'd painted the prospects in colors that came gleaming from the liquor bottles in the mirror at the back of the bar, she laced into him with such scorn he felt the hollowness of a man who hasn't eaten for three days. The next morning he went to the lawyer's office, where the old man, hardly able to believe his luck, sat in a quiver till Jack signed the contract.

"What the hell," Jack said. "Opportunity, that old bitch, don't come but once."

Although she'd been dead-set against the idea, when the time came, Penny packed up their things and acted as if she were moving up in the world. Whether or not she believed it, she worked like a demon along with Jack, running back and forth to town for paint and wallpaper and a hundred other items, arranging for loans and credit, hiring the help and getting a good write-up in the local paper, with pictures on the front page.

They turned the old dining room into a restaurant; that is, they added a few tables and printed up a menu. Then they cleared most of the furniture out of the parlor, put a bar at one end under a large gilt-edged mirror and called the rest a dance floor. On weekends they brought in a three-piece band—saxophone, violin and piano—which played with more energy than talent. But the place was lively. Folks came from town, from the Valley, even a few from fifty miles away. It was a novelty, the old hotel. People had known about it long enough to have forgotten about it. Teddy Roosevelt had lodged there, and one of the deer heads hanging in the dining room was attributed to his prowess. Even a few tourists came to spend a night in one of the four rooms Jack had managed to refurbish.

But when the summer ended, they were deeper in debt than ever. The circle of reputation was still too narrow, too limited, to appeal to more than casual curiosity. The hotel was too far off the beaten track to draw much of anybody during the week. And weekends were unpredictable. There were bars enough for the young bucks who wanted to get drunk and pick a fight; lodgings enough for tourists; resorts enough for a chosen clientele. No one came any longer for the healing powers of the springs.

By the time Jack let the regular help go and faced a winter of struggle as his family tried to gather their resources for spring, he was ready to give up the place as a bad job. He was a man of brief enthusiasms and quick discouragement, and he'd known even as he signed the papers he had taken on more than he could handle. He took a job part-time in the Valley as a bartender, and rumor had it he was fooling around with a woman in town. But curiously, Penny worked harder than ever. She made the hotel her domain, hanging on, scraping by, clinging to the place for cold comfort. Perhaps now that she was in it, she couldn't let go or wouldn't— because she'd always had a stubborn streak. At times she wanted to laugh: Jack was such small potatoes, thinking he could fool the future with his halfway measures. She could see through him all the way to his backbone: a man who could only think small, but enough for him to outsweep his talents. No wonder he was a disaster. It would have taken a certain magnitude, a flourish to bring it off: the talent for risk, for adventure. And money. She could recognize the means even if she couldn't imagine the measures. Meanwhile, she entertained her own schemes. Bad as things were, she couldn't wholly cut herself off from the sense of possibility. Suppose something should come their way, say, a land developer passing through, a wealthy investor. Till then, she honed the practical side of her nature to a fine edge. She put aside every cent she could, paying the creditors just enough to keep them at bay, scrimping on meals, piecing and patching. She stopped going to town unless it was necessary, for otherwise she'd have to take Jewel to the movies and buy her ice cream. From now on, they'd do without.

At first Jewel had been delighted by the old hotel. She went through all the rooms, opening the doors with a wonderful thrill of imagined adventure, watching motes of dust float in the light that entered through the tattered curtains. She was certain to find a fortune in gold under one of the old beds, and she lifted mattresses that had been raided by field mice for their nests and yanked open reluctant drawers. She looked for clues to an unsolved mystery such as she read about in the Nancy Drew books. But she turned up only a few stray hairpins and some fragments of yellowed newspaper. For a time she played over and over the records she found on the shelf of the Victrola in the parlor, listening to voices that sang hollowly of obsolete longings and dead loves. She tried the old piano, which had taken new felts and a tuning to bring its dead notes to life. During the summer there was the interest of seeing who'd come up the road and park in front of the old hotel. She could lie in bed and listen to the high, sweet notes of the violin, rising above those of the sax and the old piano, and listen to the last words before the car doors slammed. But after a few weeks of that, she lived only for the school bus that took her to the one-room school in the Valley. During the winter blizzards, she stared out the window at the snow and dreamed of running off to New Orleans and living on a riverboat, or to San Francisco and crossing the Golden Gate Bridge.

2.

Sometimes at night, Jewel was awakened by the howl of coyotes cutting through the indigo stillness across great distances. It was as though she'd heard their voices before, howling through her sleep, though she couldn't remember, and she wondered what they wanted, hurling their voices to the moon. Sometimes she imagined them coming in close, putting their noses to where people had walked and their ears to walls, listening to the breath of sleepers. And a shiver would go through her at the approach of their wildness. Sometimes from the room next to hers, she heard human voices, but it was even harder to tell what they wanted. Jewel would try to remember how it was where she lived before in town—the schoolyard where she played. But even when she came back to the town, she knew it had forgotten her, as though she'd been carried along by a river to another part of time and space. She wasn't sure where she lived, as though she floated somewhere between the voices of coyotes outside and the voices on the other side of the wall.

"When I married you, you said we'd be rich. And where is all that money? And all those good times. I had a better life during the war, all those boys wanting to buy a girl a drink and have some fun. And what have we got on our hands? A dead loss. I don't know why I don't pick up and go back to town, or away to somewhere with real human beings. I know about you—just leave me here to drudge while you cat around and have yourself a time."

"So that's what you were doing while I was overseas."

"What did you expect?"

Suppose her mother did leave. Then she'd be there alone. And when the coyotes howled again, Jewel heard a new note, one that went beyond any words she knew.

"All right," she heard her father protest, "let's just leave and go on back to town."

"What the hell would you do there?"

"Get a job."

"Who'd hire you after this? And how would I show my face in the street? How could I look anybody in the eye?"

Such nights succeeded those days that Penny found fault with everything, tongue lashed anyone who crossed her path, so that even the cat did well to hide. And the outcome was always the same.

"Christ!" Jack would mutter, when he again reached the point where nothing he could say would make any difference, as he already knew. And Jewel would hear the springs complain as he turned over and took refuge in silence. She'd have been glad to go back to town herself, for she was the oldest child in school and had nobody to talk to except her teacher. Miss Blackburn gave her chores to do that made her feel important and brought her books from the public library and told her she could do the best lettering of anybody she knew. Jewel painted signs for over the doors that said "Exit," and "Walk, Do Not Run," and wrote the day's spelling words in colored chalks on the blackboard, inside a border of flowers. In one of the library books, she found poems she could memorize and learned to recite all of "Paul Revere's Ride" and "The Wreck of the Hesperus." After school, if she could escape from helping in the kitchen, she scouted the land beyond the hotel for arrowheads or drew pictures of the mountains or played some of her old pieces on the piano.

Without telling Penny, Jack put the hotel up for sale, but no buyer stepped forward. That done, he seemed absolved of responsibility. He spent less and less time there, going off to prospect for manganese and feldspar, or sitting with his cronies at the bar where he worked weekends. So that he wasn't around when Henry Betts, a lawyer from Deming, came out one afternoon. He had a mission of some delicacy and was just as well pleased to find the wife instead of the husband.

When he had telephoned, she couldn't figure out why he should come unless it was on the wings of some disaster Jack had perpetrated. He could have traded the hotel for some worthless mining claim or delivered them to a scheme that was bound to leave them worse off than before. More likely a secret debt was about to strangle them—back taxes or Jack's liquor bill. Or even worse: by this time he could have made some woman pregnant. Her fears raced over the groundwork created by suspicion while she prepared her face for sociability. Meanwhile, the lawyer was taking his time, looking around with interest.

"I've heard about this place," he said affably, "but I never made it out here before this. My Daddy used to talk about it."

She invited him to sit down on the brocaded rosewood sofa she'd had Jack restore to the parlor, and which was her special pride.

"Lots of nice antiques you got here."

To keep herself from fidgeting, she offered him coffee, for she had some on the stove in the kitchen. When she'd done that and they'd arranged themselves and were clearly waiting for whatever had brought them to this moment, the lawyer said, "I've come to tell you about a woman who needs a home, a special kind of home."

If he'd come looking for charity, they had none to spare, but she knew enough to keep quiet till he'd finished. Miss Viny Trilling, he went on to explain, came from a good family, had grown up like you and me, but when she came to be an adult, she'd taken her childhood with her and couldn't tell the difference between what was in her head and what was happening in the world. Or didn't want to, for at times she was as sensible as you and me and other times she was crazier than a coyote. Lately, she'd seen a man from the porch she claimed had visited her in a dream and promised to carry her away to the mountains and make her his wife and give her a child of her own. Nothing would dissuade her from this illusion. And sometimes she'd slip out of her room and go roaming the streets, even in her nightgown, looking for him. Her brothers were at a loss—there was nobody at home to take care of her. They wanted her to be in a place where she wouldn't cause embarrassment but would be well taken care of. And he named a sum for this purpose that Penny could scarcely believe.

She had a hard time hearing the rest: that Miss Trilling would have to have fresh strawberries with cream when they were in season and oranges in winter, the big, sweet navel oranges from California. And there must be a feather quilt on her bed, and nobody must open her trunk but herself. Penny could only think how much she could put away and what it would take to hide it from Jack—who just then appeared, back from his latest foray into the hills: face grimed and his jeans and boots gray with dust.

"Looks like I got caught in a sandstorm," he said, trying to make light of his appearance. He came forward, a man Penny could only feel ashamed of, with his scraggly, red mustache and the apologetic stoop to his shoulders, and shook the lawyer's hand.

"Go wash," Penny said. "You aren't civilized. And I won't have you on this sofa."

He gave a good-natured shrug and retreated. He went down to the springs, threw off his clothes and stepped into the pool. He let the heat close around him and the water lave his tired muscles. Like a caress it was as he floated. He closed his eyes and almost fell into a doze. For a moment, all his troubles fell away, and he let himself drift into the pleasure of his fatigue, his body loosened from the pull of gravity. He allowed himself a certain luxury of sentiment, enlivened by the whiskey that had eased his homeward journey: things would work out. They'd go forward into the future. His girl would grow up and find her way in the world. Daddy's girl. He thought how she was growing towards the woman she was going to be, how the child and the woman were blending together. Sensation and feeling became a single glow he was melting into. Then the water became too hot for him to stay in any longer, and he emerged as though he'd just been boiled and peeled.

3.

Actually, the Whedons were visited by what at that time was a double stroke of fortune. Not long after they agreed to take in Viny Trilling, they received a letter from a certain Everett Ferril, who used to come to the hotel as a boy with his parents and had fond memories of the place. He had recently retired from his teaching position at a private school in Switzerland and wanted to spend some months at the hotel writing his memoirs. He hoped the piano was in tune because he wished to devote time to his music. And he would like to hire a horse for long morning rides into the mountains.

They spent the next weeks preparing for the boarders. Mr. Ferril appeared first, a much younger man than they had expected. Though he was impeccably dressed in suit and tie when he arrived, they didn't know what to think of him. He looked un-American, if they let themselves dwell on it: an unknown quantity, shaped by a life in a foreign place. A life that had left its marks and channels in his face as though he'd brooded over it but never resigned himself to it and that gave him a look both worldly and unsatisfied. Something intense and barely subdued played under the surface like an electrical field that made his hair go awry and gave a spark like anger to his eyes. Which were everywhere, taking all in—the hotel and Jack and Penny herself. But Penny was not to be rattled. She didn't care what he was like or what he saw as long as he paid his bill and gave her a future. Then he stepped forward, kissed her hand and gave her a smile so full of charm, she was struck by the novelty and entirely won over.

"You're right welcome," she said.

By the time he was settled in, Viny arrived. Penny and Jack went with Henry Betts to meet her at the train station in Deming, where her brother Frank had accompanied her. "Take good care of our Vinita," he said, as though he couldn't bear to part with her. "She's our most special girl."

When they arrived back at the hotel, Jewel had just come home from her last day at school and was waiting to meet yet another stranger. She was not yet used to the first and ducked around corners to avoid speaking to Mr. Ferril. He was quite a tall man and seemed to look down at her from a very great distance. A very gallant man, her mother said—who cast a spell with his foreign culture and manners. He spoke both French and German, so that his speech held a different flavor from what she knew, spiced with foreign words and the names of cities Jewel recognized from the outdated globe in her classroom. She was so awed by him, she'd laughed when he'd kissed her hand and was so embarrassed by that rudeness, she was perfectly tongue-tied in his presence. By contrast, her parents, whose speech and manners seemed suited only for a land of barren rocks where cattle foraged, didn't seem to care about the difference.

Viny Trilling was another matter. She was a child, newly born every second. When she looked at Jewel with unclouded eyes that seemed more violet than blue, a moment's terror overtook her, for her eyes seemed to draw Jewel into a territory that was both familiar and tantalizing, but one she dared not enter for long. Jewel could hardly take her eyes from Viny's face: the pure brow, the unspoiled complexion without freckle or blemish, just the faintest touch of pink along the cheeks. She was like a china cup, but with a stubborn tilt to her head and a stubborn set to her jaw. She was twenty-eight years old.

"You can show her where her room is," Penny said, after Viny had offered a surprisingly strong, frank hand all around.

"I'll want to see the kitchen first," Viny said.

"Whatever you like," Penny said. "Jewel will show you everything."

She's used to having her way, Jewel thought enviously.

"I'll put away her things," Jack said.

"You be careful with that trunk," Viny said. "And mind you don't open it. It's got my things."

Jack required the help of Mr. Ferril to carry a large brass-bound trunk to her room.

"I traveled to Europe with one like that years ago," Mr. Ferril offered. "Didn't know anybody still used them."

"Break your back, don't they," Jack said, glad to set it down.

Meanwhile, Jewel took Viny towards the kitchen.

"Where do you keep the dishes?" Viny wanted to know.

"In the dining room."

"That's what I want to see."

Jewel opened the china cabinet so that Viny could survey the stacks of plates and bowls and saucers. "I'll need a special bowl for my strawberries."

"I know one," Jewel said, and brought out a little china bowl with lavender flowers around the edges that she had often used herself, it was so light and elegant.

"Amaranths," Viny exclaimed. "The perfect thing."

"It's yours then."

And Viny smiled with such radiance Jewel had to look away.

During the rest of that late spring, she and Viny and Mr. Ferril were treated to strawberries and cream every morning for breakfast. Viny always took the longest to eat hers, saving one until the very last. They teased her about it—she only did it so that they could envy her and she could lord it over them. She'd laugh with pleasure, hold up the strawberry on her spoon for all to admire, put it in her mouth and close her eyes, shutting them out of her exquisite pleasure. Jewel envied her; yet she always ate hers right up. Viny the Hoarder, Jewel the Greedy, they called one another. And Mr. Ferril—what was he? What did they want to call him?

They hadn't thought; he went on so quietly while they teased each other and laughed. They never considered him part of the game, he was too—grown-up. And they both had to look at him, as though they needed to discover more than how he ate his strawberries. Though he chatted and told anecdotes that made them double over with laughter, he seemed quite beyond them, as though he could, if he wanted, refer to some private store of superiority. He treated them all, Penny, Viny and even Jewel as if they were ladies, but quite impersonally, as if he adored them all and would have extended this courtesy to any woman, even if she stood before him in rags. He praised Penny's cooking, though it was of the meat-and-potatoes variety, mediocre and overdone. He went round the old hotel with a memory attached to every object and corner, piano and Victrola and porch and dining table. How extraordinary, that he could remember so much about all the mere objects of their daily existence. He told about former guests, whom he remembered in vivid detail. It became clear that, even as a boy, he could recognize human frailty and turn it to ridicule. Jewel liked his way of making fun of people because he made fun of himself as well. With his presence, together with Viny's, the place grew lively, glowed with a life borrowed from somewhere beyond it.

But he never said much about his present circumstances: there was no mention of a wife or family, or a home he came from. He'd grown up in Michigan, but had lived all his adult life abroad. He had a low opinion of the students he had taught: rich men's brats, he called them—like pieces of spoiled fruit. He didn't explain why he had left Switzerland or where, as a man in his forties, he might be going. He must have money, Penny was fond of saying, implying that he also had everything else—good looks, nice clothes—and what was he doing here?

Mr. Flight, Viny called him.

It was a peculiar summer. Just at the point where Jewel was about to close the door on her childhood she was asked to live it all again. Penny had taken her aside. "You'll have a job this summer," she said. "And you'll be paid for it. Ten dollars a month in your bank account." She could buy clothes for the fall, when she'd be going into town for school. Meanwhile, she was to be a companion for Viny. Jewel readily agreed; she'd never had so much money before.

The summer was an invention, created from whatever fell to hand. When they discovered a litter of kittens in the shed, apparently abandoned, they fed them with eye droppers until they could eat on their own. They sewed little dresses and caps for them and made elaborate visits to one another and invented conversations for their babies. They explored the attic as well and took down tables and chairs to make a special house in one of the unused rooms. Sometimes at night, Jewel slept with Viny and they lay awake late like girls at a slumber party. Though once Viny woke her up in the middle of the night, moaning and crying out.

"What's the matter?" Jewel asked her. "Did you have a bad dream?"

"I'm the matter," Viny said, sitting up. "Why was I born?" she moaned, rocking back and forth. "Oh, don't turn on the light, don't let me wake up." She sat blinking and rubbing her eyes when Jewel did so. "Where will I go to find my love? He was here and then he was gone."

It was peculiar, her living in a dream that way, and Jewel wondered that she should have miseries like that when she hadn't a trouble in the world and didn't have to do anything she didn't want to. She could let each day go wherever she wanted and do as she liked. She didn't have to cut up vegetables or help with the dishes, though mostly she shared whatever chores Jewel had to do.

What particularly took Jewel's fancy was the trunk of clothes Viny had brought with her, all old: cloche hats of velvet and stiff ones with broad brims; hats with plumes and bunches of feathers and rings of pearls and artificial flowers and veils. Dresses of crêpe de Chine and taffeta and velvet and scarfs and shawls embroidered with peacocks and roses. Gowns that trailed the floor and silver shoes and beaded slippers. Her dress-up clothes.

Since her arrival, Jewel looked forward with quickening interest to what the day would bring, as though each day were to be lived without the burden of the previous one. And time flowed without being time. It made her feel guilty somehow, like living off the fat of the land. If, now and then, she was seized by a moment of misgiving, she would go to the mirror to remind herself that she was growing up. The first thing she would buy was a bra. The summer would come to an end and she'd be ready.

"How do you like Viny?" Jack asked her one day, out of idle curiosity.

"She's okay," Jewel said with a shrug, and immediately felt she'd betrayed her.

While they went on their way, Mr. Ferril sat at the piano in the parlor, limbering up with scales, then filling the hotel with music. Jewel envied him. Though she'd taken lessons up till the time they'd moved into the hotel, nothing she played was ever perfect. And now she was a year away from her music. The teacher had let her work on songs in the songbook to play while the younger children sang, but what she knew kept slipping away. Mr. Ferril could play pieces like "Clair de Lune," which Jewel thought was the most beautiful music she'd ever heard, and works by famous composers. Sometimes he struck chords that filled the whole place with sound. Rachmaninoff, he would tell her, one more of his foreign words. When she looked at the music he left open, it appeared so complicated and difficult she could only wonder how anyone played it.

One morning after she and Viny had admired themselves in the full-length mirror Jack had helped them move from the hallway into their special room, Viny wanted to attend a ball in the parlor and dance to music on the Victrola.

"But Mr. Ferril is practicing," Jewel said.

"We'll wait until he's finished," Viny said reasonably.

Jewel didn't want him to see them, and when it was quiet, she took off her gown to go and see first that he was gone. But as Viny was dancing to the music with an unseen partner, he appeared. Jewel felt a sudden rush of shame: she was too old to be caught like this. But curiously, he went up to put the next record on the Victrola and said to Viny, "My name is first on your dance card, ma'am. I hope I may claim the honor."

"Of course, Mr. Flight," she said, and gave him a gloved hand and allowed him to lead her to the center of the floor. They sailed around the room as though an admiring crowd were witnessing them. Viny's dress swirled out around her, in a sheen of pink silk. Movement filled the tune of the waltz and made it less plaintive, and for a moment it was possible to imagine other dancers, other voices. Jewel envied her and the way the pink dress curved across her breasts and fitted her waist and flowed to the floor. She'd yet to have her first formal, and she wanted one, and to go to a prom like they had in high school. When they finished the waltz, breathless, laughing, they grasped each other around the waist. Mr. Ferril's forehead glowed.

Then he started the record over again and asked Jewel to dance.

"I can't," she said. For though she counted steps and concentrated, she always tripped over her partner's feet.

"Just follow me," he said, taking her hand, looking at her in a way that intimidated her.

"Just put yourself inside the music," Viny said.

She clutched her dress up into a knot so that it wouldn't trail, and tried to follow, blindly, stumbling, till her face was hot and her hands were moist.

"A little practice is all that's needed," Mr. Ferril said kindly. "It's all anything needs," and he squeezed her hand.

She couldn't bear it. She stood there in the silver shoes that slipped against her heels and felt the summer collapse beneath her.

Viny plucked her sleeve. "We're late," she said. "The carriage is waiting."

She was glad to flee from Mr. Ferril's gaze, but she couldn't put from her mind the picture of Viny dancing.

"We'll teach you to dance," Viny said when they were alone together.

"I can't," Jewel said, without understanding why. She knew

she would adore dancing with Mr. Ferril if she could dance like Viny. She'd seen films of Ginger Rogers and Fred Astaire, and she could imagine being whirled around a ballroom. But it was possible to imagine herself doing it only if she didn't attempt it.

It was more than she could bear to see Mr. Ferril almost every time she turned around. Though he practiced the piano in the mornings after breakfast and sometimes worked in his room, he seemed to have a great deal of time on his hands. He had bought a new car, a Hudson with silver fenders and a wide body, not long after his arrival, but when he'd taken them for a brief excursion and they'd reveled in the newness of it, he apparently had nowhere to go. It sat in front of the hotel.

"So what'll we do today?" he asked them one morning after breakfast, as though he had so far advanced into their company they were a threesome. Jewel looked at him uncertainly, but he appeared to be waiting for his answer from Viny.

"Let's go on a picnic," Viny said, clapping her hands eagerly. "We can pack sandwiches and go on an excursion and eat outdoors."

"The car," Jewel said, hoping she wasn't being forward. "We can go in the car."

"Absolutely," said Mr. Ferril, as though he'd now been given a commission. "A wonderful idea."

Penny then packed sandwiches for them and made a thermos of iced tea, and they drove off for the City of Rocks, a few miles from the hotel. It was not so much a city as a chaos of rocks, as though the earth in a mad moment had flung out boulders in every direction. They made a great heap on a small rise where they'd been pushed above the ground, and the soil having settled among them, grasses and mesquite and a few small cedars grew out of their midst. They gleamed white in the sun as the picnickers approached. The sky was brilliant and cloudless, with a solitary hawk cruising above.

"I'll bet anything could live here," Jewel said, as they surveyed the boulders, "snakes and mice and rabbits and scorpions and—"

Viny was momentarily startled by a lizard.

"It's weird," Jewel said. "I wouldn't want to be here at night."

"I didn't think you'd scare that easily," Mr. Ferril said, teasing her.

She ignored him. "Let's climb on the rocks," Jewel said to Viny. "I can go highest, I'll bet." She scrambled up among the boulders to the point where she could look out over the desert, and down at Viny and Mr. Ferril standing together. "Come on," she yelled, "it's not hard. You can see everything."

They reached her finally, took in the view of the mountains and sat down on the rocks to catch their breath.

"The world's out there somewhere," Jewel said.

"And luckily we're here," Mr. Ferril said, "and it can all go hang."

That was the way with adults, it seemed: they were ready to condemn something before you had a chance to try it out, almost as though they wanted to keep it for themselves and never let you know.

"I'm going down," he said. "My stomach is about to digest itself."

Jewel didn't care.

"Do you think it's a grand place?" Viny asked, gesturing toward the expanse.

"Yes," Jewel said. "I want to see Paris."

"I saw a picture once," Viny said, "of a tall tower—they said it was Paris." They climbed down to the base of the rocks, where Mr. Ferril had spread a cloth in the shadows of some cedars.

"What could be better?" Mr. Ferril said, taking a bite from a ham sandwich. "Sky like this and sun and rocks. You never know how good food can taste till you eat it out in the air."

They ate and drank hungrily, then Jewel jumped up again, ready to explore.

"What energy!" Mr. Ferril said. "All I want to do is sit here forever and watch the clouds." He leaned back against a boulder.

"That would be boring," Jewel said, "with nothing ever happening."

"What do you want to happen?"

She shrugged. "I don't know. Something. There's all this waiting—and nothing happens."

"The same wherever you are," said Mr. Ferril. "All this waiting for something that never happens. And if it does, it's too late."

He reached down and broke off a blade of grass, put it between his thumbs and tried to blow on it. "I used to do this when I was a kid." She hated him just then, throwing out something mean and then playing with a blade of grass. Speaking from that superiority of his that she had no defense against. She looked at him as though he'd spoken a curse. She made a face, so he couldn't get away with it. She was sure it wasn't true.

"I want to go to school," she said emphatically.

"Yes," he said, in a dull voice, "I suppose you do."

Jewel was mortified that she had revealed herself so openly.

"Itching to run out in the world, are you? Well, it's not all it's cracked up to be, and there are things I've done in it I wish I hadn't." He cracked his knuckles, then picked another blade of grass. "Grass is wonderful stuff," he said. "Trample it down and up it comes."

"You've seen lots of things," Viny said. "You see there and there," she said, reaching over and running her finger over the lines of his forehead. "Those are all the things."

He smiled and took her hand. "I'd rather be here with you than to have seen any of them."

Jewel had heard men say things like this in films, only knew it was false even when you wanted it to mean something—even though everything came out with happy endings. Mr. Ferril was lowered another notch in her opinion.

"You don't know anything," she said, going off. He'd put her in a bad mood, and she wanted to take a swipe at him. She went around a boulder to chew on a long grass stem and dream about school starting and the clothes she wanted. She was impatient now for the summer to be over; it always got so boring. She wanted to forget about Viny and Mr. Ferril and take her thirty dollars and go shopping. If he wanted to sit there with her and Viny when he could be off speaking French and walking along the Seine and seeing the insides of cathedrals, he must be like the donkey that wanted horns instead of ears. Or like a monk or a man shipwrecked on an island. Only he'd come to this place out of his own free will. So he must be crazy. Or maybe wicked. It occurred to her that he might indeed be wicked, but she didn't think he'd killed anybody.

She'd been watching the way he acted in the hotel, as if he'd come to stay and wanted everybody to like him. Easy and familiar with the women, as though he had crossed some invisible boundary and gained their territory. She'd never seen a man act like that before. With her mother, for instance. Touching her arm, or putting his arm around her shoulder when he asked for something, making a little joke and laughing when she laughed. It was shocking, though her mother seemed not to mind at all, but even to welcome it. A change came over her mother then, like the sun moving out of a cloud, and she joked and laughed till the color rose to her cheeks and she looked warm and pretty and pleased. Between her parents there was no such intimacy. They either moved behind a cloud of indifference or acted as though they had the goods on one another and would give no quarter.

Mr. Ferril was gentler with Viny, more tender, occasionally taking her by the hand and saying, "Look here, isn't this lovely?" and showing her the sunset or a rock with veins on it. And she would smile at him, her eyes glowing with pleasure, but it was the same pleasure she had for the sunset or the other things that gave her delight. Though sometimes she would scuffle with him the way the kittens tumbled with each other.

With Jewel, it was different. He'd never touched her except when they had danced, but she found herself wanting him to look at her, wanting him to laugh with her the way he did with her mother. And when he said to Viny, "Isn't it lovely?" his voice touched a nerve that made her shiver. Sometimes she wanted to kick her legs and bang her head on the floor just like a child to make him look at her. She was awkward in her desire to please him without knowing how—angry that it should matter because he was such an old man, and she disliked him besides. When he did look at her, she pretended she didn't notice.

Towards the end of the summer, Viny's brother Frank and the lawyer, Henry Betts, came out to the hotel for an afternoon's visit. They all ate in the dining room, a small group in a room of empty tables. Then Viny insisted that Jewel come to sit in the parlor with them. When it was nearly time to leave, Viny and her brother hugged one another as though they never wanted to separate; then Frank held her at arm's length to look at her again. "My darling," he said. "My rose of Jericho."

"The name of this place is solitude, Brother," Viny said, "and its song is sung by the coyotes."

"She's a genius," Frank said to Penny and Jack afterwards. "Only she's never had a place to be it before. She lives differently from you and me."

That night Jack had a brainstorm and lay in bed under the rush of his enthusiasm. Think of it, he told Penny, they had a real start this time. With Viny there year-round and Ferril staying on indefinitely, they could attract other boarders. Build up the summer clientele. With a little luck, they could make a real go of it.

Penny could see him lying there, an ill-defined lump under the covers, eyes wide open to receive the gleam of the future. All caught up. He was such a fool, she could almost pity him. She tried to be patient. Surely, she argued, they ought to let well enough alone and see if, for once in their lives, they could get a little ahead. What was the point of taking on risks they couldn't cover?

"But we've got a chance, don't you see?"

"Birdbrain," she said, and turned over and went to sleep.

Jack lay awake a little longer, staring into the dark. Then he turned over as well and folded his arms across his chest. He wasn't about to fight her. He'd go back to his cronies and his mining claims and his woman in Deming. Penny could do as she liked.

4.

Penny had it in mind that the dawn of one of these days would find her far from the hotel. She saw a woman sitting alone on a train, in hat and dark dress and pumps—stylish without being conspicuous—while the vortices of travel whirled away behind her. She could almost watch herself looking through the window at towns speeding by while the wheels thundered out distances. She kept putting money away into the secret hoard she'd started even before that image of herself possessed her fantasy. But now that it was there, she let it carry her forward to different cities and to other men. She wanted to go somewhere in the world where nothing would hang on to her. She wanted to shed this life the way a dog sheds water, leave the hotel and all the things that had gone awry to fade beyond memory, sealed up in a room she'd never open. Even Jewel didn't belong in this picture of herself because Jewel could only remind her of where she'd been. And Jewel would be old enough to fend for herself one of these days. Jack wouldn't let her starve—he and his whore. They could all do as they liked.

In some ways, they were two of a kind, she and Jack, and at times she looked at him as though he were part of a conspiracy. He'd done all right, wandering among his cronies and whores, going off on his fruitless hunts for manganese and feldspar. Anything that would take him away from the hotel and to the price of the next drink he'd do. Short of stealing—and maybe that, too. He'd never need a cent more than he had. But her little hoard was growing. She even gave Jack a crumb now and then for the sake of good will and a clear path to the future. And because he couldn't let her get the better of him, he'd put a little cash her way when he had it. He'd gotten himself a partner, a worthless sort of blowhard, who knew everything about the country and had only till now—

which meant at some indefinite point in the future—avoided being rich for the sake of some obscure principle.

But fall was coming and the moment she'd have to look Jewel in the eye and deny her what she'd been counting on. For if Viny was their bread, Jewel was their butter.

Indeed, it was coming on September, but nobody'd taken Jewel to town for school clothes, though she kept nagging about when they were going. The plan had been that she would stay in town with the Folsoms and go to high school. Though she was only thirteen, Miss Blackburn had said she was ready. But every time Jewel mentioned it, Penny put her off.

Finally, knowing she couldn't dodge the question any longer, Penny made her come back to the bedroom and closed the door and told her. "I know you've been counting on going to town and boarding out this year, but you've got to understand that we're hanging by a thread and can't afford it."

Jewel couldn't believe it. "But I could work, I could baby-sit and wash dishes and—"

Penny shook her head. "Maybe next year, when you're high-school age anyway. Besides," she added, "those schools don't teach you anything you can't put off for a year. Besides," she added further, as though this time she had the real clincher, "you'll get a better education right here. I've talked to the principal and to Mr. Ferril, and he's agreed to be your tutor. You can go on with your piano and he'll teach you French—said it was a good way for him to keep in practice. Why, you'll have a real European education."

But Jewel was not mollified. All she could think about was being in town, where she could go to the movies with girls her age and giggle over boys and have skirts to wear instead of jeans.

She went off in a fury that was new to her, and made Viny cry because she told her to go away and leave her alone. She sat in her room in a stupor of disappointment, then went out back where Jack was killing chickens, a job he hated. She stood by while a headless chicken jerked and flung itself around the floor of the shed, the other chickens nearby clucking their distress.

"Daddy," she said, following him to the pump, waiting till the water washed over his hands. "Daddy," she said, trying to keep her voice calm, "how come I can't go to school like we said?"

The fumes of the day's whiskey fuddled his brain, and the hand that held the ax belonged to someone else. Then anger burned him: he felt unhinged by circumstance, and the look in her eyes made his own eyes moisten. He'd have enjoyed the luxury of giving way, of sitting right down with a good drink and huddling his woe with an endless compassion.

"I could work. Mrs. Folsom said she'd be glad to have me, and Jonie's there."

"Young girls need their folks," Jack said, suddenly convinced of this. Young girls wanted to wander off by themselves, and all heedless they went down dark streets without knowing what was waiting for them.

He concentrated his small, red-rimmed eyes on his hands, lathering them up, rinsing them off, examining the stubborn dirt under the nails. "Why, you got the chance of a lifetime right in your own backyard. That Ferril will teach you things that'll take your breath away."

"I want to go to high school," Jewel wailed.

"Actually, the principal was against it," Jack said. "Didn't want to set a precedent. He said, 'That young gal should wait a year'—he was thinking of you doing your best. And meanwhile, you won't have to leave Viny. Because it would break her heart, you know." He gave her a direct look. "You wouldn't want to do that, would you? She'd take it mighty hard." He walked back to the shed to pick up the headless chicken.

Jewel had been momentarily silenced. Of course, she'd have missed Viny. More than her parents—though she didn't like to admit it. Viny took up a space that no one else could fill. But that didn't change anything. "I'll have to go sometime," she said. "Viny has her own life."

"Well, and you got yours, puss," Jack said kindly. "You don't have to rush it all at once." Time enough to know what a hard place the world was. He felt he was doing the right thing by her, protecting her for her own good. There were usually good reasons for doing almost anything. And he tested that theory on the basis that he felt better than he expected to, found himself on solid ground for a change.

Jewel ran off to her room, her head full to bursting. Suppose she just ran off to town, took the money in her bank account and hitchhiked across the country. Suppose she killed herself. But though she tried, she couldn't live in her disappointment. Her consolation, such as it was, came a few days later when they went into town and she bought a new skirt and sweater with her savings. Then she and Viny went to an adventure film while Penny went to the stores and shopped. Viny put her head down whenever the hero was in danger.

From that time on, Jewel nursed a grudge against Viny, as though it were her fault she wasn't going to school. She knew it was wrong, but she couldn't help herself. Viny had created her circumstances without knowing it—had helped create the net that bound them all, tied up the knots of possibility. The hotel bound Jack and Penny; they held on as though it were their invention out there in the desert. And now she had been pulled into the trap. Viny was free—she could travel in any space and come back and be what she was. She would never be hustled out of her domain to be locked in the narrow, closed space that Jewel resisted and that everyone she knew had entered. Had it been possible to hate Viny, Jewel would have been glad to do it. But Viny was without malice; her only harm lay in being what she was.

She tried to put herself at a distance, as though Viny presented a treacherous quicksand that would keep her from moving where she needed to go. But it was impossible to get away.

"I've got something to show you," Viny told her one afternoon in her usual way, recognizing no change between them.

"What is it?" Jewel said, without interest.

"Come and I'll show you."

They went to her room, where she opened a drawer and pulled

ARGVGLADYS SWAN

out a small leather pouch. From it she took out a rabbit's foot. "I thought I'd lost it," she said joyfully, as she held it up.

"Is that all?" Jewel said cruelly.

But Viny paid no attention. "It's a coyote charm," she said.

"To keep them off?"

"No, to bring them," she said.

"Why would you want to go and do that?" Jewel said, her interest quickened, though she said, "It's just an old rabbit's foot."

Viny didn't answer for a moment. Then she said, "They're part dog gone to the devil, and you can't tame them. They howl for the part that used to lie in front of the fire, only they can't have it. They'd be too comfortable, and the desert's the only place for them. So they howl for the sake of what they are."

"What's the point of that?" Jewel said. "And who'd want them close anyway?"

"They make you remember being out there with them."

Jewel gave a shrug, tired of the game.

"It works by moonlight, by the full moon," Viny said, picking up the charm. "We can go out then."

"It sounds dumb," Jewel said.

"You see this hotel," Viny said, as though she hadn't heard. "It's under a curse."

More nonsense, but she could almost believe it. "Why?"

"Because it's here and it has no soul."

"You think it ever had one?" Jewel said in a mocking tone.

"Of course it did, every place has one. You have it for a while, then you have to let it go wandering on. You can't hold on to it. And if you try without it, everything goes out of whack."

In some ways, Viny was uncanny. "I don't know what to do," Jewel said, in a rush of misery.

"Here," Viny said, holding out her hand, "I'll give it to you."

"That's all right," Jewel said, putting her arms around her. "You don't have to give me anything." There was nothing Viny or anyone else could offer her.

"It'll be a secret between us," Viny said.

242

5.

Jewel did take refuge in her piano lessons, though not at first. When she took out the yellow-covered John Thompson music books and tried her old pieces at the keyboard, she made so many mistakes she wanted to tear up the music. Afterwards, she ran off to weep in her room. Mr. Ferril kept telling her she had real piano hands because she could reach a whole octave, and he told her she was very talented. He bought for her the notebooks of Anna Magdalene Bach, and she practiced when she could, Viny sitting in a chair beside the piano, quiet, not disturbing her, as though it were nothing for her to hear the same piece played a dozen times.

They created a schoolroom as well, moving the bed out of their special room and moving in a secretary. Jewel was learning French and reading *Ivanhoe* and *Julius Caesar* and *Romeo and Juliet*. Sometimes they read passages aloud so that Jewel could get practice in public speaking, with Viny for the audience. And so that Jewel would learn how to use words, Mr. Ferril made her write poetry. He kept pushing her; the more he pushed, the harder she tried. He was inviting her to go somewhere beyond anything she knew, but she had no idea where he was leading her. She had come to idolize him and was afraid that she wouldn't live up to his expectations. At the same time, a kind of quarrel lived in her, ready to flare up into rage.

"There's an eight-year-old girl in France who writes poetry that puts philosophers to shame," he said once. "Don't you want to do something like that?"

"I'm not eight years old," Jewel said.

"That's not what I'm saying."

She didn't want to write poems—they sounded stupid. But she learned to play "Für Elise" and "Malagueña" with such aplomb that Mr. Ferril kissed her on the top of the head and called in Jack and Penny to listen. "Mighty fine," Jack said. "Nice touch, don't you think." And Penny said the other kids would be jealous if they knew.

She could have spent hours at the piano. She had caught on finally, and it came easily, the notes in her mind moving her hands.

She skipped through the pieces one after the other. When she played particularly well, Mr. Ferril put his arm around her and said, "That's my girl."

He went to town to buy her a book of Mozart's sonatinas, and that evening they went to the piano to try the first. She was very excited.

"Here, now," he said, "come with me. I'll get you some music paper, and you copy it out. That way you'll know it. You sleep with that music in your head and let it take hold of you. That way you'll play it. Do you understand what I'm saying?"

She didn't think she did, but she wouldn't admit it. She was filled with uncertainty: she wasn't sure what he wanted of her, something more than playing the piano.

"The passion is there—all that remains is for you to let it out."

She remained silent.

"Look at me," he demanded.

She was beginning to feel suffocated by his presence there in the room. But then he smiled, and gently pushed the hair away from her face. "A lovely girl," he said gently. "Young and lovely and full of promise. Kiss me," he said.

She leaned over and kissed him on the cheek.

"Now on the lips," he said, and this time bent forward and kissed her lightly on the lips. "You see," he said. "That's a kiss between friends. It's a little doorway to be entered. Whole realms and countries to be imagined.

"Kiss me again," he said.

But she turned away.

"I'm trying to help you," he said. "I'm trying to make something of you. You're young, but you're not stupid. Try not to be stupid." She turned to leave. "You want the world, don't you? You may as well get it on your own terms. At least before they beat it out of you."

She had no idea what he was talking about.

He gave a little laugh. "I suppose I'm frightening you—maybe that's a good thing. Think of me sometimes," he said, before she closed the door. "Tomorrow Mozart. Both purity and passion—you can't get better than that."

That night she lay in bed, reliving the kiss like a tune that played itself over and over in her mind. She felt it on her cheek and against her lips. She could call up the sensations in those spots that linked with others and collected in a place she wasn't sure about. Because when she touched it, she was sure she shouldn't, yet it seemed all sensation flowed there and made her feel more herself. She didn't want him to kiss her; she wanted him to kiss her until she didn't want any more. She'd do anything not to be drawn to the next kiss. And she touched the place that seemed itself a doorway, herself a doorway that things might enter. She didn't know what to do. It was the first time she'd been kissed on the lips. Now it was something she didn't know how to live with, for it led beyond itself. To honey and anguish. She wanted something desperately, but had no idea what. Not Mr. Ferril and not music and yet those, too. He had an idea about her that she resisted, but she had none about herself.

"Do you want babies?" Viny asked her a few nights later, when they slept together.

"I don't think so," Jewel said. "I think they'd be horrible, crying all the time and having to be changed and fed."

"A child is real," Viny said.

"Of course it is, but you and I are real."

"It jumps and plays, and that's different from what's in your head."

"Of course it is. Lots of things are real."

"Yes," Viny said, touching her forehead. "When I do this, I know it's all in my head and outside it's real. Only it's different with a child because it lives in its head, but it's outside. And you can talk to it—and say what's in your head. And it knows. It's different from other people. And if you had a child, it would be yours."

"I don't want one," Jewel said.

"What do you wish when you break a wishbone?"

"To get away from here," Jewel said.

"I want to marry Mr. Ferril," Viny said.

Jewel lay in silence. "You can't do that," she said.

"Why not?"

"Just because. Suppose he doesn't want to marry you. Suppose he has a lady somewhere else. It's a stupid thing to say."

She wanted to pinch Viny and make her cry and push her out of the bed. She wasn't supposed to want Mr. Ferril. He belonged to her, only she didn't want him.

"Besides," she said, "he's a wicked person."

"He's a wicked person," Viny said, "but he's a good person. He takes me down to the river to look at the birds. We're going to catch a bird, he said he would."

"That's stupid," Jewel said. "What would you want with it?"

"To have it," Viny said. "Like the kittens. Only a baby would be better."

The lessons went on, but though she thought everything would be changed by that kiss, Mr. Ferril acted as if nothing had happened. He seemed to have lost interest in her, to have lost the focus of his idea. He never said, "Don't you want to be a great musician? Wouldn't you like to play all over Europe?" or any of the notions he'd teased her with. Her playing went badly; the harder she tried, the worse it got. And after the lesson ended with his putting a record on the Victrola and dancing with Viny, she sat there glumly, full of disgust. If he'd asked her, she'd have refused, though she wanted him to ask. If she could only play the piano better than anyone in the world, then Mr. Ferril would give her all his attention. She watched Viny laughing and clinging to his arm, their hugging afterwards, and it was more than she could bear. If only she could lie on the floor and kick and scream, but she couldn't do that either.

Suddenly it occurred to her, what if they went off together and took off all their clothes down by the river? Viny wouldn't have cared. She hadn't thought where Viny and Mr. Ferril went on their walks together while she practiced. Maybe Mr. Ferril had kissed Viny a long time ago because Viny was beautiful and they could dance together like Fred Astaire and Ginger Rogers. When they went out that afternoon, she left the piano and watched them disappear up the road. She wanted badly to follow them and spy on them. The next day when they were going to take the silver Hudson into town, she deserted the piano and ran out to the car because she couldn't bear to be left behind. Mr. Ferril accidentally closed the door on her finger, and she cried. She knew she was being allowed to go because of her finger. They ate dinner at a Mexican restaurant, but she didn't enjoy it. Her finger wasn't broken, but it would be a few days before she could go back to the piano. That meant she could go with them on their walks. She saw that Viny and Mr. Ferril held hands and let their arms swing as they walked.

But even after her finger healed, the lessons went badly. Mr. Ferril's mind seemed to be elsewhere. He was virtually silent over breakfast, and when he went into town, it was by himself. For the first time since he arrived at the hotel, he'd received several letters, all in one week. He started to use the telephone once, but thought better of it, jumped into the Hudson and went into town.

"If you have a baby," Viny said one night as they lay together, "you can tell it words, and it will say them back, and then it will make up things to say. Isn't that fun?"

"Are you going to have a baby, Viny?" Jewel asked, pushing herself up on her elbow. "Tell me, are you?"

"Mr. Ferril says I can have one if I want."

"But you can't do that, Viny," Jewel said. "It would be wrong."

"No, it wouldn't."

"You're not even married."

"I don't care," Viny said, stubbornly. "He has to go away first. But if I have a baby, it will be real."

"Who does? Mr. Ferril? Where's he going?"

"I don't know," Viny said, "but he'll come back."

"Does he love you, Viny?" she asked shyly. Perhaps that, too, was something that entered a doorway.

"He says so."

"But if he doesn't come back, what'll you do then? It will be terrible," she said, as though it had happened already, and she knew she'd gone too far.

Viny whimpered softly beside her. "A baby would be real," she said. "Don't tell," she pleaded. "It's a secret between us. Promise— you have to."

No matter what she did, it would be wrong somehow. If she told, Viny would cry and tell her she was mean and maybe never forgive her, and Mr. Ferril would hate her. And Penny would blame her for not saying something before. If she kept the secret, she'd be miserable and never know a moment's peace. But suppose Viny only imagined a baby without ever having one, or suppose Mr. Ferril came back and married her. That way she could go to school and everybody would be happy. She was willing now to let Viny have him.

6.

Mr. Ferril left them soon after, saying he'd been called away on business, but that he'd return as soon as everything was settled. He took only a small valise and left the rest of his things and paid his room and board for the next month. He kissed the women on both cheeks, as the French do, he told them, and drove away up the road. Viny waved to him until the car disappeared.

After he left, the hotel settled into dullness. Jewel let her music go and only played when she was seized by the fear she would forget everything. Her French and math books lay entirely unopened. Penny didn't say a word to her about studying. Lethargy took hold of everything. Even if something needed desperately to be fixed, it was let go. The sink got plugged up and the dishes went undone for days before they called the plumber. Jack slipped in and out without anyone noticing. Penny could tell Jack a dozen times to nail a loose board, but when it got fixed was another matter. Sometimes things ran out, like bread or eggs, but Penny didn't seem to care. Jewel and Viny spent a lot of time playing checkers and listening to soap operas on the radio, or if it was Sunday, to Jack Benny and Edgar Bergen and Charlie McCarthy.

Jewel ignored Viny much of the time, but Viny didn't seem to care. Viny moped around the hotel, played with the cats and sang to herself. She had a hard time getting up in the morning and looked pale and irritable over breakfast. Not even the advent of the large, sweet navel oranges from California revived her. She looked at the brilliant fruit and pushed the plate aside. For long periods she sat in her room and stared out the window.

Then the lethargy was pierced by voices. Penny and Jack seemed to spend half their time quarreling.

"If anything's going to get done around this place . . ."

"Sand down a rathole."

"It's what I hate about you," Penny said. "Like you've forgot Viny's here and keeping food on the table."

"I know all about it, but I got things to do. And Viny's being taken care of."

Their exchanges were as brief and fruitless as they were necessary to their existence. Jewel stayed clear of them because it was like entering a crossfire to come between them. But then something created a tension in the air that was almost like a purpose. Jewel wasn't quite clear what was going on. Whatever she overheard was fragmentary and inconclusive, but clearly it had to do with Mr. Ferril.

"I never liked that man," she heard Penny say. "Not from the first moment I laid eyes on him. I figure it was in him to do something like that."

"You'd never know it the way you two carried on."

"Listen, he was our bread and butter, and all I did was be nice to him."

"Yeah, I'll bet. I had him figured for a ladies' man from the very first go."

"Just what do you have in mind, Jack Whedon? When I want to go roving in the clover, you can be sure I'll make the most of it."

"I s'pose you would."

"And isn't it just like the pot calling the kettle black?"

Always just before Jewel could figure something out, they went on to their own private grievances and let her hang with a suspense that finally drove her to Mr. Ferril's room. She opened the wardrobe and fingered the cloth of his finely tailored suits, the tweed jacket he wore on walks. The smell of him still lingered in the room. She looked at the pile of books he left, the Shakespeare she had read from, a novel by Stendhal and the plays of Molière. A crystal ashtray still held ashes and cigarette butts in it. She found a little notebook with his handwriting, listing his expenses. He had a peculiar way of making a seven. As she leafed through it, a photograph that had been taped lightly to the back fell out.

When she picked it up, she saw a family. The woman, petite and slender, with her hair swept up elegantly, stood next to a young boy, almost her height. She held his arm as though she depended on him, and although he faced the camera, he seemed to glance off to one side, but whether at her or something outside the frame of the picture, it was impossible to tell. The two of them seemed linked together by the same eye that looked outward and somewhat askance and took in everything with the same humor and touch of superiority. And the same energy seemed to play in their expressions. Behind them stood a man taller than the boy. Jewel looked at them closely. These were his parents, where lay his origins—the ones who called him Everett and told him he mustn't spoil his supper and to watch out for the cactus thorns, who sent him to school and expected him to study diligently and mind the teachers. Behind the trio were the columns of the hotel, white and smooth in the sunlight. The hotel was young then, the paint still fresh, and all, it appeared, was whole and sound. Others were gathered on the porch. Jewel could make out the edge of a rocker and a man's leg extended. On the back of the photo was a date, June 1919. She wondered why he had left it behind.

The rest was negligible. A crumpled handkerchief. A fringed

bookmark. A paperweight. A mixture of French and Swiss coins on the windowsill. These Jewel examined one by one; they'd been in his pockets as he walked the streets of foreign cities. Then she put them back where she'd found them, left the room, closing the door quietly behind her, and never said a word about having been there.

At that point, with a sort of grudging truce between them, Penny and Jack kept things mostly to themselves. When Jewel asked questions, they told her Ferril had gone away and wouldn't be back. He had business matters to settle. And quietly, Jack and Penny gave themselves to speculation.

"No wonder he wanted to come here—seems strange now we didn't know anything about him."

"We never asked, you idiot."

"When I think of it—him being around our girl and all."

"Now you think about it."

"And what did you think with all the money coming in? Well, it's all catching up with him, poor guy. I don't know, though—I think he was planning to come back, even wanted to. He left all his things—there's some expensive stuff there."

"Maybe that was just his way of clearing out."

"I don't believe it," Jack said. "Maybe he just wanted to start over."

The way Jack wanted to do. His partner had just told him about the assayer's results on some rocks they'd brought down from the Black Range. If they could find an outfit willing to go to the expense of taking out the ore, they might have a good thing. And if the hotel did go under, as he thought about it now, he could put his time where it would do the most good. Penny could get a job in town as a receptionist or a telephone operator. That would carry them along until he hit paydirt. He'd have to find the right moment to put it to her. For right now, he'd bide his time.

It didn't take too much evidence before Penny got wind of Viny's secret. She cornered Jewel one afternoon and said to her,

"Maybe you know something I don't know. But the way Viny's been sick these mornings means only one thing, far as I'm concerned. What can you tell me about it?"

Jewel shrugged. "I can't help it if she's sick."

"Nobody said you could."

It was curious, though, the train of Penny's logic. If Viny was pregnant, it could be one man as well as another, and Jewel was party to yet another quarrel.

"What do you take me for? As if I'd lay a hand on her."

"Well," Penny said, "you never know."

For once Jack rose to ire. "You think a man's got no honor?" he said. "Taking advantage of a poor woman who doesn't have her stock of wits."

"Well, someone did, unless it's a virgin birth."

"And you still can't believe what's right in front of your eyes. All that high-toned culture he slickered you with." Jack gave a little laugh. "And you didn't even keep an eye on her."

"How was I to know? And say what you want, that Viny has plenty of wit." She knew how to flirt, anyway. She could play with a man like any woman, for all she was a child. Penny could see that. Even so, the bastard should have left her alone, he didn't have to stoop that low.

They blamed each other for not being more careful and blamed Jewel for not looking out for her and in the end decided there was no help for it. They couldn't take her anywhere to bring it off because it wasn't legal, and if they tried to do it illegally, Viny could die or they could get themselves in trouble and even land in prison. Nor could they just sit by and take the money and let her have the baby, though Penny'd have been glad to do that if she could get away with it. But she had enough saved up to take her to California and keep her going till she got a job. She was philosophic about it: all good things came to an end eventually, and if you could make anything out of them first, you were ahead of the game. All they could do now was call Viny's brother and let him take her. The moment she was gone, Penny would buy her train ticket.

When Penny told Jewel that Viny would have to leave, she burst into tears.

"What's the matter with you anyway?" Penny said. "You were all broken up because you couldn't go off to school. Now maybe you can go."

But it didn't seem to make any difference.

"Don't let them send me away," Viny pleaded as they lay in bed together for their last night before she went away.

"I tried," Jewel said, "only nobody will listen."

"I can't go away," Viny said, "because of the baby, and because he'll want to see it."

"But when he comes, he'll come to where you are."

"But that's not the right place," Viny said. "Let's run away."

"Where would we go?"

Viny lay silent. Then she said, "Listen, I've got the coyote charm under the pillow. I want you to take it."

"I thought you gave it to Mr. Ferril," Jewel said.

"No, I only showed it to him. I gave it to you. Here," she said.

Jewel took it and leaned over and kissed her on the cheek. She thought about it and kissed her on the lips.

"Only you have to use it, while I'm still here."

"I don't know how."

"Be quiet in there," Penny said at the door. "You can't lie there talking till all hours."

"Take it," Viny whispered, "and go outside after everybody's asleep. Just hold it in your hand and they'll come round."

Jewel was afraid of the dark. She didn't like the idea of going outside in the cold or meeting creatures in the dark. She didn't think anything would bother with her, though she couldn't be sure. But she couldn't refuse Viny on her last night.

"They won't harm you," Viny assured her.

"What am I supposed to do?"

"Nothing. Just wait."

Jewel put on her bathrobe and slippers and listened for sounds from the next room. Then she moved to the door, opened and closed it quietly and slipped down the hall to the front door. Off in the parlor sat the piano she had neglected for so long, a black rectangle in the shadows; and the Victrola under the gilt-rimmed mirror, which caught a gleam of light from somewhere. The floor-boards creaked beneath her movements, and she had to pause between steps so as not to wake anybody. The front door complained when she opened it, and she went out quickly. It was bright outdoors, though the moon wasn't yet quite at the full. She descended the steps, watching for the loose board, and walked out back, past the springs.

It was a clear night filled with stars. On the ground, a light powdering of snow had left a few traces. Carefully, she walked out through the mesquite and yucca trees far enough that the hotel was a large, irregular shadow behind her. She let the silence gather around her till she heard only the rustle of night things. And how do you know they are there? she wondered.

But as soon as she thought about it, she knew they were gathering in the bushes, circling around her. They moved on paws that were quick past stealth, their tails poised and their noses in the air. She felt the wildness behind their eyes and the hunger that went straight to the moon. The hair stood up on the back of her neck. Even though she couldn't see them, she felt the pulse of their blood. She caught her breath and pushed away fear, and let her breath out slowly. They had made a circle around her, and she stood at the center. It was as though she could feel herself entering the space, taking possession of it. She thought of all the people she knew, Jack and Penny, Viny and Mr. Ferril, and she didn't want to be any of them. I want my own experience, she thought. She didn't know how she could get it, but the circle seemed to hold all the shapes of possibility, the ones that entered dreams and those that the daylight brought to form. Dimly, if only she could catch hold of them, were projections of the future. There were hidden things, and things she could almost see, that appeared closer, moving and shaping. She had never known anything like it before, had never had a sense of the future growing out of herself. In a moment it was gone: even while she tried to capture it, the coyotes had moved away and the night took up its usual sounds.

She walked back toward the dark shadow of the hotel, past the low wall that surrounded the hot springs. A mist rose from the pool and evaporated in the air. The moon glistened on the surface of the water, but if something dark collided with the reflection, she didn't notice. She was intent on a vision of the future: she could see a time when the hotel would be gone without a trace and she'd be out somewhere in the world. And she wanted to rejoice because she was certain she would be free. And she wanted to weep as though she were mourning the deaths of all she had known, mourning something of her own death as well. But there was this she had lived. And what would remain of it for her to remember?

NOTES ON THE AUTHORS

RUDOLFO A. ANAYA lives in Albuquerque, New Mexico, where he also teaches at the University of New Mexico. He is best known for his novels, *Bless Me Ultima* (Tondtiuh—Quinto Sol International, 1972), *Heart of Aztlan* (University of New Mexico Press, 1976), and *Tortuga* (University of New Mexico Press, 1979). In 1989 he edited *Aztlan, Essays of Chicano Homeland,* and *Tierra: Short Fiction of New Mexico.* He is also editor of the *Blue Mesa Review.*

THOMAS FOX AVERILL is Writer-in-residence at Washburn University of Topeka, Kansas. His two collections of stories are *Passes at the Moon* (Woodley Press, 1985) and *Seeing Mona Naked* (Watermark Press, 1989). His recent stories have appeared in *Farmer's Market, Uncle, Bluff City, Louisville Review,* and *Prize Stories 1991: The O. Henry Awards.* "The Man Who Ran with Deer," the story in this volume, was the First Prize Story in the 1989 Roberts Awards.

RICK BASS is the author of a collection of stories, *The Watch* (W. W. Norton, 1989) and the nonfiction books *Wild to the Heart, The Deer Pasture* (Norton Paperbacks), *Oil Notes* (Seymour Lawrence/Houghton Mifflin, 1989), and *Winter* (Seymour Lawrence/Houghton Mifflin, 1991). His stories have appeared twice before in *The Best of the West:* "Chotean" in the second volume, and "Heartwood" in the third. He lives in the Yaak Valley, Montana.

ROBERT DAY is the author of a novel, *The Last Cattle Drive* (Putnam, 1977; reprinted by the University Press of Kansas, 1983), and a collection of stories, *Speaking French in Kansas* (Cottonwood Press, 1989). He is the director of the O'Neil Literary House at Washington College, in Chestertown, Maryland.

DAGOBERTO GILB's short fiction has been published regularly over the past decade in, almost exclusively, magazines from either San Francisco or New Mexico. His work has also been reprinted in several anthologies, including *The Best of the West 3*. A one-time visiting writer at the University of Texas at Austin, since the mid-1970s he has earned his living through construction work, mostly as a journeyman union carpenter. A native of Los Angeles, he lives in El Paso.

RON HANSEN is the author of *Desperadoes* and *The Assassination of Jesse James by the Coward Robert Ford* (both available in paperback from Norton), a collection of stories, *Nebraska* (Atlantic Monthly, 1989), and a children's book, *The Shadowmaker* (Harper Junior Books, 1987). His new novel, *Mariette in Ecstasy*, was published in 1991 by HarperCollins. He teaches fiction writing at the University of California at Santa Cruz.

JOY HARJO is a member of the Muscogee tribe of Oklahoma. Her most recent book, *In Mad Love and War*, won a William Carlos Williams Award from the Poetry Society of America and a Delmore Schwartz Award from New York University. She teaches creative writing at the University of New Mexico, and plays the saxophone in her own band.

LESLIE JOHNSON's fiction has appeared in *Threepenny Review, Webster Review, River City Review,* and *Appalachee Review,* among other magazines. She recently moved from California to Connecticut with her husband and two sons, and is working on a novel.

PETER LASALLE is the author of a novel, *Strange Sunlight* (Texas Monthly Press, 1984), and a story collection, *The Graves of Famous Writers* (University of Missouri Press, 1980), as well as stories in numerous magazines and anthologies (including *Best American Short Stories* and *Prize Stories: The O'Henry Awards*). He teaches at the University of Texas at Austin.

LARRY LEVIS's most recent collection of poems, *The Widening Spell of the Leaves,* was published in 1989 by the University of Pittsburgh Press. A book of short stories, *Black Freckles,* will be published by Peregrine Smith Books in 1992. He lives in Salt Lake City, where he directs the program in creative writing at the University of Utah.

KENT MEYERS's fiction has appeared in *The New England Review/ Bread Loaf Quarterly, The Southern Review, The South Dakota Review,* and other magazines. In 1990 he won *The Black Warrior Review*'s Literary Award for best story published in that journal during the year. Two of his stories were included in the midwestern writer's anthology *As Far as I Can See* (Windflower Press, 1989). Meyers lives with his wife and three children in Spearfish, South Dakota, and teaches at Black Hills State University.

ANTONYA NELSON received her MFA in fiction writing from the University of Arizona in 1986. Her first book, *The Expendables,* won the 1989 Flannery O'Connor Award for Short Fiction. Her second book, *In the Land of Men,* is forthcoming from William Morrow. Her stories have appeared in *Esquire, Playgirl, The North American Review, TriQuarterly, Antioch Review,* and elsewhere. She has received grants from the Illinois Arts Council and from the National Endowment for the Arts. She currently teaches creative writing at New Mexico State University in Las Cruces, New Mexico.

MELISSA PRITCHARD, co-editor of *The American Story, The Best of StoryQuarterly,* received the Flannery O'Connor Award for Short Fiction, the Carl Sandburg Literary Arts Award, and a PEN/Nelson Algren's honorary citation for *Spirit Seizures,* her first collection of short fiction (University of Georgia Press, 1988, and in paperback by Collier Macmillan, 1989). Her novel, *Phoenix,* will be published in the winter of 1991 by Cane Hill Press. Her stories have been anthologized and cited in *The Best American Short Stories, Prize*

Stories: The O. Henry Awards, and *The Pushcart Prizes.* She lives in Taos, New Mexico.

KEN SMITH is the author of *Decoys and Other Stories* (Confluence Press, 1985). His newest collection, *Angels and Others,* is due out later this year from that same publisher. His fiction has appeared in *The Atlantic, Crazyhorse, TriQuarterly,* and other magazines. His story "Meat" appeared in *The Best of the West 2.* He teaches in the creative writing program at the University of Tennessee at Chattanooga.

GLADYS SWAN's third collection of short stories, *Do You Believe in Cabeza de Vaca?* was recently published by the University of Missouri Press. Her first novel, *Carnival for the Gods,* was published in the Vintage Contemporaries Series, and her second, *Ghost Dance: A Play of Voices,* is forthcoming from the LSU Press. Recent fiction has appeared in *The Kenyon Review, Colorado Review, Ohio Review,* and *Writers' Forum.* Her story "Lucinda" appeared in *The Best of the West 2.*

THOM TAMMARO's chapbook, *Minnesota Suite,* was published by Spoon River Poetry Press in 1988. His poems have appeared in *South Dakota Review, Midwest Quarterly,* and *North Dakota Review.* He has edited several anthologies, including *Common Ground: A Gathering of Poems on Rural Life* (Dakota Territory Press, 1988). He teaches at Moorehead State College in Minnesota.

RON TANNER's fiction has appeared in *Iowa Review, StoryQuarterly, American Fiction,* and other magazines, as well as in *The Pushcart Prize XIV,* and the anthology *20 Under 30.* He lives in Baltimore, where he teaches writing at Loyola College.

OTHER NOTABLE
WESTERN STORIES OF 1990

Lee K. Abbott
"Sweet Cheeks"
Harpers, October

Rick Bass
"In the Loyal Mountains"
Southwest Review, Summer

Louis Berney
"One Hundred Foreskins"
Ploughshares, Fall

Mary Clearman Blew
"The Snowies, the Judiths"
Four Quarters, Spring

Dan Chaon
"Going Out"
TriQuarterly, 76

Jane Candia Coleman
"Mirage"
South Dakota Review, Summer

Richard Dokey
"Lana's Place"
South Dakota Review, Summer

Jamie Diamond
"Hacienda del Sol"
Ploughshares, Spring/Summer

Millicent Dillon
"Oil and Water"
Southwest Review, Spring

Jeanne Dixon
"Down Among the Gilly Fish"
The Missouri Review; no. 1

Alan Cheuse
"The Rose and the Skull"
Story, Autumn

Ed Dee
"The Tailman"
Mississippi Review, 55/56

Sarah Elmendorf
"Shark Ranch"
Mississippi Review, 55/56

Louise Erdrich
"The Bingo Van"
The New Yorker, Feb. 10

K. C. Frederick
"Ambush"
Carolina Quarterly, Fall

Robert O. Greer, Jr.
"The Can Men"
Writers' Forum, Fall

Katherine Haake
"The Woman in the Water"
Iowa Review, no. 3

Laura Hendrie
"Calliope at Night"
Taos Review

Pam Houston
"A Blizzard Under Blue Sky"
Lodestar, November

Wayne D. Johnson
"gama'giwe'binigowin
(the snake game)"
The Antioch Review, Winter

Walter Kirn
"Keeping Donna Faithful"
Esquire, July

Mark Lindensmith
"What the Thunder Said"
New Letters, Summer

David Long
"Blue Spruce"
The New Yorker, Nov. 12

Tia Maytag
"The Way Things Are"
Sonora Review, #18

James P. Moran
"Hawking"
High Plains Literary Review, Fall

Robert S. Nelson
"Ronnie Big Wolf Tooth"
North Dakota Review, no. 4

Joyce Carol Oates
"Shot"
The Ohio Review, no. 44

Carolyn Osborn
"The Gardener"
Shenandoah, Summer

Paul Ruffin
"The Grave"
American Literary Review, Spring

Lisa Sandlin
"Speaking to the Fish"
Shenandoah, no. 1

David Sims
"His Daughter's Horses"
South Dakota Review, Autumn

Steven Schwartz
"Other Lives"
The Literary Review, no. 2

Darrell Spencer
"Song and Dance"
High Plains Literary Review, Fall

Gladys Swan
"In the Wilderness"
Writers' Forum, Fall

Elizabeth Tallent
"Ciudad Juarez"
Mississippi Review, no. 52

Paul van Zwalenburg
"Quitting Time"
Cutbank, 34

Robert Winship
"Juan"
The Texas Review, Fall/Winter

Bill Young
"Mew"
Beloit Fiction Review, Fall

MAGAZINES CONSULTED

We regularly receive the following magazines, and consider the stories in them for *The Best of the West.*

Amelia · American Literary Review · The American Voice · Another Chicago Magazine · Antaeus · The Antioch Review · The Atlantic · Aura Literary/Arts Review · Bellowing Ark · Black Warrior Review · Brown Journal of the Arts · Buffalo Spree · Calliope · Calyx · Canadian Fiction Magazine · The Capilano Review · California Quarterly · Carolina Quarterly · Charitan Review · City Lights Review · Chiron Review · Cimarron Review · Clockwork Review · Clerestory · Colorado Review · Crazyhorse · The Crescent Review · Crosscurrents · Crucible · Cut-Bank · Descant · Epoch · Esquire · Event · Fiction Review · The Florida Review · Four Quarters · Gargoyle · Gentlemen's Quarterly · The Gettysburg Review · Grain · Grand Street · Gray's Sporting Journal · Great River Review · The Greensboro Review · Harper's · Hawaii Review · High Plains Literary Review · The Hudson Review · Indiana Review · Iowa Review · The Jailfish Review · The Journal · Kansas Quarterly · Karamu · Kenyon Review · The Literary Review · McCall's · The Madison Review · Mademoiselle · The Malahat Review · Mānoa · Massachusetts Review · Mid-American Review · Mississippi Review · The Minnesota Review · The Missouri Review · The Montana Review · Mss · The Nebraska Review · New Letters · New Mexico Humanities Review · New Orleans Review · The New Quarterly · Nexus · The New Yorker · North American Review · North Dakota Quarterly · Northern Lights · The Northern Review · Northridge Review · Northwest Review · Ohio Review · Other Voices · Paragraph · The Paris Review · Partisan Review · Passages North · Phoebe · Playboy · Ploughshares · Portland Review · Prairie Schooner · Prism International · Puerto del Sol · Quarry · Quarry West · The Quarterly · Quarterly West · RE:AL · Redbook · River Styx · Room of One's Own · The Seattle Review · The Sewanee Review · Shenandoah · Sonora Review · The South Carolina Review · South Dakota Review · Southwest Review · Sou'wester · Special Report · Stories · Story · StoryQuarterly · Sundog: the Southeast Review ·

Taos Review · The Texas Review · Threepenny Review · TriQuarterly ·
The Virginia Quarterly Review · Webster Review · West Branch · West-
ern Humanities Review · Wind · Writers' Forum · The Yale Review ·
Yellow Silk · Zyzzyva

ACKNOWLEDGMENTS

"Where West Is" © 1991 by Thom Tammaro. Reprinted by permission of the author.

"A Guide to Some Small Border Airports" © 1991 by Peter LaSalle. First published in and © 1990 by *The Antioch Review.* Reprinted by permission of the author.

"The Flood" © 1990 by Joy Harjo. First published in *Grand Street.* Reprinted by permission of the author.

"Antlers" © 1990 by Rick Bass. First published in *Special Report.* Reprinted by permission of the author.

"The Government Man" © 1990 by Ken Smith. First published in *TriQuarterly,* and reprinted by Confluence Press in *Angels and Others* © 1991 by Ken Smith. Reprinted here by permission of the author and Confluence Press.

"First Water" © 1991 by Larry Levis. First published as "A Divinity in Its Fraying Fact" by Larry Levis © 1990 by *The Antioch Review.* Reprinted by permission of *The Antioch Review.*

"Children of the Desert" © 1990 by Rudolfo A. Anaya. First published in *The Seattle Review.* Reprinted by permission of the author.

"Back in Aberdeen" © 1990 by Leslie Johnson. First published in *Carolina Quarterly.* Reprinted by permission of the author.

"The Man Who Ran with Deer" © 1990 by Thomas Fox Averill. First published in *Sonora Review.* Reprinted by permission of the author.

"Mud Season" © 1989 by Antonya Nelson. First published in *Prairie Schooner.* Reprinted by permission of the author.

"Wind Rower" © 1990 by Kent Meyers. First published in *Sonora Review.* Reprinted by permission of the author.

"My Father Swims His Horse at Last" © 1990 by Robert Day. First published, in a longer form, in *TriQuarterly.* Reprinted by permission of the author.

"Jackpot" © 1990 by Ron Tanner. First published in *The Quarterly.* Reprinted by permission of the author.

"How Love Is Found When the Heart Is Lost" © 1990 by Melissa Pritchard. First published as "Hallie: How Love Is Lost When the Heart Is Lost" in *The American Voice.* Reprinted by permission of the author and *The American Voice.*

"Ballad" © 1990 by Dagoberto Gilb. First published in *Threepenny Review.* Reprinted by permission of the author.

"The Old Hotel" © 1990 by Gladys Swan. First published in *Mānoa* and reprinted by the University of Missouri Press in *Do You Believe in Cabeza de Vaca?* © 1991 by Gladys Swan. Reprinted here by permission of the author.